"MY DEAR LORD DANVILLE, MY AFFAIRS ARE NONE OF YOUR CONCERN," KATRINA SAID ANGRILY.

"Exceedingly well put, Miss Vernon," the viscount replied in an acid tone. "'Affairs' is a good word to use!"

"I am so glad it meets with your approval, my lord. Nevertheless, pray recollect that I am not in any way responsible to you for my actions, and I resent the implication that I should be."

He gripped her wrists, and hauled her to her feet. She knew it was useless to struggle, but said in a low voice, "Release me immediately, my lord! You do not own me!"

"Not literally, no; but you are still mine. Even now you are afire with longing for me to take you in my arms, are you not?"

She closed her eyes, unable to deny it, for it was devastatingly true. Her body ached with desire to press close to him, to feel his lips on hers, to become one with him.

"Oh, Katrina," he breathed. "For God's sake, stop fighting me, for you can never win . . ."

∽THE∽
VISCOUNT'S WAGER

Elizabeth Barron

WARNER BOOKS

A Warner Communications Company

WARNER BOOKS EDITION

Warner Books, Inc.
666 Fifth Avenue
New York, N.Y. 10103

 A Warner Communications Company

Printed in the United States of America

First Printing: February, 1986

10 9 8 7 6 5 4 3 2 1

To Kerr, Katherine and Iain
with love
and in loving memory of my grandmother,
May Barron,
who taught me that 'History is People.'

Chapter One

Heavy rain lashed the grimy windows of the small, unkempt house in the least fashionable area of unfashionable Paddington, but so immersed in their own tempest were the occupants of the house that they noticed neither the crash of thunder nor the flicker of lightning.

Katrina Vernon sighed and burrowed further into the window seat, wishing the floorboards of the shabby parlor would give way, like a stage trapdoor, and mercifully remove her from her position as the unwitting cause of this latest domestic storm.

Her uncle stood in the center of the room, his short legs splayed, looking for all the world like a fighting bantam cock, with his wine-bright eyes. "And I inshisht that Katrina shall go to the ball with you!" he roared, his speech slurred by secret indulgence in his favorite port wine.

"The girl has nothing to wear," retorted her aunt, darting a venomous glance at Katrina over her husband's head.

Katrina took a deep breath and slipped down from the window seat to join them. "Not only do I have nothing to wear, Uncle William, but I am still in mourning for my father, as you well know. I could not possibly go to Lord Merriot's ball."

She spoke firmly, trying not to reveal her agitation. Since

1

her father's violent death four months ago, she had striven to conquer her despair, to regain her naturally optimistic disposition. It had not been easy living with her Aunt Bertha and her flighty cousin Letty, being treated like a charity case instead of a relation. Now Uncle William, her one ally, was threatening to destroy the uneasy truce she had so carefully built up.

"Nonsense," he was saying. "My brother would never have wished his daughter to wear mourning weeds for him. And I'll not have it said that I favor m'daughter above m'niece. If Letty goes to the ball, then so shall you, Katy, and that's the end of it."

Meeting her aunt's furious eyes, Katrina was not so sure about that. Only when he was the worse for drink did her uncle stand up to his wife—invariably regretting it the next day.

She was about to plead with him when she heard Letty's voice from the hallway, high-pitched with excitement. The next minute Letty herself bounced into the room, dangling her green velvet bonnet by its strings. The hem of her fur-edged pelisse was soaking wet and stained with mud.

"Ma! You'll never guess what Sir Harry said when we were driving in St. James's Park! He—" She paused, her blue eyes widening. "Lord, you all look so serious. What is happening?"

Her father shifted unsteadily on his feet and held out his arms to her. "Nothing to trouble your pretty head about, my pet. Come and give your papa a kiss, little doll."

And a doll she was, with her china-blue eyes and blonde ringlets tumbling about her face. She ran to her father and kissed him, but then pushed at his snuff-stained waistcoat, forcing him away.

"Phew! You smell of stale wine, Pa." She brushed past Katrina as if she did not exist and was about to dart out of the room again when her mother spoke in her cold voice.

"Your father insists that Cousin Katrina come with us to Lord Merriot's ball tonight, or you will not be permitted to go."

"Katrina!" Letty spun around in the doorway, her mouth dropping open in a most unbecoming fashion. "But—but she can't. Sir Harry gave us only three invitations. Besides, how could she possibly be seen out in Society with her hair like that? And she has nothing to wear."

Katrina gave her cousin a faint smile. "Exactly, Letty. That is what I have been trying to tell Uncle William."

Her uncle gripped her arm. "I care nothing for your cousin's hair," he told his daughter, his mouth set stubbornly. "I have no intention of going to this ball, so she can use my invitation." He turned to his wife. "As for you, Bertha, you treat my brother's only child as if she were no better than a servant. You will find something for her to wear—something bright and cheerful. See to it!"

Before his wife could reply, he lurched out of the parlor and across the hall to his study. They heard the study door slam and the click of the key turning in the lock.

Katrina looked at her aunt and gave her a rueful half-smile. "I am sorry, Aunt. I—"

"Sorry!" her aunt snapped. "No doubt you have been whining to your uncle behind my back, complaining and carrying tales to him."

"No, Aunt. I have not," Katrina said firmly.

"She cannot go," wailed Letty. "She will disgrace us with her hair such a shocking mess and her hands all red."

Katrina raised her eyebrows at her cousin. "Scrubbing floors with sand does tend to roughen one's hands, you know, Letty," she said softly.

"Enough of your sauce, miss," said her aunt. "Your uncle's set on it, so there's nothing to do but get you presentable for this evening. Heaven knows how it'll be done, but we'll have to make the best of it!"

That evening, looking at herself in the tarnished mirror in its rickety walnut stand, Katrina reflected ruefully that "the best of it" could not have been worse. Her chestnut-brown hair, which had been cut short in debtors' prison, was neither short nor long; "straggling" was the word for it. If she had known she would be going to Lord Merriot's ball, she might at least have slept with it in papers last night. Even the black ribbon threaded through it hung limply.

And her dress! Dear God! If her old friends in Dorset could

see her now, they would be unable to recognize her in her plump aunt's discarded gown, a hideous deep mauve satin—"A perfectly suitable color for mourning wear!" her aunt had retorted in response to her protests—and so long that it had to be pinned up at the waist. "You look a sight!" her aunt had said. "But there's no time now to take up the hem." To top it all, the bodice was cut too low for her present figure. She did not seem able to gain back the weight she had lost in prison. With her slight body and garish gown, she reminded herself of one of the child harlots who stood beneath the new gas lamps in the London streets; not at all like the vivacious twenty-one-year-old who had been a general favorite in the small town on the Dorset coast, and her father's darling.

Oh, Father, she cried inwardly, but instantly pushed away the image of her father's wasted body, trying to calm the sick shivers the memory continued to evoke. Would it always be like this? Would the memory never fade?

"Are you ready?" called her aunt from the landing. "Sir Henry's here. Lord knows what he'll say when he sees you."

What indeed! thought Katrina dryly, as she drew on her long black cotton gloves. Most probably he would give not one jot, considering it was Letty's virginity he was after, not her hand in marriage. Even in rustic Dorset she had met enough young sprigs to enable her to recognize in Sir Henry Pemberton a young blood more interested in beddings than bridals. But she knew she dare not broach the subject with her aunt nor, for that matter, with her uncle. She had hinted at it to him, but he had pooh-poohed the suggestion, telling her that her experiences had made her cynical, and that young Sir Harry was obviously head-over-heels in love with his beautiful Letty.

"Niece, are you coming or not?" shouted her aunt from the hallway, and then the door slammed.

Katrina hastily fastened the gold locket with her mother's miniature about her neck—it was the only piece of jewlery she had left—and then ran downstairs, careful not to tread on the hem of her gown.

"Hurry, child," said her uncle, bundling her wrap around her. "They're waiting for you in Sir Henry's carriage. Enjoy yourself, Katy; and remember, your father would have wished to see you happy.''

Smiling at him through sudden tears, Katrina pulled her plain woolen cape over her shoulders and ran through the rain down the flagstone path to Sir Henry's carriage.

The journey from Paddington to fashionable Grosvenor Square seemed far too short. Seated opposite Aunt Bertha and Letty, both glaring at her, Katrina decided it would be best to feign sleep, but the swaying and jolting of the carriage, with Sir Henry on the box trying to show off to his ladylove by springing the high-spirited horses, set her stomach churning. Even that was preferable to facing the ton of London. With little of her former poise and confidence in her talents to cover her natural reserve, she was dreading the forthcoming ordeal.

By the time she was inside the Merriot mansion and had encountered rude stares and giggles behind fans in the ladies' cloakroom, she knew that this was certain to be one of the worst evenings of her life. Feverishly she tried to pin a tuck in the bodice of her gown, but it still fell away whenever she bent down. She would just have to sit bolt upright all night. Damn Uncle William! Had this been the old days, this whole debacle would have sent her into fits of laughter. But then she would have been surrounded by friends, and now her friends were lost to her, as good as dead.

She leaned forward to look at herself in the mirror, holding her gown to her breast with one hand. How pale she was, the pallor making her large hazel eyes look even larger. She pinched her cheeks to put some color into them.

''Come along do, cousin.'' Letty was almost dancing with impatience. ''I feel positively sick with excitement. Sir Harry says he must sign my dance card first or there won't be any dances left for him.''

As they walked along the gallery, lined with portraits of Merriot ancestors, Letty prattled away like a child bubbling with excitement at her birthday party. Although she considered her cousin featherbrained, Katrina felt a pang; poor little bird, unwittingly being snared for Sir Harry's love nest.

They paused at the tall gilt doors as the white-wigged

footman asked for their names. As they waited to be announced, Sir Harry joined them; a ginger-haired young man of two and twenty, he aspired to be a man of fashion. His eyes swiveled to the side as he spoke, finding it impossible to turn his head because of the inordinately high shirt collar and the intricate folds of his neckcloth. This was set off by a satin coat of wide stripes of blue and gold.

Katrina was tempted to giggle, but hastily stifled it when Sir Harry cast a sidelong look of loathing at her and remarked quite audibly to Letty: "I'll be demmed if I'll stand up with your scarecrow cousin."

Letty pouted her rose-petal lips at him, and he most improperly squeezed her waist, adding: "No, my poppet, not even for you will I do it. Hang it, Letty! That's asking too much of a fellow."

Katrina felt her cheeks redden, not so much because of what he had said but because he spoke so loudly that many heads turned, and she felt herself burn under their haughty stares. Silently consigning them all to the devil, she squared her shoulders and followed their party down the staircase, praying that the pins at her waist would hold. She had no wish to fall headlong down the stairs before this glittering assembly.

As soon as Sir Harry had presented them to Lord and Lady Merriot, who greeted them with icy courtesy and barely concealed contempt, he bustled them to a quiet corner of the large ballroom.

"I never did see so many splendid costumes, did you, Katrina?" said Letty, clapping her hands together. "But why do we have to hide away in this corner, Sir Harry? I cannot see anything here."

What Letty really means, thought Katrina wryly, is that *she* cannot be seen.

"I thought your mama and cousin would prefer a quiet spot to sit in, out of the way of the dancing." He tucked Letty's hand into his arm. "With your mama's permission I shall first find you a dance program and then beg the first dance, before all the others get the chance."

Before Letty's mama had a chance to speak, he had

whisked Letty away. Katrina in truth could not blame him. Aunt Bertha was not an appetizing sight in her puce and black round-waisted satin and blonde wig, with the purple turban atop it. *We must make an interesting pair,* she thought.

"That young man may be exceedingly rich and the son of a lord, but he has the manners of a country yokel," fumed her aunt. She opened her fan and angrily flapped it to cool her perspiring face.

"At least it is cooler here, Aunt Bertha."

"Nonsense! This place is like a steam bath. I wonder that—Oh! There is Lady Hendricks. You remember, niece; I told you I met her in the Pantheon last week. Oh, Lady Hendricks—"

To Katrina's chagrin, her aunt loudly accosted the surprised lady and, familiarly taking her arm, walked away with her to the refreshment salon. From the ramrod stiffness of Lady Hendricks's back, Katrina surmised that she was not at all happy to have her slight acquaintance with Bertha Vernon renewed.

She sighed and settled herself in the square-backed chair, content to sit and watch, fascinated by the fashions, many of them new to her. A young girl of about seventeen passed by, talking animatedly to her escort. She was dressed in a short-waisted gown of champagne-colored satin, the bodice and hem trimmed with bands of rose-pink velvet ribbon. As became a young girl, the hem ended above her ankles.

How pretty she looks, sighed Katrina to herself. She felt even more conscious of her vulgar, ill-fitting gown.

"Pray excuse me, ma'am."

She had been so immersed in observing the assembled crowd that she jumped when she heard the voice at her side. She looked up to find a tall gentleman before her, dressed in a dark coat of impeccable cut with a waistcoat of silver-gray satin. His dark hair was cut short, curling at the sides, and so pronounced was his fashionable elegance and air of superior breeding that at first she glanced around to see if his bow and greeting were intended for someone else.

His penetrating gray eyes danced a little at this. "I must beg your pardon for approaching you without an introduction, but it seems you are an unknown here in town." His voice was low and musical, but it bore the firm tone of one accustomed to having his commands instantly obeyed. "Justin Benedict, Viscount Danville, at your service, madam."

Katrina rose and sank into a curtsy, remembering just in time to clap her hand to the bodice of her gown. She gave the Viscount a quizzical smile, wondering why on earth he should be approaching her. "Katrina Vernon, my lord," she told him. "You are correct. I have lived most of my life in Dorset. I am here with my aunt and cousin as guests of Sir Henry Pemberton, my uncle being unfortunately indisposed."

"Ah. That would be Mrs. Vernon and her charming daughter, would it not?"

"Then you know my aunt?"

"But who does not know Mrs. Vernon and the exquisite Letty?"

She looked for ridicule in his eyes, but he was busying himself with his enameled snuffbox. She sat down again and watched the long fingers and the immaculate white cuff-bands at his wirsts. He replaced the box in his waistcoat pocket and looked down at her with an enigmatic half-smile.

"Perhaps, as your aunt is not here to grant her permission, you would do me the honor of allowing me to be your partner in the next dance? I see you do not have a program, but it is, I believe, a cotillion."

"I—" She felt her cheeks grow warm beneath his steady gaze, knowing that it was the Viscount who was bestowing the honor upon her. "I regret that I cannot dance with you, my lord," she told him softly.

One dark-winged eyebrow arched in surprise. "Would it be an impertinence to ask your reason, Miss Vernon? It could not possibly be that you consider your dancing ability inadequate for such a gathering. I can assure you that—"

"Not at all, Lord Danville," said Katrina, bridling. "It is nothing of the sort. I adore dancing and have been considered quite an accomplished dancer. But I—I am still in mourning for my father."

Although she was looking down at her clasped hands, she was conscious of those cool gray eyes examining the hideous mauve satin. She lifted her chin and looked up at him defiantly. "It is my aunt's gown. I had nothing suitable to wear."

The harsh lines of his darkly handsome face seemed to soften slightly, and a hint of amusement lurked at the corners of his mobile mouth. "It is, I believe you will agree, Miss Vernon, a gown more suitable for walking than dancing, walking perhaps where the lighting is most subdued."

Instead of feeling insulted, she gave a crow of laughter. "Is it not hideously vulgar? My aunt would insist upon my wearing it. As it was, I did not wish to come to the ball in the first place." She opened and closed her paper fan, trying to forget the ugly scenes with her aunt.

"Now that you are indeed here, albeit reluctantly, permit me at least to walk with you and perhaps procure you some refreshment." He offered her his arm and gave her a strange smile, as if he had thrown down his challenge and was waiting for her to take it up.

For one moment she hesitated; although he had given her no cause to mistrust him, there was an aura of danger about the Viscount that both repelled and fascinated her. Then she stood up. Surely it could do no harm merely to walk with him. As her fingers slid into the crook of his arm, she became keenly aware of the warm proximity of his lean, muscular body. She was also aware that the eyes of everyone in the ballroom seemed to be fixed upon them as Lord Danville led her out to the enclosed terrace overlooking the gardens.

Chapter Two

The glassed-in terrace was dimly lit and pleasantly cool after the heat of the ballroom; Katrina drew her wrap more tightly about her shoulders. Lord Danville led her to one of the secluded anterooms, which were divided from the main part of the terrace by lacquered screens and tubs of large plants.

It was perhaps a trifle *too* secluded, and from the giggles and whispers close by she guessed that the terrace was a trysting place for lovers. For a moment she felt a qualm, wondering if it were not foolhardy to allow herself to be escorted here by a stranger, unchaperoned. It was possible that she was forgetting how to behave in Society after being so long away from it. Before she had time to protest, however, Lord Danville handed her to a large ottoman in a corner of the room and seated himself beside her, not, she was relieved to see, too close.

"Have you resided with your aunt and uncle for long, Miss Vernon?" he asked.

"For only four months, my lord."

"And before that?"

Her stomach lurched. She had not spoken of her father or the prison to anyone but her uncle since the day of her arrival in Paddington. She shivered as she recalled her aunt's hostile

reception and the reluctant agreement to allow her to stay:
"But only if you work for your keep, mind." Why on earth
would she even consider telling this stranger her melancholy
history? "I would prefer not to—"

"Pray forgive me, Miss Vernon," he countered hastily. "I
did not intend to pry."

She raised her countenance to his, sensing in him a change;
his presence seemed a source of the warmth and comfort of
which she was so desperately in need, and her strange desire
to tell him her history overruled her better judgment.

"I am afraid you would find it a sordid story, but not a
particularly uncommon one." She looked into his shadowed
eyes, unable to gauge their expression. Yet something about
him encouraged her to continue. "In truth I do not know why
I should tell you, but—" She turned from him and looked
down at her clasped hands and then, drawing a deep breath,
launched into her tale.

"My father was the youngest son of Sir Cedric Vernon of
Castlewater, in the county of Dorset. My mother was Scottish.
We lived in Dorset, but not with my grandfather; my father
had been estranged from him and his eldest brother since he
was a young man. When I was twelve, my mother died.
Fortunately, my father and I were very close; he imparted to
me his love of Shakespeare and Chaucer and the great poets,
but most of all we shared a deep love of music. I often sang
to his accompaniment in the homes of our friends in Dorset."

She paused, feeling the cool breeze from the partially open
window on her back and listening to the far-off screech of
peacocks on the lawn. Although she did not look up at Lord
Danville, she was intensely aware of his presence.

"My father eked out his small allowance by tutoring the
Duke of Branscombe's three sons in the classics and English
literature. His Grace was kindness itself. My father was
treated in a manner befitting a gentleman, and we were both
made part of all the happenings at Branscombe Castle; the
card parties and balls and theatricals. . . . But then the last boy
went to Oxford and my father became ill; he had never been
strong, and his annual bronchial attacks weakened his lungs.
His allowance was but a pittance, certainly not sufficient to

cover the extra costs of physicians and medicines." She hesitated, not wishing to continue, but also aware that she had gone too far to be able to stop now.

She drew a shuddering breath. The man beside her did not speak, but as she struggled to regain her composure, he took her hand and held it lightly between his. The gesture of sympathy spurred her on to complete her story.

"My father was proud. He forbade me to approach His Grace the Duke for financial assistance and made me swear that I would not tell any of our friends, and particularly not his eldest brother and father, of our difficulties. He was determined to journey to London to seek assistance from my Uncle William, not knowing that my aunt holds the purse strings. When it comes to money matters, my uncle is even more at sea than my father. And so eventually my father went to the moneylenders—"

The Viscount moved closer, so that she could hear his breathing, and his hands tightened on hers.

She began to tremble. "He used the money to speculate heavily—and lost just as heavily. I begged him to allow me to take a post as a governess or companion, anything to tide us over until we had enough put by to live upon. But, no, he would not permit it. 'This time we shall make a killing on the 'change,' he would say; this time and this time . . . and all the time he was wasting away before my eyes. I took in small assignments of music-copying, working secretly while he slept so he would not see me. Then came the time when he could no longer pay the exorbitant interest those—those bloodsuckers exacted from him. He was shut up in the debtors' prison, and I went with him, of course, to care for him."

Although she was reliving the nightmare of that time, she was still aware of the grip of his hand, of the powerful shoulder and thigh pressing against her side. "It was not very clean in the prison," she said, running her hand over her head. "My hair had to be cut off. But it was not all misery, you must understand. We met with perhaps more kindness and compassion there than we did in the outside world; and, of course, it was not the same as a criminal prison. I was permitted to come and go as I pleased. But there was a man—I cannot call him a gentleman, although he was by birth—'' She stopped short, a moment of panic making it impossible for her to continue; and then she drew in a deep breath and took up her narrative again. ''There was a man who made several unwelcome advances, until one day—''

Her hesitation was due not only to the sick horror the memories evoked, but also to the fact that it was not possible to tell the Viscount the story exactly as it had happened. Indeed, she wondered why she was telling him at all, for she had learned, to her cost, one lesson in prison: No man could be trusted. Shaking, she sat stiffly upright, determined to finish as quickly as possible. ''Until one day, my father discovered what was happening. His remonstrances were greeted with insults and mockery, which so goaded him that he attacked the man, who flung him to the ground. When I ran to my father,'' she continued in an anguished voice, ''I found that he was paralyzed. He never recovered from the stroke and died two weeks later in my arms.''

Now desolation engulfed her at this reminder that she would never again see her father, and she wept openly at the thought of his wretched death, not even attempting to cover her face or turn it away from the man beside her.

For a moment he did nothing. Despite her grief, she was aware of the tension in his body, like a greyhound ready to spring from the leash. Then she felt the strength of his arm about her, drawing her head to his chest, his other hand caressing her face and hair with a tenderness that surprised her. ''Poor child,'' he murmured, and she felt his cool lips brush her forehead, gentle as the touch of a butterfly's wings.

She lay against him, her sobs gradually easing. It seemed such a long time since anyone had held her close, yet, as she grew more calm, she began to experience a stirring of uneasiness at the feelings his proximity was invoking. All her senses seemed to be heightened; she became conscious of the aromatic smell of musk from him and of the sharp edge of his snuffbox pressing against her breast. Her skin, her entire body became unbearably sensitive, dreading and yet aching for his touch.

Surely he would hear her heart, it was beating so hard. As if in response to this thought, she felt his long fingers fleetingly brush the side of her breast, then draw away. She looked up at him and was startled to see how close his face was to hers. A sweet languor stole over her as he murmured her name. Unable to resist, she closed her eyes and felt his mouth upon hers. At first the kiss was gentle, but when she pressed closer, responding to him with a yearning hunger, it became deep and searching, his lips bruisingly hard on hers, forcing them apart.

He stook up and pulled her to her feet, close to him, his body pressed against hers, the touch of his hands like fire on her back, her breasts. Her nipples grew erect beneath his caresses.

"Katrina," he said, deep in his throat. "Katrina."

The sound of his voice broke the spell. Shivering, she drew away from him, imbued with sudden fear and shame. Before the time in prison, no man had ever done more than kiss her hand or, if he were an old friend of her father, her cheek. Her experiences in prison had corrupted her beyond redemption. She had allowed a stranger to touch her, to caress her body, to kiss her with passion, to hold her so close that he must know every line of her body as she did his. Her face flamed at the thought, and she edged away from him.

"I must go in, my lord," she said, distractedly smoothing her skirts and her hair. To her consternation she was trembling violently and close to tears, for all the world like a missish schoolgirl.

Lord Danville was breathing hard, and when she glanced at him she saw that his eyes had darkened. He was like a thoroughbred stallion, his muscles tense, his eyes glittering and wild. Then he drew in a deep breath as if to compose himself and stepped back from her, inclining his head in a slight bow.

"I beg your pardon, Miss Vernon," he murmured. "That was inexcusable of me." The tone of his voice sent a chill through her. He bowed again. "Allow me to procure you some refreshment: a glass of wine, perhaps, or lemonade? Or would you prefer to remove to the refreshment salon?"

She nodded, and he went to speak to the liveried servant at the door, allowing her a moment to run her hands over her disordered hair.

Again he stood before her, tall and unbending. "I have reserved a table," he told her, and took her hand. Although her fingers barely brushed his sleeve as he led her through the ballroom, she could feel the tension in his arm. Yet when she looked up at his face she saw that his expression had changed to infinite boredom.

Was it her imagination or did a sudden hush fall over the ballroom as they walked through? All she knew was that he must have sensed her concern, for he looked down at her with a sudden, warm conspiratorial smile which made her feel that only he and she existed in this vast room.

How strangely changeable he was! It was impossible to keep up with his moods.

The crowded refreshment salon was brightly lit by the lights in wall sconces and the many-branched chandeliers, but he had managed to procure a quiet table in a more softly lit and secluded alcove at the end of the room. Although they were certainly not hidden from view, at least it was unlikely that they would be overheard. When she sat down, he stood with one hand on the rosewood table, his tall figure looming above her, and she sensed that he was anxious to depart.

"You need not remain with me, sir," she told him, her eyes fixed on the orange ice and tall glass of lemonade before her. She was ill at ease with him, miserably aware that she had behaved with absolute impropriety. To have gone to the terrace with him was folly enough, but to respond to his advances with such abandon was infinitely worse. But he, too, she reminded herself with indignation, had been guilty of conduct entirely unbefitting a gentleman.

He glanced at the gold carriage clock on the mantelshelf, hesitated, and than sat down beside her. "If it is your desire that I leave, I shall immediately do so. Otherwise, pray permit me to remain and perhaps atone for my reprehensible behavior."

He spoke in low, earnest tones, and her eyes wavered beneath his steady gaze.

"Please remain if you wish, my lord," she murmured.

"Then I am forgiven?"

Her eyes locked with his. "I am as responsible as you, my lord. Shall we talk of something else?"

The silence between them seemed to stretch interminably, fraught with tension, then: "Tell me now, Miss Vernon," the Viscount said brightly, "what are your plans for the future? Will you remain with your relations in Paddington or—?"

Eager to follow him in this move to a safer topic of conversation, she set down her glass. "That is the one thing that has occupied my mind during this past month. As you must have guessed, I am not at all comfortable with my aunt." She raised her eyes to his and smiled ruefully.

"I had already surmised that your present circumstances could not possibly be conducive to your happiness. But what of your uncle?"

"My uncle is kindness itself. But you must understand that he cannot always be fighting my battles for me. He is frequently away from home, in search of books. Although, like my father, he has a small allowance from the family estates, he is in fact a bookseller; his shop is in High Holborn. So, of course, he is not always at home. Besides, it is impossible for him to be always squaring up to my aunt in my defense."

"I understand." Again that enigmatic half-smile, which could denote either sympathy or amusement. And again he glanced up at the clock and this time confirmed the time with the wafer-thin gold watch he drew from the pocket of his waistcoat. "Continue, Miss Vernon," he then said. "What of your grandfather, Sir Cedric? Would he not assist you?"

She gripped her hands together, anger surging inside her at the thought of her grandfather. "He would not help my father; is it likely he would help me? When in desperation I wrote to him, despite my promise to my father, he refused to see me, pleading ill health. No. I have decided that I must seek a post as a governess or music teacher. I am not quite sure how to set about it, but I could give lessons in voice and pianoforte. And perhaps then, once I was known, I could give little recitals. I sing and play reasonably well."

"Which, from you, probably means exceeding well," he

said with a warm smile. "So, Miss Vernon, you have hidden talents. I had already conjectured that there was more to Miss Vernon than the gauche-appearing miss to whom I first introduced myself, but you continue to surprise me." His gray eyes danced, but she refused to be drawn into a flirtation with him and busied herself with finishing her water ice, which was fast becoming an orange puddle in its glass.

"And marriage? What place does marriage have in Miss Vernon's plans for the future?"

"I have no plans for marriage." She looked directly into his eyes. "I am not exactly what you might call an eligible match, my lord: the daughter of a pauper who died in a debtors' prison, no fortune, not even a dowry or a settlement! And not exactly a beauty, especially now when I have lost my figure, and my hair is still trying to grow!" She lifted her chin defiantly, challenging him with her eyes.

"Now, there I must take issue with you. You may not be endowed with a fortune, but you have other gifts. I find your candor wonderfully refreshing, your natural manner delightful and as for you hair, that gamin style is quite charming, far more so than Caro Lamb's. You could make it the rage of London."

She looked for mockery in his eyes, but to her amazement he ran the side of his hand down her hair, brushing her cheek, and then took her hand and carried it to his lips, kissing it lingeringly, his eyes never leaving hers. Even then, he did not release her hand but held it in his—here, in this bright open room, where everyone could see them together! And why, in God's name, was she permitting him to do so? Her mind no longer seemed to govern her actions. It was as if he were the famous Dr. Mesmer and she his willing patient. Yet somehow she did not care, and she allowed her hand to lie comfortably in his.

"My dear Miss Vernon, you have quite the most expressive eyes I have ever been privileged to gaze into; and your lips! Ah, what lips are there!" He leaned closer to her ear. "Your soft mouth was made for kissing," he whispered, "as I should well know!"

She was well aware that he was expecting her to blush and

hang her head, but instead she laughed out loud. "Oh, now you are really trying to bamboozle me. I pray you, sir, do not continue in that vein!" She smiled, and caught a responding glint of amusement in his eyes.

"But tell me, Miss Vernon." He sat back, swinging his quizzing glass on its black riband, his mood changing once again. "Since you are so candid about yourself, pray tell me, what is your opinion of me?" he drawled.

"Of you, my lord?"

"Yes, Miss Vernon. You have surely formed some opinion of my character during this past quarter—no, almost half an hour in my company. I beg you, Miss Vernon: your opinion of Justin Benedict, tenth Viscount of Danville."

"No, my lord, I could not possibly do such a thing!"

"Come, come. The truth, Miss Vernon!"

"Very well, sir, if you insist," she said with a little laugh. She glanced around, certain that those at the table nearest them were straining to overhear their conversation. She lowered her voice when she spoke. "You are obviously a gentleman of high fashion, my lord, but I believe that in reality you hold the world of fashion in contempt."

For a moment she was sure she had angered him, for his eyes narrowed and his lips clamped in a thin line. Then he raised one eyebrow and smiled. "Quite so! Most perceptive of you, Miss Vernon. I follow only those fashions I set. But come, a little more of the personal. What of me, myself?"

"I beg your pardon, my lord, but I do not know you well enough."

"Come, come, Miss Vernon. Anyone seeing us together would think us intimate friends."

His emphasis on the word *intimate,* accompanied by a tightening of his hand on hers, sent a flush of warmth coursing through her body.

She looked down at their clasped hands with a little smile. "I cannot fathom you, my lord. You veer so often from one mood to the next that I find you inscrutable."

"Inscrutable! I? Never say it!"

She looked up in time to catch a wry, mocking smile that

made her uneasy. "I do say it, my lord. Do not press me further, I beg of you."

He withdrew his hand, and when she looked up again it was to find him glancing at his watch once more, an expression of such brooding anger on his face that she drew back from him, startled. Immediately the dark look disappeared, and he gave a light laugh.

"Upon my soul, Miss Vernon! I have enjoyed the pleasure of your company so much I had quite forgot my appointment with Lord Merriot in the gaming room. Pray forgive me, but I must beg leave to escort you back to the ballroom."

"Of course, Lord Danville. Pray forgive me for having detained you." She gathered up her wrap and fan and reticule, and put her hand through Lord Danville's arm. There were curious looks and whispers as they progressed through the room, but Katrina ignored them. The Viscount had chosen to spend half an hour in her company, and no amount of idle gossip could change that.

Once the doors of the salon had closed behind them and they stood alone in the hallway, Lord Danville turned abruptly to her, his face a mask. "It is most unlikely that we shall ever meet again, Miss Vernon. Will you therefore permit me to offer you a few words of advice?" He clamped his lips shut in a grim line, and his eyes blazed with a curious light. He did not wait for her to reply. "Do not remain with your relations in London. If you wish to enter Society again, be sure that you have allowed enough time to elapse before you return; enough time for this, your first entry, to be forgotten. And, most importantly, do not be quite so trusting. People are not always as they seem, especially in Society. You are like an innocent lamb amidst a pack of wolves."

The hard expression in his eyes and the sudden sardonic smile chilled her to the bone. She resented the implication that she was incapable of being at home in Society although, remembering her outward appearance, it was perhaps justified. Yet she detected a deeper meaning behind his words which she could not fathom.

"I thank you for your advice, my lord, and for honoring

me with your company," was all she could think of to say to him. He nodded to the footman to open the doors to the ballroom, and a wave of music and laughter and the swishing of skirts broke in upon them.

Chapter Three

Noise and heat and a pungent mixture of scent and warm bodies assaulted Katrina as Lord Danville escorted her across the ballroom to the corner she had left just one half hour ago. Was it really only half an hour? So much seemed to have happened in such a short time. Lord Danville waited while she sat down and then took her hand and bent toward her, his gray eyes searching hers. For one moment, she thought he was about to kiss her, here, in public! Then the fire in his eyes turned to steel, and he released her hand, bowing formally.

"Pray take heed of my warning, Miss Vernon. I have no wish to see you suffer the same fate as your fair cousin, although I suspect that that is not at all likely. To see you in London Society is like seeing a wild white rose in one of the hothouses in Kew Gardens."

With a cynical twist to his lips, he abruptly turned and strolled languidly across the ballroom to join a group by the far wall. His arrival was greeted with loud bursts of laughter and a general raising of quizzing glasses in Katrina's direction. Through all the obvious banter, the Viscount's back was turned to her, and so she was unable to gauge his reaction to this reception.

She settled back into the chair, trying to ignore the no longer concealed laughter and insolent stares. Questions raced through her mind. Why had Lord Danville spent so much time in her company? At first she had thought it mere kindness, the exceptional courtesy of a gentleman taking pity on a lady in unfortunate circumstances. But then his moods had changed so erratically. . . . And that last look outside the salon had been one of a devil, a satyr. A shiver ran across her shoulders as she recalled the cold eyes and sardonic smile. Yet at times he had seemed genuinely concerned about her, especially when she had spoken of her future. And she had enjoyed his rapier mind; had she known him better, she might have scored one or two hits herself. Most of all, she remembered the probing warmth of his mouth on hers and, even as she thought of it, flickers of newly aroused desire ran through her as she experienced again the feeling of his arms about her and his taut body against hers.

Why? Why had he chosen her? He was indeed unfathomable, inscrutable as she had told him. He had not liked that. Perhaps there was an image he preferred to project and she had penetrated it? She did not know. Situated as she had been on the fringes of high society in Dorset, she had met her share of unusual men, but never anyone like Lord Danville.

Her musings were broken into by the chatter of two women who stood nearby, their bright eyes watching her above their painted fans.

"Danville is the devil's disciple, I swear it," said one. "But surely to escort that vulgar creature in Society and to honor her with his company for such a time is going too far. Society will shun him."

"Nonsense!" replied the other. "They will think it nothing but one more of Danville's quirks, and make it the *on-dit* of the town."

Katrina's heart pounded in her breast. Cheeks flaming, she lifted her chin and cast a haughty glance at the women. Unfortunately, this only caused them to giggle even more.

Staring defiantly ahead of her, she sat on the edge of the chair, holding her spine so straight it ached.

Suddenly her aunt and cousin appeared before her. She

jumped up in alarm when she saw the tears sparkling in Letty's eyes and the furious expression on her aunt's face.

"Sit down, you little slattern," hissed her aunt, pushing her down into the chair.

Katrina felt as if her face had been slapped. "What is it, Aunt? What in God's name is the matter?"

"You have disgraced us all," her aunt whispered harshly, her eyes bulging with fury. "Because of you, we shall never again be able to move in Society circles."

Letty gave a little sob and glared at Katrina.

"What in heaven's name have I done?" asked Katrina. "Will you kindly tell me, Aunt, what I have done to deserve this?"

"You surely did not think Lord Danville had taken a fancy to you, did you? It was a wager!" Her aunt spat out the word. "A wager! To think that I should live to endure this. And you, miss—you with your high and mighty airs, you played right into his hands. They all thought you such a freak that someone wagered Danville five hundred guineas he would not spend one half hour in your company. He, having no concern for his reputation, accepted."

"But he balked at the kiss," said Letty, with an ugly laugh.

"The kiss?" whispered Katrina.

"Yes," hissed her aunt. "Someone offered to double the wager if Danville kissed you in public. But it appears he could not bring himself to do that, despite his love of gaming!"

Katrina closed her eyes and clenched her hands together in her lap to still their trembling. "Can we go home now, if you please?" she whispered, feeling very sick.

"We are going home, but you will sit here until we have left this room. Only then may you follow us. I refuse to be seen in your company after what has happened."

Katrina's eyes flew open. "Oh, no, Aunt, I beg of you, do not leave me here on my own." She clutched desperately at her aunt's sleeve but was roughly shaken off.

Her aunt bent over her, thrusting her face close. "If you

dare to rise from that chair before we have quit this room, I swear I shall cast you out into the streets this very night."

Katrina, seeing the hatred in her aunt's eyes, could well believe it of her. She lifted her chin and sat up straight, giving her aunt a cool, unwavering look. "Very well. I shall wait."

With a great show of bravado, Aunt Bertha, with the sniffing Letty trailing in her wake, stalked out of the ballroom, nodding to her left and right as she went, as if nothing had occurred.

Katrina felt like a tiny sailboat in the center of a raging sea, which she had to negotiate before she could reach safe harbor. As the doors closed behind Letty and her aunt, she cast one quick look of loathing across the room at the Viscount's back, and then placing both hands flat on the seat of her chair and praying that her shaking legs would support her, she stood up.

For one horrible moment the room swung around her, and she was afraid that she would faint. "Don't be such a ninny!" she told herself sharply. She had never in her entire life fainted and was not about to now. She took a few deep breaths, as she used to do when she was about to sing at Branscombe Hall and, lifting her head and gazing directly in front of her, she began to walk slowly toward the stairs; they seemed to be miles away from her. For a few seconds panic engulfed her, and she had to fight the desire to pick up her skirts and run.

Although the music for a quadrille was playing in the background, the sound of shuffling feet was stilled, and the whispers seemed magnified to shouts in her ears. Someone laughed loudly and others tittered. Katrina's stomach twisted into a knot, but with legs that seemed weighted with lead and her heart pounding so hard she thought it would burst, she continued on, carefully mounting the stairs until she reached her goal. The two footmen opened the gilded doors . . . and then she was out in the hallway, with the doors safely closed behind her.

For a few moments she stood there, head swimming, but

then she straightened up and approached the footman at the head of the entrance stairway.

"Mrs. Vernon?" she asked. "She was departing in Sir Henry Pemberton's carriage, I believe." She was breathing heavily, as if she had indeed run the length of the ballroom.

"I'll ask the porter, madam," said the man. He returned almost immediately.

"Sir Henry gave orders that he wouldn't be leaving yet," he told her. "He put Mrs. and Miss Vernon in an 'ackney coach. They've gone, miss."

"Gone?" Katrina's heart plummeted. "You must be mistaken. They said they would wait for me. Inquire again, if you please."

"No mistake, miss. They've gone all right," he replied, giving her an insolent grin. She knew immediately that the story of the Viscount's wager must have already spread to the servants.

"Kindly have my cape brought to me and arrange a hackney for me," she ordered him in a cold voice, fighting the panic that threatened to swamp her. How could her aunt do this to her! Any moment now, others might leave the ballroom and find her there. "Hurry!" she told the footman.

"May I be so bold as to ask if you've any cash to pay for the coach, miss?"

"No, you may not," she said with icy fury. "And my name is Miss *Vernon*. Fetch me my cape and order me a coach immediately, or I shall report your insolent conduct to your superiors."

The footman was about to reply, when the ballroom doors opened and group of people came out, laughing.

"But the kiss, Danville. Damnation, the kiss!" someone shouted. "You reneged on the kiss!"

Katrina froze, and her hands gripped the balustrade rail.

"My dear Belmont," drawled a voice. "Although I am prepared to do almost anything you care to name for money, I must surely draw the line somewhere."

It was the Viscount's voice, but so changed that she hardly recognized it. The clear, incisive tones had been replaced by a languid drawl indicative of extreme ennui.

Intense shame swept over her as she remembered how she had poured out all her deepest feelings to him. At the same time she was assailed by bitter rage. How dare he humiliate her before everyone. Drawling, cynical devil! How she loathed him! She turned her back as furious tears filled her eyes.

"Your cape, miss," said the footman in her ear, and handed her the woolen cape with one extended hand and a sneer upon his insolent face. She waited until the group surrounding Danville had disappeared into one of the gaming rooms before she put on the cape.

"No 'ackneys to be 'ad, miss; nor chairs."

"There must be. How else will I get home?"

The footman shrugged. "Sorry, miss." He turned away to attend to another guest.

"May I be of assistance?" A corpulent, middle-aged man of distinguished appearance addressed her with a smile.

"I thank you, sir. But I—I am hoping to procure a hackney or perhaps a chair."

"You cannot be thinking of traveling alone without servants at this time of night, Miss Vernon."

Katrina stiffened. He knew her name, which meant that he, too, was most probably part of this whole cruel conspiracy. By now she was so wrought up that her mind was filled with visions of rapine and white slavery.

"Thank you, sir," she said icily. "I shall manage."

"I beg your pardon," said he. "I should have introduced myself. I am Sir Matthew Bainbridge. I believe I was at Oxford with your father: Christ Church. Was he not Robert Vernon, the youngest son of Sir Cedric Vernon?"

Relief flooded over her. "Oh, yes, indeed he was, Sir Matthew. Forgive me, but—"

"You need not explain, Miss Vernon. Lady Bainbridge saw what happened in the ballroom. She asked me to offer you our assistance if it were needed, whilst she said our adieus to Lord and Lady Merriot. Ah, here she is now."

A tall, formidable-looking woman, walking with a beribboned cane, came across the hall to them. "So you found her, Sir Matthew."

"Yes indeed, my dear. And, as you thought, Miss Vernon

appears willing to avail herself of our assistance. Would you believe, m'dear, she was thinking of venturing out into London alone?"

"I thought as much." Lady Bainbridge spoke in a brusque, almost masculine fashion, but she gave Katrina a little pat on the shoulder and a kindly smile. "I do not wish to insult you, Miss Vernon, but your aunt by marriage is a harpy, a harridan, selling her daughter to the highest bidder. I regret to say everyone thought you but another one of her little packets of goods, albeit not quite so well turned out."

Katrina had to smile. Lady Bainbridge was too forthright for her to take offense.

"I do not mean to make excuses," she continued in her loud voice. "London Society is not renowned for its heart and welcomes any diversion, however bizarre. But you must understand that we do not relish having to rub shoulders with the Mrs. Vernons of this world. I knew nothing of this infernal wager until Danville returned you to the ballroom. It was only then that we learned you were the daughter of Robert Vernon." She clumped her cane on the floor, and the footman hurried up to her. "Have orders been given for our carriage?"

He was all obsequious bows now. "It is already here, your ladyship."

"Good. Now, Miss Vernon, we shall drive you to your home, which is . . . ?"

"No, no. It is most kind of you, but we are lodging in Paddington, much too far away—"

"Nonsense! It is but a little detour for us. It is easy to see you are too innocent of London ways to suggest you could travel home alone."

In less than five minutes, Katrina was comfortably established in the richly appointed carriage and wrapped in a rug to fend off the November chill. By the time they were clear of the bustling streets of Mayfair, she had told the Bainbridges her history, including her father's death and her reception by her aunt and uncle.

"If I had but known about your father," sighed Sir Matthew. "But what of your grandfather, Sir Cedric? If you are not happy with your aunt and uncle in Paddington, will he not assist you?''

"Regrettably, no. I wrote to him when my father died. His eldest son and heir, my Uncle Basil, replied with an exceedingly cold letter, saying that his father was indisposed and unable to receive me. He enclosed sufficient funds for my father's burial, and that was all. He made no offer of further assistance, financial or otherwise. In any case, I believe there is very little money in the family.''

"Either dreamers or gamesters, the Vernons—or both,'' said Lady Bainbridge. "You seem a sensible enough girl, though. Must be the Scottish strain in you. But what are your intentions if you leave your uncle's house and protection?''

"I intend to seek employment as a music teacher or a governess, my lady.''

"The devil you do! Ha! I don't at all envy you. Most ill-treated breed of all, governesses—unless you are fortunate enough to find a position with nobility. The nouveaux riches use them worse than scullery maids.''

"I have no alternative,'' said Katrina. "I intend to be independent. My Uncle William has but a small allowance from his father and has to eke this out with his bookshop. My aunt hates Uncle William even to mention it; 'going into trade' she calls it, but it is the one place he is content. In truth, I believe he goes there to escape from my aunt.''

"I should not be at all surprised,'' said Lady Bainbridge. "And forgive me for saying so, but she has little cause to talk of trade. If I remember correctly she was the daughter of a mercer in Covent Garden, and not even a rich one at that. Now, my child, one word of warning from one who has lived in this world a long time.'' She leaned forward and tapped Katrina on the knee with her fan. "Until you are safely stowed away, keep well away from the likes of Lord Danville. He's a dangerous man.''

Katrina gritted her teeth at the thought of the man who had been the cause of her humiliation. "You can be assured that I will,'' she replied. But to herself she vowed she would have her revenge if ever she were given the opportunity.

"The rakehells like the Barrymores are easily spotted, but

Danville is another kettle of fish altogether. He can put on the elegance and charm until he has caught you in his net, and then—poof! You are undone.''

"Who is he? What is his background? I know nothing of him—except that I despise him!''

'He is a member of one of the oldest families in England— an excessively wealthy landowner who cares nothing for his estates or tenants or, for that matter, anything in this world but the pursuit of pleasure—and his music, of course.''

"His music?''

"Aye, his music. Other men collect snuffboxes or paintings. Danville collects anything to do with music: old instruments, music scores, the finest musicians in Europe—he had that fellow Haydn staying with him years back. And his latest mistress is an Italian opera singer with dark, flashing eyes— Mendoza or Manzini, or something of that sort. Danville has even gone so far as to become a musician himself. They say he's a fine performer on the pianoforte, although I wouldn't know anything about that; it's all nothing but a great noise to me.''

Despite her hatred of the man, Katrina's interest was aroused. "That is strange. I, too, am a musician; a singer.''

"Aha! So now you've given Danville a reason to be interested in you, but you'd have to be good at it. Are you?''

"Tolerably. But I have not sung for almost a year. Perhaps I cannot any more; I am almost afraid to try.''

"Well, well, at least you are safe from Danville then; 'tolerably' would not do for him. But when it comes to women, apart from bedding with them, Danville's a complete misogynist. He enjoys entrapping women only to toss them aside when he tires of 'em. It's a game to him. Some say this stems from his childhood. He had a cruel despot of a father whose cruelty drove his young wife to running away with a penniless actor. Beautiful girl she was, too. Young Justin was ten years old at the time and, so they say, adored his mother. And he had another misfortune when he was a young man, but that is no excuse for his behavior.''

"As I shall no longer be moving in his circle, it is unlikely that I shall encounter Lord Danville again.''

"That is a good thing. You don't want to be another name on his list."

"His list?"

Lady Bainbridge gave a bark of laughter. "Aye, his list of conquests. They say he has a notebook in which he keeps the names of the women he has deflowered." She poked her husband in the ribs, and he awoke from his half-sleep with a snort. "Ain't that so, Sir Matthew?"

"Eh, what's that?"

"Danville's list. Don't they say Danville keeps a list of his conquests?"

"Oh, that's mere rumor. Probably no truth to it."

"Well," said Katrina, "I can assure you that my name shall never appear on Lord Danville's list. He is an insufferable man!"

"That's the spirit!" cried Lady Bainbridge. "Don't you be taken in by his charm and elegant manner. It's all playacting. Danville could out-act the late, great Garrick himself, I can tell you. No wonder they call him 'Devil' Danville!"

The carriage, which had been bowling along at a comfortable pace, began to slow down, and Sir Matthew pulled down the window to peer out into the wet, misty night.

"Ah, this appears to be Paddington. Give me the direction, Miss Vernon, and I'll tell the coachman."

Katrina gave the directions to the little lane off Sussex Place, although she was reluctant for them to see the shabby little house.

"Now, Miss Vernon," said Sir Matthew, as they pulled up outside the privet-hedged house. "Tell me how we may be of further assistance to you? Come now, no protestations. It is the least I can do for the daughter of my old friend."

She had been about to protest that they had done more than enough, but his earnest expression encouraged her to beg another favor. "If Lady Bainbridge would be so kind as to look out for a suitable post for me, I should be eternally grateful. I cannot bear the thought of staying with my aunt one day more than is necessary and am determined to be independent of her."

"That I shall willingly do," said Lady Bainbridge. "Give

her a card with our direction on it, Sir Matthew, in case she should have need of our help again. But if you lose it, m'dear, Bainbridge House, Richmond, will always find us. We spend more time there than in London, nowadays." She leaned heavily on her cane, as if she intended to rise. "Now, let us go in. I have a few words to say to your aunt about leaving her young niece to find her own way home." She gripped the cane more tightly, as if preparing for combat.

The thought of an encounter between Lady Bainbridge and Aunt Bertha was too much for Katrina after the evening's ordeal. "No, no. I beg you, Lady Bainbridge, do not trouble yourself. I am sure my uncle has already remonstrated with her. I must thank you both again for your great kindness."

She quickly grasped Lady Bainbridge's hand and, having earnestly thanked them both yet again, she jumped from the carriage and ran up the pathway. She pulled the bell hard, hearing it jangle through the house, praying that Lady Bainbridge would not follow her. The door opened; she lifted her hand in farewell and the carriage drew away.

"So you did find your way home," was her aunt's frosty greeting, as she peered past Katrina to see who had driven her. "Who brought you?"

"Yes, I am home, my dear aunt," replied Katrina, her voice cold as marble. "No thanks to you. Sir Matthew and Lady Bainbridge carried me here on their way home." She walked past her aunt and started up the stairs.

Her aunt followed her. "Don't you play the hoity-toity miss with me. There's Letty crying her eyes out, making them all red, because Sir Harry refused to bring us home. He was too embarrassed to be seen with us."

"A good thing, too!" retorted Katrina.

"You saucy cat!" Before Katrina could duck, her aunt had struck her a glancing blow across the face.

Katrina reeled and almost slipped on the stairs. Furiously angry, she was tempted to strike back, but she drew herself up and gave her aunt a look of disdain. "You will not have me to trouble you for much longer, Aunt. I am looking for a situation, and as soon as I find a suitable one I shall leave and be glad never to return."

Any hopes she might have had of her uncle's intervention were dashed by the sound of his drunken snores from the study. He had obviously fallen asleep in there after they had departed, and therefore knew nothing of what had happened at the ball.

"If I have my way, miss," said her aunt, "you'll be out of this house by morning," and she flounced away to the kitchen.

Katrina made her way up to the little garret room next to the maid's. Although the room was cold and drafty and sparsely furnished, it was at least hers, and she could escape there whenever she felt she must get away. She knelt and peered out the rain-smeared skylight, watching the clouds drift across the crescent moon. After a while, she got up and dragged off the hateful gown and everything else but her underslip.

She shivered as her bare feet touched the wooden boards, and quickly climbed into the little truckle bed and pulled the meager bedclothes around her, wishing she had the cozy rug from the Bainbridges' carriage to keep her warm.

For a few minutes she lay listening to the rustle and squeak of the mice in the skirting boards, half-remembered conversation and snatches of dance music all jumbled in her mind. Then came vivid memories of a darkly handsome face and the scent of musk, the ardent touch of a man's hands circling her breasts, and the warmth and urgency of his hard body against her. The very thought made her body pulsate and, as she tossed and fretted, unable to sleep, Katrina knew with certainty that although she would probably never meet the insufferable Lord Danville again, it was not going to be easy to forget him.

Chapter Four

The following morning, Aunt Bertha and Letty set forth on a shopping expedition. Letty's mood of deepest despair had changed to squealing ecstasy upon hearing the news that Sir Harry's servant had called while she was asleep, bearing a note from Sir Harry, inviting her to go for a drive in Hyde Park later that afternoon. Only when Katrina had completed the long list of chores her aunt had left her did she confront her uncle, who could be heard stirring in his study around noon.

She was the only member of the family who could enter her uncle's study without being met with complaints about disturbing a man's peace and invading a gentleman's inner sanctum. Even she was not allowed to clean it; and the maid was permitted only to clean the grate and re-lay the fire, nothing else. Untidy piles of old copies of the *London Chronicle* and various periodicals littered the corners of the room, and there were books everywhere: on the floor, the chairs, the tables—and one particular pile was topped by a dish bearing scraps of shriveled meat and dried-up chutney glued to it. The fumes of stale wine and tobacco permeated the air.

"Sir down, Katy," said her uncle, "and tell me what is troubling you." He waved his hand to a chair and then closed his eyes and groaned, obviously suffering from his overindulgence the previous night.

Katrina removed the large tabby cat and a pile of dusty books from the chair and sat down. In her anxiety not to hurt her uncle's feelings, she was uncertain how to begin, but sensing that he would prefer the interview to be a brief one, she plunged in. "Uncle William, I am looking for employment," she announced.

He peered at her with red-rimmed eyes. "Employment? What type of employment?"

"A live-in post—as a governess or a music teacher."

"Do you mean that you intend to leave us, to live elsewhere with strangers?"

She hesitated, then replied: "Yes. I think it best, Uncle. You, I know, wish me to remain here, but an extra mouth to feed—I am sure that Aunt Bertha is finding it difficult to manage, especially as you both have such great plans for Letty and must fit her out accordingly. It would be far better for us all if I were to find a comfortable position with, perhaps, a young family. Then I could visit you often and yet not be a burden to you."

Her uncle bent to tap the cold ashes from his pipe onto the fireplace and slowly packed the pipe full of fresh tobacco. "I have never thought of you as a burden, Katy. I only wished to make my dead brother's daughter happy." He leaned forward again to light his pipe with a spill from the fire and then peered at her though a billow of smoke. "But you are not happy here, are you?"

She sighed. "No, Uncle William. I cannot lie to you. Aunt Bertha and I do not suit. Everything I do or say seems to irk her."

He put his hand to his forehead and rubbed it back and forth. "Ah well, she's not an easy woman," he murmured. "Not easy at all."

"So, that is settled," Katrina said briskly, not wishing to discuss Aunt Bertha with him. "I shall place an advertisement in the *Morning Post* and Lady Bainbridge also promised to be on the lookout for a position for me.''

''Lady Bainbridge?''

''Yes. I—I met her last night at the ball. She was kind enough to speak to me and promised that she would advise me if she heard of a suitable post.''

Her uncle laid down his pipe and got up, gathering up the cat which had curled itself on his knees. ''Promise me, Katrina, that you'll not leave here until I am assured that the position you have found is one that will make you happy.''

Katrina went to him and kissed his cheek. ''I give you my word, Uncle William. You have been so kind to me. Please do not think me ungrateful.''

''Of course not. You remind me greatly of your dear papa; affectionate but proud. It was his pride that killed him, remember that. There will always be a home for you here, however distasteful it might appear to you. But for now, Katy, I have a proposal that will get you out of the house and, therefore, away from your aunt's sharp tongue. I must undertake an inventory at the shop. I cannot locate anything at present! Will you come and assist me this afternoon and for the next few days?''

She hid a smile. Her uncle had been talking of doing an inventory of his books ever since she had arrived in Paddington. But it would be an opportunity to escape Aunt Bertha until her temper had cooled a little.

''I should love to, Uncle. We can take the advertisement to the *Post* on the way.''

That afternoon, they took a hackney coach to Charing Cross and then walked up the bustling Strand to Fleet Street, where they deposited the advertisement at the offices of the *Morning Post*. It was a fresh day, windy but sunny, and by the time they had walked up Chancery Lane and reached the little bookshop in High Holborn, Katrina felt brighter and healthier than she had for a long time. Not only the vigor of the walk but also the relief of getting away from Aunt Bertha lifted her spirits. She began to appreciate why her uncle gained so much pleasure from his bookshop.

They halted before the shop, while her uncle searched

through his pockets for the key. *William Vernon, Bookseller* read the faded gilt lettering above the dirty bow window.

Katrina pushed down the door handle, and the door creaked open. "Mr. Brown must already be here, Uncle. We do not need a key." Her uncle ceased his search, and they went inside.

The smell of dust and mildew filled her nostrils, and she sneezed. But there were also the smells of ink and old leather and the strong aroma of coffee from the coffeehouse next door, all of which she loved. Bidding her uncle's bespectacled young assistant a bright "Good afternoon, Mr. Brown," she went through the shop to the little room at the rear and, having dusted the large table, put down the wicker basket of food they had brought for a late luncheon. Then she tied a large white apron over her dress of plain gray kerseymere and put on a cap to protect her hair from the dust.

When they had completed their luncheon, they worked for more than two hours, Katrina taking down the books from the shelves and calling out the titles to her uncle, who sat at the high desk in the corner and wrote them down. Dusting each book carefully, she riffled through the pages for any odd scraps of paper, and then passed it on to Mr. Brown to replace it on the shelves she had already dusted.

During that time they had only one customer, a student from St. Paul's School who was searching for a cheap copy of Plutarch's *Lives*, his own having been torn apart in a scuffle, he told them with a grin. Katrina's arms were aching from stretching to the topmost shelves, and she was about to suggest that they send Mr. Brown for a jug of coffee from next door, when the door bell jangled again.

"Will you see to that, Katrina?" said her uncle.

She stepped down from the stool and, pausing only to smooth down her grimy apron, went to the front of the shop. In the fading light she could discern a gentleman looking at the books in the window, his back to her. He was tall, the curly-brimmed beaver hat he wore making him appear even taller.

"May I be of assistance, sir?" she inquired.

He turned with a start, his eyes widening. It was Viscount Danville.

She gasped, as if she had been doused with a bucket of icy water.

"Miss Vernon?" Obviously taken aback at finding her there, he swept off his hat and gave her a civil bow.

She recovered her composure instantly and, lifting her chin, directed a look of cold disdain and loathing at him, despite being uncomfortably aware of her grubby apron and cap.

For a moment they both stared at each other without speaking. It was enough time for her to notice that although Lord Danville was in driving clothes—a many-caped topcoat flung casually over a plain cutaway coat of bottle-green superfine, tight pantaloons, and top boots—he managed to maintain his air of extreme elegance.

She sniffed inelegantly, feeling a sneeze coming on and, unable to contain it, she turned from him and sneezed into her apron. When she turned back, her cheeks burning, it was to find Lord Danville holding out a fine linen handkerchief to her, a glint of amusement in his eyes.

"I will fetch my uncle to attend to you," she informed him icily, ignoring the handkerchief. "Although I believe it unlikely that we shall be able to provide you with whatever it is you are looking for."

"You have very little confidence, then, in Mr. Vernon's stock, Miss Vernon?"

She glared at him. "That is not what I meant, Lord Danville. We are in the midst of an inventory here, and it is therefore difficult to locate with ease any volume you might require. May I suggest that you try Hatchards. They're better stocked and infinitely more fashionable." She managed to make the last words a sneer, which was her intention.

"Ah, Miss Vernon," he said with a bow and a lift of an eyebrow she remembered so well, "you have forgotten. I hold the fashionable in contempt."

She flushed and bit her lip at this reminder of what had happened between them the previous night. "How could you have—" she said in a harsh whisper, her hauteur shaken, replaced by a mixture of emotions, which included acute embarrassment and, particularly, intense anger. "I will fetch my uncle," she said, turning away from him in an effort to regain her composure.

"One moment, Miss Vernon." He laid his hastily removed coat on the counter beside his hat and Malacca cane and then approached her, a serious expression in his cool gray eyes. "Before you summon your uncle, there is something I must say to you." Before she could stop him, he had taken her hand, his expression changing to a look of such burning intensity that she found it impossible to look away. "I had not expected to find you here," he said in a low voice, "But—"

"Katrina!" called her uncle. "Do you need me?" He appeared from around the corner.

Releasing her hand, Lord Danville quickly stepped back from her.

"May I present my uncle, Mr. William Vernon, Lord Danville," said Katrina. "I have not yet discovered what book his lordship is looking for, Uncle William; perhaps you—" She hurriedly escaped into the back room.

Her heart was galloping in her breast; she drew in several deep breaths to calm it. Damn the man! Why did he have such an effect upon her? She had intended to give him a thorough set-down and instead he had made her feel like a fifteen-year-old chit from the schoolroom—all trembles and blushes. She brushed some of the dust from her apron, but was determined not to remove it. Let the despicable man think what he liked; she was not about to observe the niceties for him!

"Katrina," called her uncle.

"Coming, Uncle William." She cast a quick glance in the piece of mirror hanging on the wall to insure that her cap was on straight. Then, taking another deep breath to further compose herself, she went to the front of the shop.

"Katrina, my dear, I have sent Mr. Brown next door for a jug of coffee and some cups. Lord Danville has kindly consented to take a cup with us. He requires a copy of Cellini's *Memoirs*. Was that the original or the translation, my lord?"

"The original. I have but one copy, and it is at Danville Hall. I need one for my town house."

Of course it would be the original his lordship would require, sneered Katrina to herself. What a dilettante! Dabbling in music, and pretending he could read Cellini with the smattering of Italian he had no doubt acquired on the obligatory grand tour in his youth.

"Now, let me see," said her uncle. "I am certain that I have seen that Cellini somewhere. . . ." He looked about him distractedly, as if he expected the book to materialize out of the air.

Katrina took his arm. "Would it not be better if I looked for the book while you take coffee with Lord Danville, Uncle?"

"I have an even better idea," said Lord Danville. "Why do not I assist you in your search? I fear I have come at an inopportune time. It is the least I can do."

So today my lord was playing at being humble! "Not at all, my lord," said Katrina. "We should not want you to get dust on your boots or clothing." She made it sound as if it were a sin to wear fine clothing and to have highly polished boots, and once again she was infuriated to see a quirk of amusement in his eyes and about his mouth.

"No, no, indeed. You are right, my dear." Her uncle beckoned her aside. "If you will excuse us a moment, my lord," he said, and led Katrina into the back room. "I wish you to entertain Lord Danville here, Katy, where there is a comfortable chair and a little fire for him. You must give him some coffee and engage him in conversation while I look for the Cellini. I am certain I have one put away somewhere. But where, that is the question, where? Imagine Lord Danville, a renowned connoisseur, coming here!"

"Is he indeed a connoisseur of books?" she asked in surprise.

"Oh, yes, indeed he is. The library at Danville Hall is reputed to be one of the finest in the country. I wonder why he chose to come to my little shop, especially when it is so out of his way?"

Katrina wondered at it, too. It certainly had not been to see her. His start of surprise when he saw her had been genuine enough. How she wished she had not come to the bookshop today! The last thing she wanted was to have to make polite conversation with Lord Danville. Yet, for her uncle's sake, she could not show the Viscount the door, as she would have wished. His patronage might be of great value, for although her uncle had no head for business and his books were poorly displayed, she knew that he was a knowledgeable collector.

"Ah, there is Mr. Brown with the coffee," he said, as the door bell tinkled, and he bustled her back to the front of the shop where Lord Danville was engaged in leafing through one of the books from the pile on the counter. "If you will accompany my niece, my lord, you can partake of some coffee, perhaps, while you wait? Mr. Brown and I will find the Cellini in no time. Shall I inform your man that you will be a while longer?" He peered out the window at the gleaming curricle outside.

"No need," drawled the Viscount. "He will wait."

Katrina took the steaming jug of coffee from Mr. Brown, who blushed as his hand touched hers. "I shall get the cups, Miss Vernon," he whispered, and went out again.

"My lord?" She led the way to the back room and set the jug of coffee on the table. "Pray be seated, Lord Danville," she said, not looking at him. She busied herself with removing the wrapping from the square of gingerbread she had baked herself that morning. When she looked up, it was to discover that the Viscount was still standing.

"Will you not be seated, Miss Vernon?"

"Thank you, not yet, my lord."

With much bowing to the Viscount and shy smiles at her, Mr. Brown brought in the cups and poured out the coffee, to which Katrina added cream. Then, bearing two cups of coffee and two slabs of gingerbread for himself and her uncle on a tin tray, Mr. Brown scurried out again.

"I do believe that young man is smitten with you, Miss Vernon," announced Lord Danville, as soon as Mr. Brown had gone.

Katrina, who had just taken a sip of coffee, choked and was taken with a fit of coughing. "How extremely observant of you, my lord," she retorted, once she had recovered. "Would you deign to take a slice of gingerbread, or is it, perhaps, too mundane, too prosaic, too *vulgar* for you? Forgive me, I cannot offer you oysters or—"

"Not at all, Miss Vernon. Besides, I rarely take oysters with my coffee, and then, naturally, only when they are in season. Is the gingerbread of your own baking? Yes? Then I must indeed sample it. How very stimulating to find so many diverse talents in one young lady!"

Why, when she despised him, did she find it so hard not to laugh at his absurdities? She reminded herself of his cruel humiliation of her at the ball. Yet here, in the dusty back room of her uncle's bookshop, it was difficult to reconcile the gentleman with his feet stretched out almost domestically to the fire, munching on her gingerbread, with the cynical, drawling gamester of the previous night.

Unable to think of anything to say to him, she sat down at the far end of the table and occupied herself with eating a piece of gingerbread, content for a moment to forget who he was and to enjoy looking at him; his clothes were of exquisite cut, fitting his fine figure like a well-made glove. She soon became aware that he, in his turn, was watching her, and she smiled ruefully to herself, certain that she did not make half so attractive a subject to look at.

He set down his coffee cup and cleared his throat. "I trust your journey home last night was a safe one."

She jerked her head up, the blood rushing to her cheeks, and looked for mockery in his eyes; she found none. His expression was bland, as if he wished merely to exchange polite chitchat, but an air of tension pervaded the room, warning her to tread carefully. She gave him a steady look "I should prefer not to discuss Lord Merriot's ball," she informed him, trying to match his emotionless manner. In an instant, his urbane expression had disappeared.

"It must be discussed," he said passionately, his eyes blazing. "I cannot leave unsaid all that—"

She gripped her hands together in her lap and raised her eyes to his. "It must be left unsaid, my lord. If you speak one more word about the Merriot ball, I shall leave this room.

I prefer to think that it never happened, that I was never at the ball. Is that understood?''

For a long moment his eyes locked with hers, and she saw in their depths an expression of concealed violence, almost of hatred, which quickly died away even as she looked, to be replaced by a cynical smile. "I am compelled to obey you, Miss Vernon. It is understood." He picked up his cup again and took a sip of coffee, looking at her above the rim of the cup. "May I ask if you have thought any more about your plans for the future?"

He seemed to have calmed down, and Katrina, anxious to dispel the frisson of danger in the room, determined to engage him in a safe topic of conversation. "Yes, indeed I have, my lord. This very afternoon I placed an advertisement in the *Morning Post* for a position as a governess or a teacher of music. I am hoping that it will produce some replies."

"Your uncle knows of this?"

"Oh, yes. He understands. I know it is not considered quite the thing for the granddaughter of a baronet to seek employment as a governess, but it is what I must do."

"If you will permit me to say so, Miss Vernon, you are a woman of exceeding courage."

"Am I indeed, my lord?" She looked into his eyes, and then away. "That man could out-act the great Garrick!" Lady Bainbridge had said. How true! For even now she could have sworn she saw nothing but sympathy and admiration in his eyes. More fool she! Thank God she knew his true character. She had heard the real Lord Danville in Lord Merriot's hall last night, stating in his affected drawl that there was nothing he would not do for money.

"You are pensive, Miss Vernon. Do you perhaps fear what lies ahead of you?"

"Not a whit, Lord Danville. Nothing that lies ahead of me could be half as bad as that which is behind me. I look forward to the future with the fervent hope that it will, at least, be better than the past."

"I am sure of it. I am also sure that there are people in this world who will sincerely wish to assist you. Despite my warning to you last night, Miss Vernon, not everyone is to be mistrusted.''

The platitude was ludicrous, coming from him. ''Do you think I do not know that, my lord? Although I am country bred I was not kept in seclusion. Even in a debtors' prison I met with sincerity and true friendship, more so than I have found in the artificial hothouse of Society.''

Her barb of sarcasm missed its mark, for he merely replied: ''I do not doubt it, for your disposition is such that it invites sincerity and kindness.''

How despicable he was, with his flattering little phrases, his slight smile and courteous inclination of the head toward her! She watched his hands, adorned with but one ring, a heavy gold signet, as they took out and opened his gold pocket watch. The gesture reminded her of the previous night, and she remembered that these same hands had touched and held her, arousing her and sending lambent fire throughout her body. Hating herself for even thinking of it, she hurriedly stood up, and he immediately rose from his chair. ''If you will excuse me, my lord. I—''

She was interrupted by her uncle's voice, and the next moment he bustled in, triumphantly holding up a book. ''Aha! I knew it! Here it is, my lord. And a fine copy, too. Dust it for me, Katrina, if you please.''

He handed her the volume with the red-tooled leather binding and gilt-edged pages. She dusted it and gave it to the Viscount, who leafed through it and then took out his quizzing glass to examine the title page and frontispiece.

''It is indeed a fine copy, Mr. Vernon.'' He seemed surprised and genuinely pleased. ''I am doubly in your debt. How much do I owe you?''

''Shall we say five guineas?''

''Only five? Are you certain? This is a rare edition and in excellent condition.''

''I paid but three guineas for it, therefore five appears a fair price.''

''Oh, Uncle William,'' protested Katrina. ''You will never make a good businessman.''

While they were completing the transaction, she wrapped

the book in brown paper and string. As she handed the book to the Viscount, his fingers brushed hers—not by accident, she was sure—and he smiled his rare, charming smile at her. She did not respond to it, but merely inclined her head in a slight acknowledgment.

"I trust that you will soon be comfortably settled in your new situation, Miss Vernon," he said, and made her a deep bow, more befitting a duchess than an assistant in a bookshop.

Her uncle accompanied Lord Danville to his curricle, and Katrina, peering through the window, saw them shake hands and watched as the pair of well-matched grays set off at a smart pace down the street.

"What a charming fellow," said her uncle when he returned. "Even shook my hand."

"And why should he not," she replied sharply, "considering you are a gentleman."

"Yes, yes, m'dear. But he was dealing with me in my capacity as a bookseller. Many gentlemen of less consequence than Lord Danville have not acted in so courteous a manner toward me. Strange; I had heard so many diverse rumors about the Viscount, some of them quite shocking, but none of them appeared to fit the man I met today."

"Hm!" Katrina bit back a scathing retort.

"By the bye, whilst we are talking of Lord Danville, Katrina, it appeared to me that his manner toward you seemed most amicable, almost as if you had made his acquaintance before today. And yet you, I felt, behaved toward him in a manner that I might describe as verging on the discourteous. And how did he know you were seeking a post?"

She took a deep breath and stretched up to dust an empty shelf above her. "We met at the Merriot ball last night," she replied, thankful that her face was hidden by the shelving.

"Ah, now I understand. He had been, let us say, indulging a little too generously last night?" He came to stand at the foot of the stool. "Do not think I meant to offer criticism of you, Katy. I have never known you to behave in anything but the most courteous manner, unless extremely provoked. Come down now. You have done more than enough for one day."

He helped her down from the stool and then sighed and shook his head, still holding her hands in his.

"I shall miss you greatly when you leave me, Katy. I almost hope that you will not receive any response to your advertisement."

Chapter Five

Her uncle's hopes were to be dashed, for the very next evening, when he and Katrina returned from the bookshop, it was to find a letter addressed to her on the hall tray.

"Delivered this afternoon by a slap-up servant in livery," declared Letty. "And there's a crest on the seal. Do open it, cousin."

It was a wonder that Aunt Bertha had not already done so, but the seal was so heavy that it would have been impossible to open the letter without breaking it. The paper was a fine bond as heavy as parchment.

Dear Madam, read Katrina. *With reference to your advertisement in this morning's "Morning Post," I am in need of a gentlewoman of good education to act as governess to my daughter. If you are interested in this position, I shall be at home to receive you at 11 A.M. tomorrow morning, the 27th instant, at the above address, when further details will be discussed.*

The letter was signed: *Lady Helen Standish* and the address read *Belvedere House, Cavendish Square*.

Letty snatched the letter from her and squealed when she

saw the address. "Why, that's the Earl of Belvedere. Lady Helen's his daughter. You remember, Ma. Mrs. Potter told us there was some great scandal years back when Lady Helen eloped with a curate."

Aunt Bertha took the letter and read it. A sharp "Ha!" was her only comment before she handed it back to Katrina and walked away.

Uncle William crooked his finger to call Katrina into the study, and then carefully closed the door and turned the key.

"This letter from Lady Helen seems most opportune. I must confess that I was concerned that you would be unable to find a suitable situation, but this might do, it might very well do."

He seemed distracted, ill at ease, his hands aimlessly tidying a book here, an ornament there. Katrina smiled at him but said nothing in reply, unwilling to acknowledge that she was agreeably excited by the prospect of being employed by the daughter of an earl, especially after Lady Bainbridge's warning against the evils of working for the nouveaux riches. She did not wish to evince too much enthusiasm for a position for which she might not prove suitable. She had, after all, lamentably few qualifications for the position of a governess.

Her uncle paced to the bow window and back again, obviously troubled. "Katrina. I did not wish to discuss this with you in the shop today, with Mr. Brown there. Indeed, I do not know even now how to broach the subject, but . . . As you know, I was averse to your leaving us and seeking employment, but after hearing what your aunt disclosed to me last night, I believe that it is, perhaps, the best thing for you to do."

Her heart sank. She could tell from his face what it would be. Why couldn't her aunt have kept her tongue still?

"I was most shocked, nay horrified, to learn what occurred at Lord Merriot's ball. It is no wonder you spoke so sharply to Lord Danville yesterday. By God! If I had but known the half of it, he would not have set foot over my threshold! How could a gentleman of such seeming charm and sense behave in so dissolute a manner?"

"Please, Uncle," she said agitatedly. "Do not concern yourself with it. I have already forgotten it."

"I blame myself entirely for insisting that you go to the ball and for not insuring that you were properly chaperoned. But, Katy, my dear girl." He took her hands and looked earnestly into her face. "What in God's name possessed you to spend so much time alone in the company of a stranger? Bertha tells me you were even seen to be holding Lord Danville's hand. I cannot believe that!"

She turned her face away. "Please, Uncle. If you truly hold any affection for me, discuss it no more. I have no excuses, no explanations for my conduct."

"There, there, child. Never mind, never mind. I did not mean to upset you." He patted her shoulder and then turned away to polish his spectacles on his coattail before pinching them onto his nose. "But I confess that I should feel more at ease if I knew you were to be established in a household where your abilities would be valued and where you would not be exposed to such insults. I only regret that I cannot provide you with the comfort of such a home," he added sorrowfully.

Katrina flung her arms about him. "Oh, Uncle. You have made me exceedingly happy. Just knowing that someone cares for me is enough." She kissed him and looked up into his face with a rueful smile. "Let us hope, though, that the news of my escapade at the Merriot ball has not reached Lady Helen's ears."

The following morning, her uncle accompanied her in the hackney to Cavendish Square, directing the cab to go around the square twice until it lacked one minute to eleven. Only when he had delivered her to the stately butler did he leave her, promising to return for her in one hour.

She was shown into the large morning room at the rear of the huge mansion. Although the room was sunny, the furnishings were heavy and dark, and the windows draped in a dark wine velvet which she found depressing.

A tall woman rose from the sofa and came forward to greet her. She was dressed simply in a morning dress of blue-and-white-striped cambric. "Miss Vernon? I am Lady Helen

Standish. Do pray sit down. Will you take chocolate, tea, or coffee?"

"Tea, if you please, Lady Helen."

Katrina sat down on the edge of her chair and watched as Lady Helen poured the tea. She was then offered a dish of brandy snaps by the maid, which she declined. Lady Helen smiled across the occasional table. She was far younger than Katrina had expected, perhaps eight or nine and twenty, and a beauty in the classical style: tall and graceful, full-breasted, with her ash blonde hair simply but artfully dressed. But, apart from imagining her draped in the flowing robes of a Greek statue, Katrina saw that the classicism ended there, for far from being cool and remote, Lady Helen's smile was warm and her manner gracious and friendly.

"Now, Miss Vernon," she said, when she had dismissed her maid, "to business. I understand that you are seeking a position as a governess. What I have to offer is not precisely the position of governess; it is more that of a general factotum—a companion for me, a nurserymaid and governess for my daughter, all combined. In particular I have need of someone with whom I would find myself compatible."

She looked about her at the vast room with its ornate ceiling and overwhelming furnishings, and wrinkled her forehead. "Contrary to what you might think from this house, I live a very simple life. My husband, Edward, is a clergyman with a comfortable but not at all substantial living, and the parsonage is fairly small. We could offer you only a modest remuneration, for I receive but a small allowance from my mother." She looked down at her hands and then clasped them together and looked up at Katrina with a faint smile. "And nothing at all from my father, barring our sons' school fees."

"I should require very little, Lady Helen," said Katrina. "So long as I have my bed and board."

"I would hope that what we are able to afford will be sufficient to allow you to dress modestly but well. Of course, you will have your own room and will take your meals with us. You will not be considered a servant, Miss Vernon. We have two female servants: Sally our housemaid, and our housekeeper, my faithful Jenny, who was my abigail before I was married. We have two sons, Richard and George, who are both at Eton; and our little daughter, Julia, who is to be your charge, is eight years old. The only recommendation I can offer is that we all live together in an extremely contented fashion, and would hope that if you join us you would be as content as we are." Her sapphire-blue eyes sparkled with good humor.

Katrina was charmed with her simple kindness and her evident desire to set her at her ease. "You will naturally wish to see references," she said hesitantly. "My friends in Dorset—" She bit her lip and began again. "My father—"

"I know your circumstances. You need not give me any explanation. Merely tell me your accomplishments, and I will see how they befit my plans for my daughter."

Lady Helen's knowledge of her background puzzled Katrina, but she went on to list her talents, praying that they would be sufficient, for she had taken a great liking to the beautiful woman before her. "I would be able to teach all facets of music: the pianoforte, singing, history, harmony, and theory. I am reasonably proficient in sketching and watercolors, but, I regret, not at all proficient in needlework." She gave Lady Helen a slight smile. "In truth, sewing is my weakest point. My French is fluent, and I have sufficient Latin and Italian to instruct your daughter, at least for the time you would be requiring my services."

"That is splendid," said Lady Helen. Which, thought Katrina, was a rather overenthusiastic response to such a meager list of accomplishments. "We live a quiet country life, with a few pleasant social gatherings. Parochial visits and meetings seem to engage much of our time. In truth, Miss Vernon, I am as much in need of a companion as anything else, and I have the feeling that we shall suit extremely well, so long as you do not mind living quietly."

"After four months of living in London, it is what I should like above anything." Katrina looked down at her lap, brushing away an imaginary speck of lint from her black silk dress. "London has given me little pleasure," she murmured.

"Do not condemn London out of hand, Miss Vernon. It

holds many delights—the opera, theater, concerts, which you, perhaps, have been unable to enjoy. But when would it be convenient for you to come and live with us, do you think?''

The interview had taken less than half an hour, yet she was already being asked when she could take up her new position. The thought of being able to leave the shabby house in Paddington and her Aunt Bertha almost immediately made Katrina's head spin. She was about to reply when she was brought up short by the knowledge that no actual mention had been made of her past circumstances. The thought of being accepted by this delightful woman and her family only to be rejected when they later discovered the truth made her determined to acquaint Lady Helen with her background. ''I must tell you, my lady, that my father—''

Lady Helen held up a slim hand. ''If it is to tell me that your father died in a debtors' prison, you need not continue,'' she said gently. ''You see,'' she said in response to Katrina's startled glance, ''I really am acquainted with all your circumstances. Now I shall repeat my question: When would you be able to come and live with us?''

This time Katrina had no hesitation in replying. ''As soon as you wish,'' she said gladly.

''You mean you would be prepared to come tomorrow? Capital! I have been visiting my mother here; she has been unwell but is now very much improved in health. I cannot wait to leave this dark mausoleum and return to Edward and Julia. Why do not we travel together to Buckinghamshire, then, and keep each other company? That is, if you are certain you are able to leave so soon.''

''Most definitely,'' said Katrina, no longer trying to hide her delight at the prospect.

''Very well. It is settled then. I shall be traveling in my father's carriage and shall call for you at your home at eleven o'clock tomorrow morning. Then we shall reach Buckinghamshire before nightfall.''

She bent to pour more tea, but then set down the silver teapot without completing the pouring, and lifted her face which, to Katrina's surprise, was suffused with a flush of seeming embarrassment.

"There is one more matter to be mentioned, Miss Vernon, that once alluded to need never again be spoken of between us. Please believe me when I tell you that it has no bearing at all on our mutual plans for the future. I know all about your contretemps at Lord Merriot's ball."

Katrina gave an involuntary start and her stomach clenched into a knot.

"I mention it for but one purpose: that you will not be constantly concerned that it may reach my ears and jeopardize your position. I know all about it, and it is already forgotten."

"You cannot possibly know all the circumstances. I—"

Lady Helen again held up her hand. "Ah, but I do, and you may therefore put it out of your mind immediately."

"Then it must have been Lady Bainbridge who told you," cried Katrina. "And that is why you also knew about my father and the prison. Now I understand!" She gave a sigh of relief. "I wondered how I could be so fortunate as to receive a response to my advertisement so quickly. It was Lady Bainbridge!"

Lady Helen nodded and smiled her warm, sweet smile. "So now all is known between us, and instantly forgotten. I mention it only because I wish us to be friends, not merely employer and servant, you understand?"

And Katrina, warmed by Lady Helen's natural and amiable manner, was certain that they would be.

But for the parting from her uncle, the next morning would have brought Katrina nothing but joy. She had packed her few belongings in a carpetbag—her black fustian dress, her old gray kerseymere, two shawls, one wrap, her underwear, nightwear, hose and footwear, a few meager toiletries, together with three books her uncle had given her: a calf-bound volume of Shakespeare's works, a treasury of poetry, and— "To entertain you," her uncle told her—a book by an anonymous author entitled *Sense and Sensibility*.

Her uncle said little to her when they parted, and she responded in kind, her heart being too full for words. As she was leaving the study, he pressed a purse into her hands. "I wish it were more," he whispered. "Hide it, quickly," and she hurriedly tucked it into the pocket of her pelisse, gave him a quick embrace, and ran out of the room before her emotions betrayed her.

"The carriage is here," shouted Letty.

Katrina gave her aunt a quick kiss on the cheek and murmured her thanks, and then embraced Letty, who wept profusely, as if she were losing a much-loved sister.

"Do write, cousin, and tell us about your adventures," she shouted, as Katrina hurried down the pathway.

The journey was far from adventurous. The carriage, luxuriously upholstered and very well sprung, was more conducive to sleep than excitement. And after a delicious luncheon at an excellent coaching inn at Beaconsfield, Katrina did in fact fall asleep.

When she awoke, it was late afternoon and beginning to grow dark. The rolling countryside and woods of Buckinghamshire passed by the carriage windows.

"We shall soon be home," said Lady Helen, stretching her legs before her. "We passed through West Wycombe a half hour ago. I do hope Edward will be home when we arrive."

Whatever scandal had attended Lady Helen's marriage, the fact that she mentioned her husband in almost every sentence she spoke led Katrina to believe that she was still very much attached to the Reverend Edward Standish.

They were now passing a fenced park, densely wooded, which stretched to the left of the narrow rutted road. A little further on they passed great iron gates and, on a rise, the dark mass of a vast manion, sparsely lit.

Lady Helen jerked down the blind.

"What place was that?" asked Katrina.

"That?" Lady Helen pressed her lips together. "Oh—you mean Danville Hall."

"Dan—" Katrina drew in her breath and held it for a moment, her heart beating rapidly.

Lady Helen gave her a long, apologetic look before she spoke. "I had hoped you would not have to know until tomorrow," she said with a sigh. "Pray forgive me for keeping it from you. We live by the village of Danville. The

Parish Church of St. Peter's and the parsonage itself are part of the Manor of Danville, although now a separate living. But you must not let it concern you. Lord—Lord Danville has two other country establishments and is rarely seen here. In truth, he spends precious little time at any of his country estates, as the unfortunate condition of his holdings here will attest to.'' The tone of her voice expressed more regret than anger and, for the first time, her beautiful face bore the remote, cold quality of a Greek statue. "It is extremely unlikely that you will ever meet Lord Danville here.''

Katrina sincerely hoped not. She sank back against the cushioned seat, her happy anticipation of seeing her new home marred by the knowledge that it was part of Lord Danville's estate.

Chapter Six

The sound of dogs barking broke through Katrina's reverie, and Lady Helen again raised the blind to reveal an attractive village with thatched cottages and two or three timber-framed houses. The carriage had slowed to a walking pace to avoid running down the dogs that barked at its wheels, and it rumbled over the cobblestones, past a pond and a stretch of green, beyond which stood a church with a large square bell tower. Then it turned down a short narrow lane and drew up outside a stone house whose brightly lit windows issued a warm welcome.

"We are arrived," announced Lady Helen, and she laughed as the door opened and a child in a white dress with a blue sash rushed out and ran down the gravel path, her ringlets bouncing. The carriage door was hurriedly opened and Lady Helen descended the step, leaving Katrina to observe her new charge in the light flooding from the house.

Julia was plump with golden hair and a shrill voice, which was presently squealing, "Mama, Mama!" as she tugged at her mother's skirts for one more kiss. Her father, having received his embrace, smilingly watched them.

Katrina descended from the carriage, feeling somewhat of

an intruder, with a tightness in her throat at the sight of this tender display of natural affection.

A slightly disheveled Lady Helen turned to her. "Miss Vernon, please forgive us," she said, laughing. "You will be thinking us sadly ill-mannered. May I introduce my husband, Edward. Edward, Miss Vernon."

Katrina held out her hand to the Reverend Edward Standish and immediately wondered if she should have curtsied. But he took her hand in a firm grasp and gave her a gentle, almost shy smile. He was of medium height with light brown hair and eyes and dressed in a dark brown coat which was well cut but not in the height of fashion.

"Welcome to our home, Miss Vernon," he said in a soft voice. "You must be fatigued from your journey. Pray go inside, and I shall join you later when I have made arrangements for the carriage and horses."

The parsonage was not large, but the hallway and parlor were furnished with such refinement and decorated with such delicacy, with light-colored wallpapers, that the effect was that of a house of far larger proportions. "Faithful Jenny," who was introduced to Katrina as Mrs. Bateman, was a tall, angular woman with a large white cap tied beneath her chin, so large that her face, with its thin nose, peered out from within its confines like a sharp-beaked bird from its nest. She acknowledged Katrina's smile with a brisk nod, nothing more, and took her pelisse and gloves from her. Here was one person who would need to be won over!

Julia would not be such a problem, for she was even now tugging at Katrina's hand to show her to her room. "Do come, Miss Vernon. As soon as Mama's message arrived, Jenny and I prepared it for you. It's Grandmama's room when she comes to visit us. Where will Grandmama sleep now Miss Vernon's in her room, Mama?"

"Probably in the boys' room. We shall manage. I had intended to offer you some refreshment, Miss Vernon, but my daughter seems determined you will see your room, and nothing will gainsay her. Perhaps, in any case, you would prefer to freshen yourself after the journey? I will have Sally, our maid, bring you hot water and John will carry up your bag." Lady Helen took a candlestick from the hall stand and led the way up the oak staircase, with Julia bounding up behind her and Katrina taking the rear.

She was shown to a bedroom at the back of the house. An oil lamp burned brightly on the round table, warmly illuminating the room, and a welcoming fire glowed in the fireplace. "Why, it's lovely," gasped Katrina, taking in the ivory paper sprigged with pale green flowers and the bed draped in a matching fabric. She had not expected to be assigned such a comfortable and attractive room.

"The window has a good view of the river and woods of Danville Hall, which run behind the village," Lady Helen told her. "Now we shall leave you to get settled. Come along, Julia. Pray come down whenever you please, Miss Vernon. We are having only a cold collation tonight, so there is no need to change for dinner."

Which is a good thing, thought Katrina as the door closed, considering I have only one other good dress. She would have to use a portion of her uncle's money to purchase a new one as soon as possible.

Shortly after John, the outdoor servant, had carried up her bag, a knock came at the door and a shy, slight girl of about sixteen, who introduced herself as Sally, the maid, bore in a jug of steaming water. "Will there be anything more you'd be wanting, miss? " she asked.

"No, thank you, Sally." She gave the girl a warm smile and received in return a sweet smile which brightened the girl's plain and rather sallow countenance.

When the door closed, Katrina sank into the little tub chair by the fire, grateful to have a short time to herself for reflection. She was certain to be content here, she thought, as she looked about her; the room was even more pleasant than her own in Dorset had been. She smiled at the portrait above the mantelpiece: a blue-eyed child with blonde curls holding a fluffy white kitten with a pink ribbon around its neck. A likeness of Julia, perhaps; or more likely of Lady Helen as a child, for the artist, if she could read the signature aright, appeared to be George Romney. Although Julia was used to having her own way, she reflected, she seemed a malleable child, eager to please. Mrs. Bateman had been less inclined to welcome her arrival. No doubt she saw her as an intruder in the family circle, neither a servant nor a member of the family, a thankless position, as Lady Bainbridge had been so quick to point out. So, remembered Katrina, had Mary Wollstonecraft in her treatise on the education of daughters. Well, she would have to work on Mrs. Bateman. If she could learn to live with Aunt Bertha, she could adapt to anyone!

But beneath her feelings of contentment with her new home there lurked a presentiment which disturbed her, like a hand clutching at her heart. The proximity of Danville Hall, the fact that the village itself and all the surrounding property were owned by Viscount Danville troubled her beyond measure; and so also did her recollection of Lady Helen's demeanor when she talked of the Viscount, almost as if she had cause to fear him. Yet her husband was an incumbent in the Manor of Danville, albeit with a separate living. It was most puzzling.

She rose to draw back the winter curtains of pale green fustian and opened one of the windows. Outside, the wind riffled through the trees in the wood that lay beyond the large garden. She could see only the dark mass of trees stretching back to merge with the velvety evening sky. And as she listened to the sounds of early winter—the skittering of leaves across the garden paths, the sighing of the wind in the eaves—she admitted to herself that what troubled her most was that when Lady Helen had told her that it was most unlikely she would ever meet Lord Danville here, she had felt deep within her a twinge—no, a positive dart—of disappointment. The memory of his lean, hard body pressed to hers, his smoldering eyes, was still fresh in her mind. After all, it was but four days since the Merriot ball. Mentally taking herself to task for this odious daydreaming, she jumped from her chair and set about tidying herself for supper. She took up the copper ewer and poured water into the washbasin of white china decorated with pink flowers and green leaves. Memories soon fade, she told herself sternly as she scrubbed her nails. Once they had, she would be rid of the arrogant, despicable Lord Danville.

The thought was both a welcome and a melancholy one!

After a most congenial evening spent with Lady Helen and Mr. Standish, which served to strengthen her first impression that she was most fortunate in her employers, she repaired early to her room and slept tolerably well, taking into consideration the fact that it was a strange room and that she had also become unused to the sounds of the countryside. She vowed that a screech owl was perched on the roof directly above her room all night!

The next day, having attended matins in the small Gothic church and then breakfasted, she spent the entire day in becoming acquainted with Julia. She was pleased to discover that her charge had already received excellent schooling from her parents. She was also relieved to be told over dinner that evening by Mr. Standish that she need not teach Latin to Julia, as he intended to tutor his daughter in both Latin and religious studies.

"You look relieved, Miss Vernon," he said with a smile.

She returned the smile. "I am, Mr. Standish. Although my father was a master of the classics, I was not one of his most apt pupils. A piece of unseen translation I could construe tolerably well, for I always had a lively imagination, and once I had the gist of the story could guess at half the words. But Latin verbs and declensions—" She shook her head ruefully.

He laughed out loud at this. She liked Edward Standish. Although he was generally quiet and solemn, as befitted a country clergyman, there was a readiness to laugh and a twinkle lurking in his light brown eyes which made her understand how he could be attractive to some women. But she was not one of them, for as a *man* he was not to her taste; he was too quiet, too unprepossessing. It was not his lack of looks, for he was tolerably handsome for a clergyman. No, it was more his lack of drive, of ambition, of *pride*. She could never envisage Edward Standish rising to the position of archbishop, for instance, or even, for that matter, bishop. He was too modest and, had the idea been suggested to him, would most probably have laughed his warm, comfortable laugh. Marriage with the Reverend Edward Standish would be just that, warm and comfortable, but never exciting.

As she watched Lady Helen presiding over the dinner table, she wondered if she ever missed the excitement of life in London—the balls, the Opera, the theater—and decided, looking at that classic countenance, that she probably did not. Despite her beauty, Lady Helen seemed far more at home here in the small parsonage with but one indoor servant, one part-time outdoor man, and a housekeeper, than she had in her father's mansion in London. Katrina decided that although, if *she* were in Lady Helen's place, she would have missed the lively excitement attendant on being an earl's daughter in Society, there was no need at all to pity Lady Helen. She was perfectly content.

The following morning, Mr. Standish was to work on his sermon at home while Julia made macaroons in the kitchen with Mrs. Bateman. Lady Helen intended to occupy the morning in making parochial visits, taking John, the groom-cum-gardener-cum-coachman, with her to drive the gig.

It was obvious that her husband was apprehensive at her going. "I wish you would not, my dear," he told his wife earnestly, as she tied on a pretty blue velvet bonnet, which framed her face in a most becoming fashion. "You know there have been disturbances in Pudsey Lane recently, and only last week one of the gamekeepers almost caught a poacher in the man-trap in the woods, and he says he was certain it was Dick Foster, for he ran awkwardly with a limp, like Dick. I also fear the danger of disease. You should not, you really should not take such risks, for the sake of Julia and the boys, if not for me. Why not visit Mrs. Burton this morning? She, I hear, has been unwell all week."

"Mrs. Burton has a maidservant and is perfectly able to take care of herself." Lady Helen briskly drew on her plain tan leather gloves and looked into her husband's eyes. "You know I must visit these poor people," she said softly. "If I do not, who will? They need me; Mrs. Burton does not."

"May I come with you?" asked Katrina. She had been standing uncertainly in the hallway, unsure what she was expected to do.

"I am hesitant to ask you to accompany me," said Lady Helen. "You have heard already what Edward has to say. All of it, I regret to tell you, is true. The better class of tenantry have their own money to keep up their houses, but the cottagers' homes are in an appalling state, with no sanitation whatsoever but a fetid gutter running down the center of the lane, where the children play in its filth."

"Can nothing be done to improve their conditions?"

Immediately, Lady Helen's expression changed to the marble look Katrina had seen before, and she turned away to examine the large wicker basket covered with a white cloth that stood on the hall stand. At the same time Edward Standish busied himself with choosing an umbrella for his wife from the same stand.

"Surely Lord Danville has been made aware of the situation?" Katrina said hotly, surprised at their attitude.

"He is so rarely here," said Lady Helen lightly.

"His agent is aware," said Edward Standish.

To her amazement, they both shrugged, and she realized from their expressions that the subject had been brought to a close.

"I will come with you," she insisted.

"Very well," said Lady Helen. "I shall welcome the company. You had best change into old clothes, for it is not wholesome in the cottages, and our clothing must be fumigated when we return."

Katrina ran upstairs and put on her oldest dress, the same old gray wool she had worn most of the time in prison, and gathered up the old wool-flannel cloak she used to wear on long winter rambles in Dorset. She paused to look at herself in the long mirror and saw a pair of large, bright eyes beneath the short hair which curled softly around her face after her diligent use of the curling tongs before church. Despite their doubtful destination, she looked more content, more alive and sparkling than she had for a long time.

Her enthusiasm was short-lived, however, for once John had driven the gig through the village, past women who smiled and waved and men who doffed their hats to the vicar's wife and her companion, the view became more and more depressing, culminating in two rows of flintstone cottages with indifferent thatching facing each other across the "fetid gutter" of which Lady Helen had spoken. The stench was overpowering, and Katrina recoiled at the sight of a boy in a ragged shirt sailing a roughly hewn wooden boat on the stinking water.

"Would you prefer to wait for me in the village?" asked Lady Helen. "I could send John back there with you."

"Of course not. You forget I am not one of your delicate females. I am used to worse things than this."

Lady Helen smiled and squeezed her hand. "I can see we are going to deal famously together. Before we enter, allow me to acquaint you with Meg Foster's history. She is dying— of consumption, I believe. She was once a maid at the Hall and is a woman of intelligence, which makes her situation even harder for her to bear. Dick, her son, is seventeen and has a malformed hip which makes him lame. He can read and write, but, alas, can find no employment but the odd job we and some of the villagers give him; not enough to drag himself out of this place. I tell you this so you will not be taken aback, for young Dick Foster can appear most insolent to those who do not know him."

As Lady Helen descended from the gig, it was plain to see that the inhabitants of the Lane welcomed her, for their sullen faces lit up when they saw her, and they greeted her with a deference which, Katrina thought, would not have been as evident had others been visiting them—the lord of the manor, for instance. The thought of the elegant Viscount in this squalid place, looking down from his considerable height and turning up his fastidious nose at its inhabitants, sent such a wave of fury through her that she quite shook with its vehemence; and she wished she had the same elegant Viscount before her at this very moment, to tell him exactly what she thought of him!

They had to bend to enter the Fosters' cottage, which lay toward the end of the terrace. Katrina had picked up her skirts to walk down the lane, but when she entered the dark cottage she found that here, at least, the floor had been swept clean and the room smelled as fresh as was possible with two people living and eating and sleeping in it. The lad who had been sitting at the small, bare table scrambled to his feet. He was stocky and broad-shouldered, with a mop of brown curly hair, and Katrina saw as he approached that he walked with a lurching gait.

"Good day, Dick," said Lady Helen. "How is your mother today?"

"Good day, your ladyship. She's much the same. Neither bad nor good." He glanced over at the emaciated woman who lay in the small wall-bed, covered by a faded quilt. "It's her ladyship, Mother. Come to visit."

Lady Helen approached the bed and began to talk in a low voice to the woman, leaving Dick Foster to eye Katrina questioningly.

"Good morning," she said to him. "I am Miss Vernon."

He gave her a nod, but said nothing, merely indicating, with another curt nod in the direction of the only chair in the room, that she sit down; he, not waiting until she was seated, sat down again on the bench by the table and resumed his work.

"What are you doing?" she asked him, seeking to break the silence.

"Mending harness," was the brusque reply.

"Lady Helen tells me you read and write." A second later she wished she had kept silent, for her words seemed to have touched a nerve.

"Aye, an' much good it does me, miss, as you can see. What good's book-learnin' to me, I ask you? No job, nor prospect of one, nothing! With me mother sick, living in one room with water coming in through the roof." He rasped a file savagely across the metal of the harness, as if it were someone's throat he was cutting. "Once we had a right, tight little cottage with two rooms, hard by the common, where the wind blew fresh and free. An' our own cow an' chickens, with grazing rights for the cow and as much free firewood as we could gather, and freedom to snare rabbits. Now our rights are gone, along of everything else, and the common's been enclosed with paling, by order of Lord High and Mighty

Danville, and it's men they snare in the woods now, not rabbits—''

"Dick, be still," said a quavering voice from the bed. "You keep your mouth shut, Dick Foster, you hear me? Let the lady be."

"Can you not appeal to Lord Danville's agent?" Katrina said quietly, determined to pursue the matter.

"Danville's agent!" He spat perilously close to her feet. "Mr. Carlton? For one thing, he's never here, always up in London on some pretext. For another, in spite of his smarmy, kiss-your-hand ways with the nobs, he'd have us all shot down afore you knowed it, if he had his way." He leaned closer to her, and she recoiled from the wild look in his eyes. "But don't you worry none, miss. One day I'll get them both, Danville and Carlton, and it'll be worth the hanging for."

His blue eyes blazed with a fanatical expression that made her more afraid for him than for his intended victims, and she was much relieved when Lady Helen pronounced she was ready to leave.

"You see now why I warned you against Dick Foster," she said, as they drove back to the parsonage. "But he is harmless. It is merely hot-blooded yough."

"Do you think so? I am not so easily convinced that he is harmless, but I fear it is he who will be the most harmed. I feel most strongly for his unfortunate situation."

"Yes, so do I. I am afraid that giving him a smattering of education was one of the worst things that could have happened to him. Not only did it give him a thirst for more, it also made him realize the extent of his degradation. What is more," Lady Helen lowered her voice so that John could not hear, "it is said he is the bastard son of one of the late Viscount's friends, for Meg Foster was a maid up at the Hall, as I told you, and was dismissed, it is said, when her condition was discovered."

Katrina could now readily understand the reasons for Dick Foster's bitterness and, in her thoughts, she vented her indignation on the head of Lord Danville and his father, who had apparently been as dissolute as his son, to turn out a poor maidservant who had been ravished by his friend.

And as she took up a quill pen to write to her uncle in her room that evening, she was seized with a passionate determination to do whatever lay in her power to come to the aid of Lord Danville's unfortunate tenants; for, despite their evident compassion, Edward Standish and his wife seemed inclined to provide them with nothing more than soup and soothing words.

Chapter Seven

William Vernon's reply to his niece's letter was delivered to her at the beginning of December. In sprawling handwriting that was almost indecipherable, he gave her all the news of the town: The Regent had severely sprained his ankle while performing the Highland Fling—*a sight I must admit I regret not seeing!* added her uncle. Katrina smothered a giggle as she read it, imagining the now exceedingly portly Prince in a Scottish kilt. The rift between Beau Brummell and the Prince was widening, with the ton lining up in opposite camps. *But a prince is a prince whatever happens,* penned Uncle William, *and so I fear if Brummell does not soon make amends it will be the end of him.* He gave her little family news, mentioning only that Letty had been at Covent Garden with "that pup, Pemberton," the previous night, and had succumbed to a fit of hysterics when her father complained at her coming home at two o'clock in the morning. *I am sadly missing you, my dear niece,* he added, and tears sprang to Katrina's eyes as she read it. "Dear Uncle William," she whispered.

There was a hurried postscript squeezed into all four corners of the page: *Danville has commissioned me to find half a dozen or so obscure books which I shall have to travel*

*the length and breadth of England to find. He has undertaken
to cover all my expenses. By the bye, what an extraordinary
coincidence that your new post should be in his country, but I
understand he goes so rarely to his rustic estates you will
have little to fear on that account!*

Katrina had wondered at it, too, especially as Lady Bainbridge
had warned her so vehemently against Lord Danville, but
then she, too, must have known, when she recommended her
to Lady Helen, that the Viscount rarely visited Danville.

It was a dry day with a fresh wind blowing, but no sign of
rain; an ideal day for walking. And so, having spent the
morning in lessons with Julia and the early part of the
afternoon helping to decorate the church for Advent, she was
delighted when Lady Helen suggested that they walk up to
the Hall to return Mrs. Talbot's wicker baskets, which had
been sent down from the Hall filled to overflowing with
greenery for the church. Mrs. Talbot was the housekeeper at
Danville Hall, a woman of superior breeding, whom Katrina
had instinctively liked when she had first met her in church.

By the time they had reached the gatehouse of the Hall,
Julia was already complaining of feeling tired.

"Oh, Julia, you cannot be tired so soon," said her mother.
"We have walked not much more than half a mile."

The gates stood half open, but when they called out and
knocked on the gatehouse door, there was no reply.

"Smith must have been called away. Let us go in." And
they made their way up the long driveway, trying all the while
to ignore Julia's complaints that her feet were hurting and she
was getting blisters on them.

This was Katrina's first visit to Danville Hall, and she
looked about her with eager anticipation. The driveway was
over a mile in length, lined with stately poplars that stood like
sentinels all along it. On both sides were stretches of natural
parkland, more attractive to her eye than any formal garden.
But when she mentioned this to Lady Helen, she was told that
there were formal gardens at the rear of the Hall. At the end
of the avenue of trees, on a rise, stood the mansion itself; it
was not of contemporary design, but had been built by one of
the Viscount's ancestors in the early seventeenth century.

Danville Hall was three stories high and of noble proportions. Its classical symmetry of line was saved from appearing too austere by the natural warmth of the material with which it had been built, red brick that had darkened with age. And in tasteful contrast with the deep red were the white oval niches containing black marble busts that divided the windows of the ground and first floors.

They were about to mount the wide stone steps when Lady Helen clutched Katrina's arm. "Oh, good God!" she exclaimed.

Katrina turned in alarm, to find the tall figure of Lord Danville approaching from the rear of the house. "Oh, God," she whispered, echoing Lady Helen, who stood white-faced, breathing hard, as the Viscount drew near them. She felt Lady Helen's fingers tighten on her arm.

"Your servant, Lady Helen; and yours, Miss Vernon." He inclined his head to them both as if this meeting were an everyday occurrence. "And, of course, *yours* Miss Julia!" he added with great emphasis, and took the delighted child's hand and kissed it.

His lean figure was encased in riding clothes: a coat of bottle-green with biscuit-colored breeches and gleaming top boots. He had removed his hat and the winter sunlight glinted on his dark hair, which the wind had ruffled slightly, as if a woman's fingers had run through it. There was a glint, too, of amusement in his eyes as he surveyed them. How foolish we must look, thought Katrina, two reluctant females and one adoring child; for Julia had immediately succumbed to his charm and was busily telling him how they had been setting up the crib and decorating the church with branches of yew and holly boughs. To his credit, he was listening to the child, or at least gave the *appearance* of so doing. A consummate actor, indeed! thought Katrina.

She straightened her shoulders and lifted her chin, determined that he have at least one female not in awe of him, for Lady Helen seemed to have been struck dumb. "We were on our way to return these baskets to Mrs. Talbot and shall not detain you, my lord." But they were not to escape so easily, for Mrs. Talbot herself now appeared in the great doorway, with Jarvis, the butler, beside her.

'You cannot possibly walk all the way back to the parsonage without pause for refreshment and to warm yourselves,'' said the Viscount.

"No, no," muttered Lady Helen. "There is no need—"

"But of course there is need," cried he. "The poor child is cold and weary and, no doubt, hungry. Are you not hungry, Miss Julia? And, besides, there are some new kittens in Mrs. Talbot's parlor."

That was inducement enough! "Kittens! Oh, Mama, please may I see them? Please!"

Lord Danville's eyes caught Katrina's, and she had to smile at the gleam of triumph in them. The man was a devil all right; but, oh, Lord, what a handsome devil! As she followed the defeated and silent Lady Helen up the steps, she was intensely aware of the Viscount behind her. His closeness, the very scent of him, set her heart racing and a warmth flooding her body. If only we hadn't come here today! said her mind. How have I lived all this time without seeing him! cried her senses. And how glad she was that she had curled her hair that morning and trimmed her bonnet with a cherry-red ribbon, to brighten her attractively cut but colorless new charcoal-gray gown.

She had seen from the glowing look he had given her that he found her attractive, and as they mounted the last step he took her elbow lightly in his hand, his touch sending a dart of pleasure through her, a feeling that continued to vibrate even after he had released her.

When they stepped inside, their voices echoed in the great hallway. It was a striking mixture of the old and new, with a black and white marble-tiled floor partially covered by a vast Axminster carpet and, around the walls, marble statues in various states of undress.

"There is a fire burning in the library," said the Viscount. "Won't you go in? And perhaps some tea and hot chocolate, Mrs. Talbot?"

"Certainly, my lord." The housekeeper was already moving away to carry out his request.

"Thank you, my lord," said Lady Helen in a colorless voice, at last appearing to have found her voice, "but I have matters I wish to discuss with Mrs. Talbot; the parish Christmas party, you know. Why do not I take refreshment in her parlor with Julia while you show Miss Vernon the library?''

Katrina looked at her in amazement. Lady Helen must surely have taken leave of her senses to talk of leaving her alone, unchaperoned, with the Viscount in his own house! She was about to utter a polite protest when Lady Helen hurriedly added: "It is a truly magnificent library, Miss Vernon. I am convinced you will be extremely impressed by it," accompanying this recommendation with such an expressive pleading look that Katrina had no alternative but to acquiesce, while silently cursing Lady Helen's strange reluctance to be in the same room as Lord Danville.

She allowed herself to be ushered into the library, wondering if she should be concerned at the ominous thud of the heavy oak doors as they were closed by the footman who had bowed her and the Viscount in. But once inside she could not withhold a cry of pleasure. "Oh, it is magnificent!" She turned eagerly to Lord Danville, who smiled at her reaction.

"It pleases me greatly that my library should meet with *your* approval." The emphasis sent a flush into her cheeks, and she turned from him to look more closely at the room.

The library was all browns and reds. The oak paneling, the leather bindings, the log fire in the great fireplace itself, all combined in this warm color scheme. The books were stacked from floor to high ceiling and divided horizontally, at the first-floor level, by a gallery wide enough to permit chairs and small tables at intervals around it. A most intimate setting for solitary reading—or a cozy *tête-à-tête*! On the ground floor were comfortable sofas and chairs and large round tables, one with a massive portfolio of prints lying open upon it. She was tempted to dash from shelf to shelf to take in as much as possible while she was there. The very smells were warm and enticing: leather and ink and the fragrance of burning logs. The room invoked a feeling of almost sensuous pleasure in her which, she decided, could in itself be a great danger, quite apart from the threat of being alone with Lord Danville.

He spoke. "Will you not come nearer the fire, Miss Vernon?" He handed her to the sofa by the fire and stood by the fireplace with one foot on the hearth rail, displaying his fine figure to advantage, yet seemingly unaware of the mixture of grace and masculine arrogance he presented. "Your walk must have made you cold," he said.

"And hungry?" she asked pointedly, unable to resist that allusion to his seduction of little Julia.

He laughed outright, displaying even white teeth. "Touché, Miss Vernon!" A devilish look danced in his gray eyes. "She fell for it, did she not?"

"Especially the kittens. That was a master stroke!"

"I cry pax, Miss Vernon, and admit I was determined to entice you into Danville Hall."

"Why?"

"I had forgotten how blunt you can be!" His eyes darkened and a slight, sensuous smile touched his lips. "Because I wished to see how you looked in my house. Is that reason enough?"

So now he was even going so far as to consider her for the post of his mistress! She flushed but did not turn her head away. "And did I pass muster, my lord?"

"Indeed you did, Miss Vernon." His eyes caressed her while one long-fingered hand played with his quizzing glass, which he did not raise. He made an attractive picture; the elegance of his dress and deportment were not today marred by any contrived air of languor or ennui. On the contrary, the intensity of his expression, the tension of his body, the taut thigh muscles, made Katrina think of some exotic panther ready to spring.

And am I to be his prey? she wondered, and was determined to change the tenor of their conversation.

"I have been reading such a highly amusing new novel," she told him brightly. "*Sense and Sensibility*. I do not know the name of the author. It merely says 'By a Lady.' Do you know of it?"

He gave her a long look before replying, as if he recognized her stratagem, and then, conceding defeat, he cast her an amused smile and sat down in a nearby chair, crossing one long leg over the other. "Indeed I do. I have a copy of it in this room. The Regent is said to be greatly taken with it and has asked to see any more books the author might write.''

''Oh, are there to be more? I would so much like to read another, for I find her writing not only amusing, but *true*.''

''And which do you consider yourself, Miss Vernon? Sense or sensibility? Sense, I should imagine. Although at times I have the dinstinct impression your passions betray you into sensibility.''

She was determined not to be drawn into any more conversation of a personal nature and, having accepted a glass of amontillado from him, she again steered away from personalities by saying how picturesque she found the park and the exterior of Danville Hall.

''But you have not yet seen the half of it. There are the ornamental gardens and the woods and river; many acres, all awaiting Miss Vernon's inspection—and approval. Of course by now you will have seen the village and most of the nearby environs.''

Like an icy blast of north wind, a coldness swept over her. She set down her glass and picked up a book from the table before her and examined it, but her eyes registered neither the title nor its author. ''Yes,'' was her only response.

''And what is your impression of Danville?''

She could not avoid such a leading question, and yet she wished with all her heart that it was avoidable, for to answer it meant ending the warmth, the understanding that was presently between them. But answer it she must; she had made a solemn pledge to herself.

''My impression is that Danville is a paradise for the well endowed and a hell for the unfortunate poor,'' she told him in a cool, clear voice.

His eyes narrowed. ''Meaning?''

''Meaning that your poorer tenants, your cottagers—especially those in Pudsey Lane—are living in appalling conditions, in squalid hovels, whilst you totally ignore their petitions.''

She flung her head up and looked directly at him. Only by a tension about his jaw and a slight line of red over his cheekbones did he register that he had heard her words. He raised one dark eyebrow at her and assumed the cynical expression she remembered so well. Uncrossing his legs, he slowly got to his feet and leaned one elbow on the mantel-shelf, raising his quizzing glass to look at her.

She, too, tightened her jaw, mentally girding herself for battle. "You do comprehend what I am talking about?" she demanded heatedly, as he said nothing, but continued to examine her through his glass.

"Oh, indeed I do, Miss Vernon," he drawled. "You have undoubtedly been visiting my more unfortunate tenants with Lady Helen."

"Yes, I have. And if you were to inspect them yourself, I am convinced you would be as shocked as I at their condition!"

"Oh, do you really think so?" he said in his infuriating drawl. "Although I am most reluctant to argue with you on the subject of the condition of my estate, I am forced to remind you, Miss Vernon, that my affairs are none of your business. Nor, for that matter, are they mine. They are the concern of my agent, Mr. Marcus Carlton. Perhaps you would wish to give him your instructions regarding the management of my estates?"

Goaded by his sarcasm, she raised her voice. "I am amazed that even a—a man of your sort would close his eyes to the conditions of such a—a slum as Pudsey Lane."

"A man of my sort?" Again, the cynical, mocking smile. "You have an unfortunate manner of speaking, Miss Vernon, as if you yourself were a member of the inferior class you are so violently championing."

Blood rushed to her cheeks at the snub. "Do not think that by giving me a set-down you will silence me, my lord! Your holdings are in a disgraceful condition! Everywhere I go I hear complaints of you as a landlord! You enclose the common land so that your people have nowhere to graze their beasts! You keep man-traps in your woods to catch those poor desperate men whose wives and children go hungry! It is you, and those members of the ruling classes like you, who will bring about an English revolution far more bloody than the one in France!"

She knew she had become almost incoherent in her passion, but she could no more contain it than she could hold back a river in full spate.

He gave her an amused, indulgent smile, which further infuriated her, and held up his hand. "If I may be permitted one word, Miss Vernon. It is apparent you have been reading too much of Thomas Paine or, I shudder even to mention the name, some of Hannah More's claptrap!"

Grinning jackanapes! She felt like hammering at his smiling face with her fists, gouging his eyes with her nails. "You forget, my lord, that I am not one of your simpering females who has been sheltered from the real world. I have witnessed the results of the care-nothing, do-nothing attitude of the upper classes at first hand in a debtor's prison. I have myself been the victim of one of your so-called gentlemen—"

She stopped short, biting her lips together, appalled at the results of letting her passions—and tongue—run away with her. Striving to regain her composure, she swiftly rose from her seat.

He straightened up, his lips quirking into a sardonic smile, but his eyes remained cold and hard. "I see that I have been entertaining not only a bookish bluestocking but also a rampant radical."

"Entertaining!" she shot back at him.

Now even the sardonic smile was gone, and his face was as hard as granite. "Nevertheless, despite your low opinion of me, Miss Vernon, I must remind you again that my affairs are none of your concern. Speak to my agent when he returns from London, if you must, but do not speak of it again to me, ever! I will not brook such damnable interference in my affairs!"

His lips were set in a thin line as he opened the door for her, and he spoke no further word to her, pausing only to give orders for his carriage to return them to the parsonage before he strode across the hall.

What had she achieved by launching into her diatribe against him, she thought, as the carriage bowled along the driveway. Nothing! He had not even caught the gist of what she was saying, aware only of his piqued pride. And why was it only he who could goad her into imprudence? Even Aunt

Bertha had never had the satisfaction of making her so furious that she would speak without consideration first. Only he had the power to do that. Insufferable man! How she hated him! But if she hated him, why was it she was so perilously close to weak tears, as if she had suffered yet another great loss?

As she sat, grim-faced and silent, across from an equally silent Lady Helen and a sleepy, replete Julia, she preferred not to answer that question.

Chapter Eight

Nothing more was said of the visit to Danville Hall that day; but on the following day, in the early afternoon when Katrina was taking a small luncheon with Lady Helen, she quickly broached the subject.

"You may have been wondering, Lady Helen," she began tentatively, "what passed between Lord Danville and myself to make him so out of sorts at the end of our visit."

Lady Helen raised startled blue eyes to hers. "Indeed I have, Miss Vernon. When I came into the hall with Mrs. Talbot, I could hear your voice, although the library doors were closed." It was said in a tone of gentle reproach, yet even now she did not ask for any explanation.

"I taxed Lord Danville with his neglect of his holdings and the appalling condition of Pudsey Lane," continued Katrina, her cheeks glowing at the memory of it, "and he told me his affairs were none of my business."

Lady Helen's perfect lips quirked. "Quite so," she murmured. "Some more cake, Miss Vernon?"

Katrina was vexed at her seeming indifference to the plight of the cottagers. "How can you and Mr. Standish—" She bit back the heated words and began again. "Surely, as the spiritual leader of the parish, Mr. Standish must *feel* for these people?"

Lady Helen's white fingers pleated her linen napkin agitatedly, but her face bore its usual calm expression. "You know that he does, Miss Vernon; that *we* do. How can you believe otherwise? Everything that is in our power is done to assist them."

"No!" flashed Katrina. "Carrying soup and physic is not enough, don't you see? I cannot pierce Lord Danville's impenetrable hide, but perhaps Mr. Standish could. Oh, can you not see that?"

She realized at once that she had gone too far. Lady Helen rose majestically and rang the bell for the table to be cleared. At the doorway she turned and confronted her. "What passes between you and Lord Danville is your own concern, Miss Vernon, although I advise constraint. I do not wish to be receiving complaints of your behavior from him. But I am reluctantly forced to remind you that you are in our employ. It would be most unfortunate if you misconstrued our desire to befriend you as license to criticize our conduct."

With a glacial look, she swept from the room, leaving Katrina to bitterly reflect upon the dangers into which her quick tongue had led her. Many an employee would have been instantly turned off for less. And yet she still churned with indignation at the Standishes' passive acceptance of the Viscount's indifference to their parisioners' distress. It was not as if their living was in Lord Danville's hands, although it had been, she believed, when Edward Standish had first been appointed to it. In addition, after two weeks in their employ she had not gained the impression that Edward Standish was a weak man. On the contrary. She opined that his quiet, modest exterior hid a steely determination and a firmness of character, which he occasionally used to quell Julia when her high spirits carried her too far for even a doting papa to condone.

Her mind still working on the puzzle, she went upstairs to her room and splashed her burning cheeks with water to cool them. She must fetch Julia from the kitchen, where she was most likely being plied to excess with Mrs. Bateman's goodies; the child was spoiled by every member of the household, but fortunately she was so good-natured it affected her very little. Before she left her room, however, Katrina was determined to take a little time to calm herself and gather her thoughts. She sat in the cushioned window seat and looked out over the beech woods of Danville, watching the few coppery leaves that still clung to the branches shivering in the breeze.

It was patently obvious that the Viscount held some threat over their heads. Some hold he had on Edward Standish or Lady Helen, or both, that forced them to keep silent, to go about their duties without challenging him. "Devil" Danville, Lady Bainbridge had called him. Devil, indeed! And yet her whole being still ached for the mere sight of him. A touch of his hand could set her shivering with delight. Even that she could understand, for had not Lady Bainbridge said that he set out to add the names of conquests to his notebook? No doubt he employed all his considerable demonic powers of seduction; and, once conquered, his victims were tossed aside, forgotten in the excitement of the new hunt. It was no wonder that his touch thrilled her; he had diligently studied the art of seduction, both in theory and practice.

But had he not hinted at more yesterday, when he said he wished to see how she looked in his house? The idea of being his mistress was somehow even more repugnant to her than to be seduced and abandoned. To be kept by him, like a horse or a hound . . . No, not even as valued as that, for there was always the threat of his tiring of her within a week.

"I shall be neither his victim nor his mistress," she said aloud, and with this vow she briskly combed her hair, straightened her dress, and set off to remove a reluctant Julia from the kitchen to practice her scales on the pianoforte.

The next day was a Saturday, and Julia was excused from lessons, except for her music lesson with Katrina and scripture studies with her father; Katrina would have the morning practically to herself. Lady Helen had greeted her with perfect courtesy at breakfast, as if nothing had transpired between them. She spoke of the plans for the parish Christmas party and of how much she was looking forward to seeing her two sons—although, as they were spending Christmas with her parents in Norfolk, that would not be until the New Year. Then she proposed a visit to the dressmaker that afternoon to arrange for a new gown for Christmas.

Katrina went up to her room, planning to pass the morning in writing three letters: to her uncle, to Lady Bainbridge, and to the Duke of Branscombe, her father's former employer, to acquaint him with the change in her situation, for she had received the kindest letter from him after her father's death, chiding her for not having acquainted him with their straitened circumstances, and admonishing her to be sure to apply to him if ever she should need assistance. *If your damnable Vernon pride will permit you to do so!* he had added.

She had just completed the first letter, to her uncle, when there came a scratching at the door and she opened it to find Julie there, holding out a letter to her.

"Mama said to give you this, and Lord Danville's coachman is waiting for a reply."

"Lord Danville?" Katrina quickly took the letter. It bore a heavy crested seal and was addressed to her in bold black handwriting which she had no doubt was the Viscount's own.

"Come inside, Julia," she said to the child, who was standing on tiptoe, craning her neck to peer at the letter. "Help yourself to a comfit—only one, mind—and be still while I read Lord Danville's letter."

It was brief and to the point.

Dear Miss Vernon: I owe you an apology! Consultation with various people has better acquainted me with the condition of the Danville estate. Your assertion that there has been gross mishandling in its management is not far off the mark. I can only express gratitude for it having been drawn to my attention and deeply regret that in doing so you were subjected to my insults. Forgive me! Mrs. Hamilton, the wife of the retired sea captain who has recently moved into Allardyce House, has apparently been angling for an invitation to see over the Hall. I have therefore invited Captain and Mrs. Hamilton here this afternoon. Will you accompany them so that I may personally convey to you what this letter so briefly touches upon? If your answer is in the affirmative, my coachman will be there at three o'aclock. The bearer awaits your reply.

Your humble servant, etc.
Danville

The sense of amazement—and relief—was so powerful that she was forced to sit down, the strength gone from her legs. That he should not only apologize but also agree that there had been mismanagement of his estate was marvelous indeed! Immediately following the amazement and relief came a heart-hammering excitement mingled with panic at the thought of meeting with a contrite Lord Danville.

Don't be such a hen-witted ninny! she told herself and, taking a few deep breaths, soon regained her composure and got to her feet. "Julia, will you kindly take this letter to your mama and ask her if I may go to Danville Hall this afternoon with Captain and Mrs. Hamilton?" She was reluctant to present herself to Lady Helen until she was entirely composed.

Taking the letter, Julia ran from the room. "Walk, Julia, walk," admonished Katrina with a smile. And Julia slowed to a ladylike walk until she had crossed the landing; then she could be heard running down the stairs, taking the last two steps with a jump.

A few moments later, to Katrina's consternation Lady Helen herself came to her door. "Oh, my lady, I did not intend—"

"I was coming upstairs in any case. Here is your letter." Lady Helen handed it to her and then pressed the palms of her hands together, rubbing them against each other in a gesture of indecision. "Are you certain you wish to speak to Lord Danville again?" she asked presently. "Is it wise, after your last encounter?" She seemd to need reassurance that she would be acting correctly in permitting her to go to Danville Hall.

"Yes," replied Katrina in a measured tone. "I truly believe I can achieve some good by speaking with Lord Danville again. If only," she added with a wry smile, "I can learn to bridle my tongue."

Lady Helen smiled at this and then, to Katrina's surprise, took both her hands in her own and looked into her eyes. "If

Lord Danville is in earnest, you have achieved more than I ever thought possible. It is in your power, perhaps, to bring not only relief to his people but also to save his very soul." Her blue eyes brimmed with tears, and she turned away to dab at them with her handkerchief. "That is why we shall permit you to visit the Hall, although convention would demand otherwise," she said in a muffled voice. "Shall I tell the coachman you will be ready at three?"

Katrina nodded, but said nothing, remaining in the center of the room as the door closed. She was amazed by this revelation of Lady Helen's motives. To save his soul! That then was the reason Lady Helen permitted her to go to the Hall. She had it in mind that Lord Danville could be persuaded to undergo some momentous religious conversion! How naive of her, how blind she was not to see that the Viscount was a hardened case, far beyond redemption.

At least, thought Katrina, with a rueful smile, my violent attraction to him has not closed my eyes to his true character. But she would play him at his own game and achieve her objective while she held the advantage.

Meanwhile, she must prepare herself for this meeting. She heated the curling iron in the fire and parted her hair in the center, pulling it forward at both sides and curling it gently. Thank heaven it had at last grown a little and shone with the luster of good health, like polished chestnuts. Her figure, too, was filling out again and as she smoothed the charcoal-gray, trimmed with black velvet bows, over her hips she was aware of the firm swell of her breasts against the fitted bodice. She chose an emerald-green ribbon to thread through her hair, and she would wear the new face-framing bonnet with the jaunty feather. Although she must conform to the convention of mourning, she knew her uncle had been right in saying that her father would not want her to dress forever in black for him.

Captain and Mrs. Hamilton were all delighted anticipation at the thought of seeing the Hall. The captain had a rough, wind-worn countenance and a bluff manner to accompany it, both of which betrayed his naval connections, but his plain way of speaking pleased Katrina far more than Mrs. Hamilton's affected manner.

They were greeted in the hall by the Viscount, who was all grace and superior manners as he showed them first the library and then the portrait gallery, which had paneled walls lined with oil paintings, mostly of Danville ancestors in various modes of fashion, back to the days of Charles I. So engaged was Lord Danville in answering Mrs. Hamilton's questions that he had spoken nothing more to Katrina than the "I am glad you have come" she received when she arrived, accompanied by a glowing look and a squeeze of his fingers.

She did not mind it, for it gave her time to collect her thoughts and to observe him as he patiently responded to Mrs. Hamilton's numerous frivolous questions. He was dressed in a coat of dark blue superfine, which fit his broad shoulders with such precision that Katrina wondered how long it must have taken for him to be assisted into it! His neckcloth was a masterpiece of snowy-white linen; his waistcoat was of gold and ivory striped silk. Over the close-fitting pantaloons he wore gleaming Hessians with gold tassels. She was so intent upon the pleasure of looking at him that she was startled when she heard him speak her name.

"I was informing Captain and Mrs. Hamilton that you had a particular interest in music, Miss Vernon, being a musician yourself. I propose showing you my music room and, to save their being bored to distraction by two prosy aficionados of the art, I am placing them in Mrs. Talbot's capable hands for a while, Mrs. Hamilton having evinced a special interest in seeing the old disused kitchens and the chapel. Would you be so kind as to wait for me here?"

Without waiting for her reply, he escorted the good captain and his loquacious wife down the wide staircase and, before Katrina had time to do more than glance into the gilt-framed mirror to make sure her hair was still neat, he had returned.

"There," he said with a smile and a little sigh of relief. "I have settled the Hamiltons, and poor Mrs. Talbot will be engaged in answering questions for at least the next hour. I must remember to avoid my amiable housekeeper for the remainder of the day, for I shall not be in her good books for having foisted Mrs. Hamilton upon her!''

Katrina smiled in response to the laughter in his eyes. How attractive he was when he was in a good humor!

"I propose that we speak together first, and then I shall take you to the music room, for once we begin to talk of music it will quite take out of my head all I wish to say to you." He offered her his arm. "Shall we walk along the gallery, or would you prefer the library, where it is warmer?''

She hesitated for a moment. The long gallery was more public and therefore more safe, yet the memory of the library, despite their confrontation yesterday, was a powerful inducement. "The library, I think, for I am a little cold." She drew her shawl more closely about her and accompanied him down the stairs and into the library, all the time aware of the warmth of his arm as he held it.

This time she felt no pang of apprehension when the library doors closed behind them, although perhaps she had even more cause today, with Lady Helen not in the house. But Lord Danville's note—and Lady Helen's words—had not only surprised her but also given her cause to think that perhaps there might be some tiny part of him that was yet inviolate.

Two sleek greyhounds lay before the hearth and sprang up at their entry. Despite her protests that she liked dogs, the Viscount put them outside the door and, having again closed it, handed her to the sofa. He poured her a glass of sherry and offered her a plate of almond biscuits, and then stood gazing at her with such a warm expression in his eyes that she should have avoided him by turning away, but did not.

"How well you look!" he exclaimed. "Despite the many disadvantages of Danville, its air seems to agree with you. You have positively bloomed since I last saw you in London."

She smiled at this. "I am happy here. My employers treat me more like a friend than a servant. I am accepted by the people of the village as one of them. Little Julia, although a trifle indulged, is a delight—intelligent and eager to learn. Yes"—she raised her eyes to his—"Danville does agree with me."

"It gives me great pleasure to hear it," he said with emphasis. He gestured toward the empty space beside her. "May I?" he asked, and at her affirmative nod, sat down next to her on the small sofa, his knees pressed against hers, though she was not sure if it was intentional. The nearness of him caught her breath and hurried her heartbeat, but she made no move to draw away. He cleared his throat as if uncertain how to begin, and then said: "Before I speak to you of the results of our conversation yesterday, there is one other subject I must broach, and nothing can gainsay me this time."

The intensity of his expression, the darkening of his eyes and his hurried breathing denoted his passionate determination to continue; she knew before he began what his subject would be.

He took her hands in his, forcing her to turn toward him, and bent upon her a searching look as he spoke. "When I accepted Fanshawe's wager at the Merriot ball, you were a stranger to me, a member of the notoriously vulgar Bertha Vernon's family, cousin to that little bird of paradise Letty Vernon, and outlandishly dressed to boot. A perfect subject for a wager! Imagine my consternation when I discovered that my victim was not only a lady of quality but also one whose circumstances demanded sympathy and respect, not to be laid open to the ridicule of the entire room."

The memory of her humiliation swept over. "Please do not continue," she whispered. "I cannot bear it,' and she turned from him, tears filling her eyes.

His hands clasped hers even more tightly. "You must allow me to finish," he said passionately. "For the first time in many years, I deplored my own actions and realized how they could make others suffer. By then it was too late to extricate you from the consequences of my folly, but I could at least have escorted you from the ballroom, away from the prying eyes and the derision. Instead, my damnable alter ego continued the cruel farce, even after I had discovered not only that you were in need of sympathy but also that I was damnably attracted to you. Did you in all honesty believe that I would have embraced you thus if it were not so? And then to discover, later that evening, that you had been abandoned by your aunt and left to find your own way home!''

So agitated was he by the memory of it that he jumped up from the sofa and paced about as he continued to speak. ''Shamed and appalled by the consequences of my actions, I determined to speak to your uncle, to explain all to him, offer him my most abject apologies; and then, I hoped through him, to reach you. You know the rest. I arrived at the bookshop to find you there and, to my utter dismay, you forbade me even to mention the subject of the Merriot ball. It has been festering inside me ever since.''

He ceased his pacing and again sat down beside her, taking her face between his hands and gently turning it toward him. ''Oh, my dearest love, do not weep. I wish I had never been at the damnable ball—but for one thing: had I not been there I might never have met my adorable Katrina.''

She looked at him through a watery haze and then closed her eyes, tears spilling down her cheeks when his mouth touched hers. He drew her close to him, his touch not as intimate as it had been at the ball, infinitely more tender, and she allowed herself to succumb without fear. It was as if here, in his arms, was the only right place for her to be. His restrained tenderness surprised and delighted her, and she was content to rest against him, her head on his chest, as he gently kissed her wet eyelids and her face before returning again to her eager mouth.

Eventually, with a regretful sigh, he drew away. ''I fear time is passing, and we shall be discovered here by the Hamiltons without having seen the music room!''

She reached for her reticule to get a comb to tidy her hair, but he put his hand over hers and drew her to him again. ''Say you forgive me,'' he whispered against her mouth.

''I forgive you with all my heart,'' she whispered in return, and their lips met again in a passionate seal on their reconciliation.

Now he allowed her to comb her hair and powder her face, which glistened with the result of tears and kisses, even going to the intimate extreme of borrowing her comb to neaten his own ruffled hair.

When they were both made neat, he sat down in the wing chair by the fire, saying it was safer not to be too close to her. "Now, my dear—my dearest Miss Vernon, to the subject of the management of my estate. Once again I must beg your forgiveness. My pride is taking a sad bruising today," he added, with a wry smile.

She smiled in return, and for the first time in a while spoke a coherent sentence. "Shall we agree, my lord, that I acted in an importunate manner two days ago and that you, not unnaturally, responded in kind?"

"Very well put, Miss Vernon. Then we shall say no more on that account. What I will say to you is that, importunate or not, your accusations were well founded, and I am determined to carry out several investigations before Carlton, my agent, returns from London."

"Then you will be remaining at Danville awhile longer?" She was concerned as soon as she had spoken the words that they sounded too eager.

"I shall indeed. A great deal longer. Will that please you?" He gave her a searching look.

"Yes, it will," she replied calmly. "But how can you bear to be away from London, when you are so seldom in the country, my lord?"

"I shall do my level best to bear it with your assistance, Miss Vernon! But come, let us go to the music room, or we shall be caught out." He took her hands and raised her from the sofa, holding her for a moment and looking tenderly into her eyes before releasing her. Then, offering her his arm, he led her up the staircase again and through the gallery to the music room.

When they entered, she stood in the doorway surveying the room with delight. Danville Hall was a veritable palace of delights! How could he bear to spend so little time here?

The music room was decorated in white and gold, with hangings and wall coverings of eau-de-nil brocade. A carpet patterned in delicate shades of pale rose, gold, and eau-de-nil covered the floor. Two pianofortes stood, one at each end of of the room, and there were also a spinet, a golden harp, glass-fronted cases containing various musical instruments—

many of them ancient in design—and several gilded music stands. The shelves in the embrasures on either side of the mantelpiece were lined with books, all no doubt on the subject of music. On a large round table were spread several leatherbound portfolios of music.

There was a slightly musty atmosphere in the room, as if it had been rarely used, but this had been dissipated somewhat by the scent of apple-tree logs that burned in the fireplace and also by the blast of cold air which blew in through one of the full-length windows, which Lord Danville immediately closed.

He took her on a brief tour and then said, abruptly: "You say you sing, Miss Vernon. It would give me the greatest pleasure to hear you."

"Oh, no, my lord. I have not sung a note for many months. I could not." Her mouth went dry at the thought of singing again.

"Nonsense! Once learned, music is never forgotten. Come. We are private here. No doubt your voice will prove a trifle rusty if you have not been exercising it, but you must begin again sometime."

"I am afraid to," she said quietly, not wishing to appear like some simpering female having to be coaxed into performance. "I believe truly that I have lost my ability to sing."

"You will never know if you do not at least try," he said gently. "You need not think I will be sitting in judgment upon you." He leafed through some of the portfolios of sheet music while she gripped her hands together, wishing she could calm the sickening hammer of her heart. "Giordani? Do you know *'Caro mio ben'*? It is a simple air but needs—"

"Of course I know it!"

"Very well then. Let us begin."

He sat down at the pianoforte, opened the lid, and began to play. She could tell even from this simple accompaniment that he played well, but could not distinguish how well, being too preoccupied with her part in the song to think of his. To her great relief, the voice was still there, but her breathing was extremely ragged and, therefore, her phrasing suffered. Lord Danville confirmed this in an uncompromising manner, which pleased her; she wanted no sops to reassure her, but good advice she was prepared to accept.

"But you have a delightfully expressive voice with a lovely dark quality to it," he added, after he had completed his criticism. 'It is obvious that you have received expert tutelage. Who was your teacher?"

"Signor Bartini. He was a regular guest at Branscombe Castle and usually stayed there for long periods of time."

"Bartini! I bow to you, Miss Vernon. I had no idea I was entertaining a pupil of the great Bartini."

"I was his pupil until his death two years ago."

"I recollect hearing his last performance at the opera. The voice was still robust and expressive even then. Well, well. You owe it to your distinguished music master not to neglect your voice. Come, some Handel to regain the flexibility."

Their cozy *tête-à-tête* in the library was not forgotten but put aside as they set about the making of music in a professional and dedicated manner; a manner which at times led to slight disagreements between them as to tempo and phrasing, but never amounting to anything that could cool the warm rapport between them.

It was after an all-too-brief but most enjoyable and invigorating session of music-making that the Hamiltons broke in upon them with regrets that they must now depart. So disappointed was Katrina at having to leave that she half hoped the Viscount might suggest he would drive her home. But now it was he who seemed to care more about the conventions than she, for he made no such suggestion, and parted from her with only an expressive look, a tender smile, and a squeeze of her hand as he shook it, to remind her of what had passed between them.

Chapter Nine

At the beginning of the following week, Lady Helen received a note from Mrs. Talbot asking if Julia would care to have one of the kittens and, if so, would she prefer to come to the Hall to choose one for herself? Lady Helen sent word in return that Miss Vernon would bring Julia to the Hall the next afternoon. A twinkle of amusement shone in her blue eyes when she told Katrina about the invitation.

"I wonder what other justifications Lord Danville will find to bring you to the Hall once he has exhausted the inducement of the kittens." She smiled openly at Katrina's consternation. "Forgive me for teasing you, but Mrs. Talbot is exceedingly loquacious, you know. You may take Sally with you to help alleviate the gossip that is bound to attend your visits to the Hall."

Despite her embarrassment, Katrina was extremely grateful for the excuse to go to Danville Hall again, for she was looking forward with excitement, not only to seeing the Viscount, but also to singing with him again. During the hymns in the three church services on Sunday she had sung out with renewed vigor, no longer afraid that her voice had gone. She had even received several compliments on the beauty of her voice afterward. The thought of making music with Lord Danville again invoked a feverish excitement that remained with her the entire day.

Two days had passed since her last visit to the Hall, and during those two days she had been attempting to consider dispassionately what had transpired between her and the Viscount. For a very brief while on the evening of that meeting, she had allowed herself the luxury of thinking that Lord Danville might even be considering marriage, but she soon scoffed herself out of such nonsense by repeating out loud the bitter words of Mary Wollstonecraft, herself a governess and hired companion: *"Few men seriously think of marrying an inferior!"*

Few men indeed! And least of all a man such as Lord Danville. In any case, the pleasures of connubial bliss were not for such as she. The most she could hope for from him was a proposal to become his mistress, and *that* her pride would not permit her to accept. The least she could hope for was an attempt at seduction to add her name to his little book, if indeed such a book existed, and *that* she would never undergo, however tempted she might be by his embraces. She determined to live for the present, to secure through her own good offices relief for the poor of Danville, and to enjoy the pleasures of Lord Danville's company for as long as he was prepared to accept her on her own terms: her company, even her kisses, but nothing more. She was not about to relinquish her security as a well-esteemed member of the Standish household for the insecurity of Lord Danville's bed until he grew weary of her embraces. The thought of the future without him was a melancholy one; therefore, she would not think of the future, only of the present and its inherent pleasures.

"At what time are we to go to the Hall for my kitten?" asked an impatient Julia on the morning of the proposed visit.

"This afternoon, at three o'clock, when I return from visiting Mrs. Foster and little Ned Green with your mother."

"Oh," sighed Julia. "Not until three. How shall I bear to wait?"

"You will bear to wait by practicing your new pieces on

the pianoforte and by writing out the list of irregular verbs we have been studying," replied Katrina. "And I shall ask Mrs. Bateman to make sure you are not idling your time away."

During the past weeks, Mrs. Bateman's chilling manner had gradually thawed. Once she had discovered that Katrina had no intention of undermining either her authority in the household or her uniquely warm relationship with Lady Helen, she accepted Katrina's presence with equanimity and was even beginning to address her in more than brusque monosyllables.

The visit to Meg Foster was a harrowing one. The woman was in the final stages of consumption and, despite the blankets and extra fuel Lady Helen had provided, could never get warm enough. As Dick Foster greeted them at the door, his manner was even more sullen than it had been on previous visits, and he sat at the scrubbed table whittling at a stick with a long-bladed knife while they changed Meg's bedclothing.

When they had completed their task, Katrina went to the table while Lady Helen fed the woman the rich broth she had brought with her.

"No better, is she?" Dick jerked his head in the direction of the bed.

"No, Dick. I regret not." Katrina sat down on the bench opposite him.

He continued to slash at the stick with more intensity, as if the energy of his entire being were concentrated in the strokes of the knife.

"But take heart, Dick. I believe his lordship is going to make an investigation very soon, when his agent returns from seeing to his business affairs in London, and then you will see some changes. I am certain of it. With the roof mended and the chimney repaired so that it no longer smokes, this room will at least be more comfortable to live in."

"Whatever he does, it'll be too late for me ma. And, any road, I'll believe he'll do summat for us when pigs fly!" He muttered imprecations beneath his breath, most of which Katrina could not catch, which was probably for the best, apart from "his danged lordship!" When he looked up at her again, she saw the glint of tears, and instinctively she reached out to cover his rough brown hand with hers.

"Bear up, Dick," she said softly. "I intend to do everything in my power to help you and all the cottagers."

He sniffed loudly and wiped his nose on his sleeve, but for a moment she caught a glimpse of a fleeting smile that quite transformed his sullen face.

"Thank 'ee, miss," he muttered. "You'm powerful kind. She's all I got, you see. I've none but her, and when she goes—" He jerked back the bench, scraping it on the stones in the earthen floor, and lurched outside.

The memory of Dick's misery hung over her throughout the day, so that when, at last, she was alone with Lord Danville in the music room, she was forever searching for an opening in their conversation to renew the subject of the cottagers in Pudsey Lane. But it was the Viscount himself who provided the opportunity, by looking up from the music score they had been discussing and saying: "My pride is in serious danger of being bruised again, Miss Vernon, for your thoughts are most definitely not on our conversation nor, I regret, upon me, but have wandered away. Am I so very tedious?"

Katrina gave him a wry smile. "Of course not! But you are indeed correct in thinking that my thoughts are elsewhere. It is just that—" She hesitated, afraid that he would be angered if she talked again of the condition of his holdings.

"Come now. I do not bite, you know."

His relaxed, teasing manner encouraged her to share with him her concerns about the Fosters. "The woman is dying, and although she is past all curing, I believe that her last days at least could be made more confortable if a few repairs were made to the cottage."

He had frowned at her words but exhibited no signs of anger. "I wish you need not go with Lady Helen on these visitations. She goes of her own volition, but you as her employee have no choice."

"Oh, no. You are quite in the wrong there! It is my decision to go with her, and she herself has often voiced her reluctance to expose me to the dangers of disease. I am not in any way compelled to go.''

"Except by your own powerful sense of compassion or," he added, with a quirk to his leps, "perhaps in your capacity as a radical crusader?''

She gave him a look that was half amused, half baleful, and he threw up his hands in mock surrender.

"I cry you peace, Miss Vernon. But in all seriousness, I had intended to personally inspect Pudsey Lane with Carlton when he returns next week from London, but if you feel so strongly about the state of my cottages, then I shall go there sooner.''

"You will take care, my lord!'' She was suddenly alarmed at the thought of the bitter feeling against him that existed among the cottagers.

"I am deeply flattered by your concern. Perhaps I should take you with me for protection against my own tenantry?'' He said it in a teasing manner, but she responded in earnest tones.

"The feeling against you there is so very strong, it might be best if you had someone like Mr. Standish accompany you, someone who is respected by the cottagers.''

"Very well. I must confess the thought of hiding behind a lady's skirts when I visited my tenants did not appeal to me, but clerical bands I shall accept!''

"Oh, will you be serious! This is not a matter for amusement. You would be no use at all to your cottagers if you were dead, my lord!''

A flash of anger shot through his eyes, reminding her that she must still tread carefully with him. "And is that the reason for your concern for my safety, Miss Vernon? That if I were dead, my cottagers would receive no assistance?'' The lightness of his tone was negated by the dangerous glint in his eyes.

"Do not be ridiculous! You know very well that is not my only concern!'' She bestowed upon him the warmest of looks and was rewarded by a softening of his expression. "But come, my lord. We must make a start if we are to have time for even one song before Julia has chosen her kitten.''

"The devil take Julia and her kitten!"

She gave him a roguish smile. "Ah, but without Julia and her kitten I should not be here, my lord."

"No, indeed. I am forgetting! The heavens bless Julia *and* the kitten!" With laughter now lighting his eyes, he took her hand and pressed his lips to it. Then, turning it over, he kissed the palm lingeringly so that her heart also turned in her breast.

She gently withdrew her hand. "To music, my lord," she reminded him.

"Ah, yes. To music. What shall we perform today? Do you sing any Mozart?"

"A few of his songs and the two Zerlina arias from *Don Giovanni.*"

"Excellent! I am, as you will learn, a devotee of the sadly neglected Mozart, and have been ever since I heard him play in a salon in Vienna."

"You heard Mozart play? How marvelous! He was, I have heard from Signor Bartini, a prodigious pianist."

"Prodigious is too mild a word," he said with fervor, his whole body tensed with the excitement of his subject. "I was a boy of but fifteen at the time, studying music in Vienna. Mozart was no longer lionized as he had been in his younger years, but there were still the loyal *cognoscenti* who acknowledged him the master of all time."

"What was he like?" Katrina asked eagerly.

"In appearance? Small; powdered blond hair; pale complexion. His strongest feature was his eyes, which animated his countenance with fire and passion; and his hands were never still, always in motion. But it was at the pianoforte keyboard that he came into his own, for there those small hands had complete control and played with ease and fluidity some of the most difficult passages ever written. He was also an incomparable improviser."

She had never before seen the Viscount so animated on any subject. His eyes, his entire countenance, glowed with the memory of the great musician. "You were indeed fortunate to see him," was her only comment.

He responded as if his thoughts were still at a great

distance. "I was indeed. But although several devotees of music banded together and issued him an invitation, many invitations, to come to England and reside for a time as a guest in a country in which he was still appreciated, the offer came too late, for he died that same year and was buried in a pauper's grave."

This man never ceases to astonish me, thought Katrina. For now the dilettante who played the pianoforte tolerably well was brought close to tears by the memory of a musician who had died nigh on twenty years before.

He took out his fine lawn handkerchief and blew his nose. "Come, Miss Vernon," he said briskly. "You have caught me on a raw spot. Let us proceed with our music before it is too late even to begin." He sat down at the keyboard, saying with a devilish smile: "Something must be done about our never having enough time together." He immediately played the opening bars of *"Batti, batti,"* before she was able to reply.

They had time for only three pieces before Katrina heard the carriage clock on the rosewood table strike four. "Oh, good Lord, is that the time! Julia will be half mad with impatience."

He closed the lid with a sigh and, when he stood up, detained her by taking her hand in his. Until then, he had made no move to kiss her, and she was not sure whether to be grateful or sorry for it. But now he carried her hand to his lips and, casting a hurried look behind to insure that there were no servants visible, drew her to him and, lifting her chin with one hand, bent his head to kiss her, his mouth warm and still on hers.

At first she responded in kind, her lips pressed against his, but unmoving. Then his mouth softened and became more mobile, and she instinctively opened her lips, while pressing closer to him.

Eventually, with a shuddering breath, she pulled away, her mouth soft and damp from his kisses, and she gave him a tentative smile. He ran his eyes over her face and then groaned and drew her gently to him again. "Oh, my love," he breathed, his mouth against her hair. "Something must indeed be done about this."

She stiffened and drew away from him again, this time moving to the table to pick up some sheets of music. She was determined at all cost to avoid an invitation to become his *chère-amie*, although she recognized that it could not be postponed indefinitely. She wished to prolong their present status for as long as possible, for once he voiced his proposition, their relationship, both personal and musical, would be at an end.

When she turned back, it was to catch a hurt expression in his eyes which quickly turned to teasing. "I do believe Miss Vernon permits me to kiss her solely because she wishes my musical services, nothing more!"

"Exactly!" she responded, delighted to find the conversation turning to a lighter vein. "I charge one song per kiss."

"Ah, but then you must avoid at all cost asking me to play you an entire opera. What would you consider fair recompense for an opera, Miss Vernon?" His eyes challenged her to find a suitable reply to the trap he had prepared.

She chose to ignore the question, but a warm tingling coursed through her veins at the thoughts he had aroused.

Laughing, he tucked her hand into his arm and escorted her along the gallery and down the stairs.

"Why do you come so seldom to Danville Hall?" she asked him, as they crossed the tiled hall.

"Because the countryside bores me," he drawled. Then, catching her disapproving look, added quickly, "No. You are correct. There is more. The Hall revives old, best forgotten memories."

She sensed by the tension in his arm and the averted head, that she was treading on dangerous ground, but, foolhardy as it might be, she felt impelled to pursue the subject. "But surely the best way to erase unhappy memories is not to fly from them, but to replace them with new and happier ones?"

He stopped short and gave her an intense, searching look, which she met with equanimity, although inwardly she quailed expecting him to erupt into a passion at any moment, or at the very least to retire behind his cynical façade. But he did neither, only sliding his hands down her arms to hold her wrists in a light grasp. At the same time, his face softened into a smile. "You are, of course, correct, Miss Vernon. But then, I suppose, not even my old remembrances of this place are entirely unhappy ones. It was once my favorite home. I recall that when I was a young boy it looked like a forest at Christmastime, with boughs of holly and fir and other evergreens. I would go with the servants to cut them, and we'd drag them in from the woods in a great sheet. I recollect the spicy aroma of plum pudding and roast goose and tables groaning with flummeries and syllabub and shivering blancmangers and . . . Miss Vernon," he interrupted himself with a glowing look and sudden excitement catching his voice, "you are a witch, a veritable witch! But a good one, I hasten to assure you! I shall both replace and renew old memories by reviving the Danville Christmas ball, and we shall have houseguests by the dozen and even the rambunctious Christmas party for my staff and tenants. You hear that, Jarvis?" he shouted.

Jarvis, the butler, who had been intently studying the pattern of the carpet beneath his feet, looked up as if surprised and said: "I beg your pardon, my lord?"

"Come, Jarvis, do not be pretending you are more deaf than you really are."

"No, Mr. Justin, I mean, my lord." Jarvis gave his master a broad grin, and his faded eyes looked at Katrina with new respect, as if he were seeing her in a different light.

Katrina was delighted that she had inadvertently been the cause of the Viscount's extraordinary enthusiasm.

"And, my dear Miss Vernon," continued Lord Danville, "we shall have a concert, with the leading musicians in the land to perform, and you, my dear, sweet Miss Vernon, shall be one of them."

"Oh, no, I could not possibly—"

"You can, and you shall."

His enthusiasm was exceeded only by Julia's when they entered Mrs. Talbot's parlor.

"She has been all impatience," whispered Mrs. Talbot to Katrina, "but at least she has had an abundance of time in which to make her choice." Her kind but shrewd eyes looked at Katrina speakingly.

Katrina turned quickly to Julia to hide her flush of embarrassment. "Which kitten did you choose, Julia?"

"This one. The fluffy gray one with the pretty face. And it's a girl kitten, Sally says."

"And why did you choose that one in particular?" asked Lord Danville.

"Because she was the one who came running to me when I sat down."

"Ah, so *she* chose you, then."

"Yes, she chose me." Julia appeared even more enthralled at the idea that the kitten had chosen her.

The kitten was wrapped in an old towel and Julia clutched it to her chest, whispering endearments in its furry ear, as Lord Danville announced that he would drive them home in the gig. Katrina hid a smile at the thought of the elegant slap-up Viscount driving a humble gig carrying a governess, a maidservant, and a child with a mewling kitten.

As they were about to depart, he turned about and said to his housekeeper: "Oh, by the bye, Mrs. Talbot, we shall be reviving the Christmas ball and the servants' party this year and I intend to invite several houseguests. I shall discuss the whole with you and Jarvis as soon as I return, as we have precious little time for preparation."

The expression on Mrs. Talbot's face as she bobbed a curtsy and uttered a stunned: "Very well, my lord," was one of the high points of Katrina's day.

Chapter Ten

The Viscount was as good as his word. Within three days, gilt-edged invitations addressed to the Reverend Mr. Edward and Lady Helen Standish and Miss Katrina Vernon were delivered to the parsonage. They were at breakfast when Mrs. Bateman carried in the cards with due ceremony on the silver card tray and placed them before Lady Helen. "Lord Danville's coachman brought these," she said, her abrupt manner rather spoiling the effect.

Katrina, guessing what they were, watched Lady Helen's face as she took them up one by one, only an almost imperceptible tightening of her face muscles betraying her. "For you, Miss Vernon," she said, handing Katrina three of the invitations. She sat for almost half a minute, saying nothing, but giving her husband an unfathomable look. Then, drawing in a deep breath, she took up her cards and opened them with the silver letter opener.

Katrina now turned to peruse her own cards. One was an invitation to attend a private concert given by Lord Danville. A concert, she thought wryly, at which she was to perform, much against her own inclination, for she was convinced that his guests would be far more knowledgeable about music than the average persons of quality; and although she had been used to performing in such company at Branscombe Castle, the voice was, as Lord Danville had said, a trifle rusty and, what was more, she had lost the self-assurance that was so essential for performance.

The second invitation was to a ball to be held three days before Christmas; the third, to a party on Boxing Day for the Viscount's tenantry and the local servants, farmers, gentry, and nobility.

As she perused her invitations, Katrina was aware of the conversation that was taking place between Lady Helen and her husband, both of whom had retired to the window recess, their backs to her. They were conducting their conversation in low voices so that it was impossible to hear what they were saying, but it was clear that Mr. Standish was trying to persuade his wife into doing something which she did not wish to do.

Please, God, thought Katrina, don't let them refuse the invitations; for if they did, it would be imposible for her to attend, and although she would not be able to dance at the ball because of her situation as a governess-companion and the fact that she was still in mourning, the anticipatory excitement of the concert and meeting the Viscount's friends and seeing the Hall come alive had buoyed her up for the past three days.

It was Julia who mercifully put an end to her anxiety by asking, on learning what the pretty cards were: "Will you and Papa be dancing at the Hall, Mama? Will you buy a new dress for the ball?" She bounced up and down in her chair, her blonde curls bobbing around her pretty face.

Lady Helen turned from the window. "We shall see, Julia. But it will certainly be necessary for Miss Vernon to have a new gown."

"Yes, indeed," echoed Mr. Standish, a warm smile replacing his troubled expression, and they both looked toward Katrina.

"I have your permission to accept the invitations, then?" she asked.

"Of course," replied Mr. Standish. "And if, for any reason, we are prevented from attending, you can be sure that someone from the neighborhood will be glad to have you accompany them, for you have become a general favorite in our small parish, Miss Vernon.''

The warmth of his tone and the kind look he gave her made her wonder, as she did at least once a day, at her good fortune in being accepted into such a household. But at the same time she was astonished that her employers would contemplate permitting her to attend the activities at Danville Hall without them. It was unheard of for a governess to appear in company alone, and although she doubted if Lady Helen would wish to go to the Hall if Lord Danville were there, Katrina very much hoped that Mr. Standish would be able to prevail upon her to do so.

"We mean what we say," Lady Helen continued. "This very morning I wish you to accompany me to Mrs. Brown's, for there is not sufficient time for us to make an evening dress ourselves. If it is to be ready for the concert, there is no time to be lost."

"But I—"

"No 'buts,' if you please! This is to be our gift to you in recognition of your good services to us all."

Katrina was all confusion. "I could not accept such generosity. I have been here for such a short while." Tears stung her eyes at the thought of their kindness, in contrast with the mistreatment she had received from others, particularly Aunt Bertha.

Julia's warm, sticky hand stole into hers. "Don't weep, Miss Vernon. Mama and Papa aren't vexed with you."

She bent and hugged Julia's plump body to her breast. "I know they aren't, my dearest Julia. I'm weeping from happiness."

"Oh, that's all right then." Julia gave her a kiss and bounded away to play with her precious kitten by the fire.

Within the hour, they were inside Mrs. Brown, the dressmaker's, snug establishment in the High Street, and the morning flew past in the delightful pleasures of looking at patterns, fabrics, ribbons, trimmings, and buttons.

"It is really too bad that we cannot deck you out in lace and bright silks and flowers," sighed Lady Helen. "As the wife of a clergyman, such fripperies are unsuitable for me, of course, but they are beautiful, are they not?"

Katrina had to agree. She ran her eyes longingly over a high-waisted ball gown in palest green silk, the low décolletage trimmed with gold-spangled lovers' knots.

"Must it be black, my lady?" inquired Mrs. Brown. "There's so little can be done with black."

"Oh, I think not, do you, Miss Vernon? You have been wearing day-dresses of gray."

Katrina nodded. Although gray was far from being her favorite color, it was infinitely preferable to black, which was so dull with her hazel eyes and chestnut hair. She longed for the time when she could wear her favorite greens again.

Mrs. Brown showed them fabric bales of different shades of gray, and Katrina was immediately taken with one, a pearl-gray satin which had a soft, silvery sheen to it, but she was certain it would not be considered suitable for a governess. To her surprise, the pearl-gray was the one Lady Helen picked out and said, a smile in her eyes, "This is the one you like, is it not, Miss Vernon? I think it will be most suitable."

When the measuring and the draping and pinning were completed they had fixed on a pattern which was to be adapted to the decorous necessities of Miss Vernon's station.

"The neckline a little higher, I think, but delicately trimmed to give it emphasis." And the small, birdlike figure of Mrs. Brown darted here and there, holding up and taking away spools of ribbons and cards of lace and braid trim as Katrina stood patiently, with the pearl-gray still draped around her.

In the end, all three were extremely satisfied with the results of their efforts, although Katrina was very much afraid that the dress was prohibitively expensive and not at all the simple gown a hired governess should wear. But then, how often did a governess receive an invitation not only to a concert but also to perform at that concert?

The evening dress was finished within a week, and on the very morning of the concert it was sent up to the parsonage with all the final alterations completed. As Katrina drew it out of its folds of tissue, Julia emitted a squeal of ecstasy. There was an audience of four in Katrina's room to see the new gown: Lady Helen, Mrs. Bateman, Sally, and Julia.

"Put it on, please, Miss Vernon," cried Julia. "We want to see it."

"Hush, Julia," said her mother. "We shall see it tonight."

"You'll look a proper vision it it, that's what!" Katrina was not quite sure how to take this pronouncement from the redoubtable Mrs. Bateman, but smiled her thanks in case it was meant as a compliment. "Sally, you go on down and peel those potatoes," said the formidable housekeeper. "Come along now, Mis Julia. Your mama wishes to talk with Miss Vernon alone," and she marched the reluctant child from the room.

Katrina immediately surmised what was to come and wished she could save Lady Helen embarrassment by saying so, but it was not her place to outguess her employer.

"Miss Vernon," she began, and then halted for a moment, rubbing her palms together in her habitual nervous gesture. "Edward and I have decided not to attend the concert tonight. He has his sermon to prepare and I, as you know, am suffering from the beginnings of a cold in the head."

Katrina knew nothing of the sort, but held her tongue.

"We deeply regret not being able to hear you sing, but—" Lady Helen held out her delicate hands in a gesture of resignation.

"I deeply regret it, too, my lady. But are you certain you still wish me to go? If neither of you is to be there, will it not appear exceedingly presumptuous of me to attend alone?"

"You will not be alone. Lady Kettering has undertaken to allow you to accompany her and her daughter to the concert. It has all been arranged, so you need not concern yourself any further." She gave Katrina a gentle smile. "Pray do not look so troubled, Miss Vernon. I would not permit you to do anything that would damage your reputation or that of our household. You do wish to go, don't you?" she added with a sudden anxious frown. "I would not for the world have you think we are coercing you into going! It is just that, although you once held Lord Danville in great loathing, I now begin to feel that—"

Katrina colored and hastily intervened. "I should like to go above all things, so long as you and Mr. Standish consider it proper.''

"Indeed we do, Miss Vernon. You may go to Danville Hall secure in the knowledge that your presence there will not be censured by anyone.''

"Very well, my lady. I thank you. And,'' she continued, gesturing to the dress lying in the folds of tissue, "I have even more cause to thank you for your most generous gift.''

"Pray say no more about it.'' Lady Helen looked down at Katrina from her superior height and took her face between her hands, as if she were a mother and Katrina her child, although only a few years separated them. "Be happy, Katrina,'' she said, and hastily left the room.

How unfathomable Lady Helen could be at times, and yet how warm and uncondescending. That was the first time she had called her by her Christian name, and the little gesture of friendship left Katrina with an inner glow.

As the day progressed, however, the excitment she had been feeling slowly changed to dread at the prospect of not only appearing in polite society again after her former ignominious debut with her aunt, but also of performing.

It was more than a year since she had sung in public, and although Lord Danville had reassured her that she was perfectly ready, that he would not throw her to the wolves or make himself appear ridiculous by doing so, she was seized with dread at the thought of performing before such distinguished company as Lord Danville must have assembled.

They had met but once in the past week—before his guests had arrived—for a rehearsal of the two seventeenth-century Italian songs which she was to perform.

"No Mozart!'' he told her firmly.

"Ah, I collect that you do not wish me to mutilate your favorite?'' she replied smilingly, though inwardly vexed that he did not consider her sufficiently able to essay the Mozart songs and arias they had practiced together the previous week.

"Not at all. There will be others who will be performing Mozart. You do not wish to appear repetitious, do you?''

"No, indeed I do not.''

He had not said who these "others" were to be and refused to allow her to draw from him the names of his concert performers or, for that matter, the names of any of his guests. All that week, carriages had wheeled in from London—slap-up phaetons and curricles and more sedate barouches—depositing their owners at Danville Hall, and on the two occasions she was in the village she had passed fashionably dressed strangers in the High Street, ladies with huge ermine muffs and elegant pelisses, one wearing startling crimson half-boots. Katrina wondered for a brief moment if she might be the opera singer of whom Lady Bainbridge had spoken, the Viscount's mistress. The thought had sent her back to the parsonage with a heaviness of spirit that had not lifted for an entire day. But at the end of that day she was sufficiently recovered to berate herself for being such a ninnyhammer as to think that the Viscount would bring down to Danville Hall the mistress he intended to cast off in favor of his new *chère-amie* and, what was more, to have the two meet beneath his roof!

But although she had been able to convince herself that she would be spared that particular embarrassment, it occurred to Katrina that Lord Danville's guests might wonder at her relationship with the Viscount, for if he were to exhibit even the slightest degree of warmth toward her, a penniless governess, in public, she would be instantly marked as his new conquest. Indeed, she was convinced that her very presence at the concert without her employers would, despite Lady Helen's assurances to the contrary, brand her as fast and extremely presumptuous. She determined, therefore, to keep herself politely but cooly aloof from him and to behave at all times as befitted her station, to reply to him with downcast eyes, with "Yes, my lord" and "No, my lord" at the required moments, if, indeed, he deigned to speak to her at all.

The thought of such behavior was a potent dampener to her enthusiasm and also sapped what little self-confidence she had left, so that by the time she had completed her toilette and was putting on her underslip, she was feeling quite nauseated with apprehension.

To her surprise, Mrs. Bateman had offered to help her

dress, and she accepted the offer with alacrity, expressing her gratitude effusively enough to sweeten the crusty housekeeper. It was Mrs. Bateman who carried the dress up from the washhouse, where it had been hanging all day to steam out any creases, and now it was Mrs. Bateman who assisted Katrina into it, with Sally's help. As the satin slid sensuously over her shoulders and down her body, Katrina breathed in the fragrance of the dried lavender which had been sprinkled among its folds while it lay in its box.

"Now stand still, miss, and let me do up these tarradiddling buttons," and, muttering imprecations against dressmakers who put in dozens of tiny buttons to make other people's fingers sore, Mrs. Bateman proceeded to fasten the back of the dress. "There now, let's have a look at you."

Katrina obediently turned around, smoothing the gown from the high waist to her hips as she did so. How soft it felt against her body, and the satin whispered as she walked to the mirror stand to look at herself.

She hardly recognized the creature who stared back at her from the glass. Mrs. Bateman, who had been Lady Helen's dresser before she was married, had dressed her hair in a simple but artful style, with a cluster of curls on the crown and more curls on her forehead and over her ears. The only decoration was a length of silver ribbon, edged with black and trimmed with imitation seed pearls, wound around the cluster of curls and tied in a bow at the back.

"Mrs. Bateman, you are a woman of not only many talents, but also exquisite taste!" declared Katrina, and bestowed a hug on the bony figure, which stiffened at this unlooked-for contact.

"I'll fetch her ladyship and Miss Julia to see you," was the only response, and she stalked out. But Katrina knew she was flattered by the compliment.

She smiled at an awed Sally and looked in the mirror again. The dress was exquisitely fashioned in a deceptively simple style, with a neckline high enough to be decorous, but low enough to display her white neck and the dainty neckace of seed pearls which Lady Helen had kindly lent her. The bodice and hem and half-sleeves were trimmed with scrolls of black velvet trimmed with imitation seed pearls. She slipped her feet into the pale gray kid slippers and took the long gloves of white silk from Sally and drew them on.

"Oh, you do look a proper picture, miss," breathed Sally, a mixture of awe and envy on her face.

"One day you shall have a lovely dress to wear, too, Sally," Katrina said, her heart going out to the shy, thin-faced girl. "Do you have a beau?" To her surprise, the girl's face flushed a fiery red and her eyes filled with tears.

"No, miss," she whispered.

Katrina was about to say more when the door opened and Julia burst in, followed by her mother and Mrs. Bateman.

"How extremely becoming it is on you!" exclaimed Lady Helen above Julia's squeals.

"And how crushingly expensive it must have been!" replied Katrina. "My lady, how can I accept such a gift? And the shoes and silk stockings and—How can I ever thank you enough?"

"You can thank me by never mentioning it again," replied Lady Helen, severely. "Now, my dear. Something to keep you warm, for it is, of all things, beginning to snow outside." She opened up the black shawl with a heavy fringe which she had carried in on her arm, and deftly arranged it around Katrina's shoulders. It was made of a soft kerseymere as fine as gossamer and yet, at the same time, exceedingly warm.

"There's the carriage now," said Mrs. Bateman, and hurried from the room.

"Have I forgotten anything? My reticule!" Katrina turned in a panic as Lady Helen gathered up her reticule and fan and placed them in her hands.

Once downstairs, having embraced the clamoring Julia and graciously accepted Mr. Standish's compliments upon her appearance, Katrina turned to her benefactress and once again voice her gratitude.

"We need no thanks, my dear girl, when we see your happiness." Lady Helen took her hands and then kissed her cheek. "Edward will take you to the carriage. Give my compliments to Lady Kettering and her daughter and—"

The rest was lost in the whistle of the wind, and, taking

Mr. Standish's arm, Katrina hurried down the pathway, which John was even now clearing of snow ahead of them, and then climbed up into the carriage.

Edward Standish stood by the carriage door for a moment to express his wife's compliments, but Lady Kettering cut him short by sharply reminding him that he would catch his death standing out in this weather without a hat or coat. She cast a quelling look at Katrina as she said this, as if to imply that the death of Edward Standish would be laid at her door.

As he ran back into the house, the carriage started off, and Katrina sank back against the cushions, brushing the snow from her hair, her heart beating fast at the thought of what lay ahead.

Chapter Eleven

Before Lady Kettering had uttered one word, Katrina could tell from her haughty expression that she thoroughly disapproved of her gown, her hairstyle, and, most of all, her astounding presumption. No doubt she had been persuaded much against her better judgment to take Lady Helen's governess to Lord Danville's concert. Her daughter suffered not only from a remarkably plain countenance, but also a tendency to dress in fashions more suitable for a dainty girl of sixteen than a gangling, large-boned female of more than five and twenty. Her bony shoulders rose out of a cloud of pink and white ruched silk, her low décolletage displaying nothing but a flat, white chest with not a hint of a curve. She, too, looked down her considerable nose at Katrina, aping her mother's sneer.

"I understand from Lady Helen that you are to entertain us at the concert tonight, Miss Vernon," said Lady Kettering. "Is that not so?"

"Yes, Lady Kettering."

"Well, well! We *shall* look forward to that pleasure. I also hear that you have been—ah, *practicing* with Lord Danville?"

The devil take her insinuating tone and her hard, calculating eyes! Katrina had not realized that the gossips were already at work on her. No doubt the blame could be laid at the door of the well-meaning but over-loquacious Mrs. Talbot.

She was greatly relieved to see the lights of the Hall twinkling through the blowing snow. The mansion was aglow with candlelight, a doubly welcoming sight on such a cold and blustery evening. They were greeted by footmen gamely holding on to umbrellas, the wind threatening to gust them out of their hands, and then hurriedly escorted up the stone steps and into the great hall, which echoed with voices and laughter and the strains of music.

As she stood behind Lady Kettering and the Honorable Miss Millicent Kettering, Katrina suddenly felt decidedly out of place, and her heart began to pound and her mouth go dry, the memory of the Merriot ball swirling in her mind. She lowered her eyes as she followed the ladies upstairs, fearful that she would see someone who might remember her from that ghastly night. When she entered the upstairs chamber that had been reserved for the ladies, she was aware of the censorious looks being cast her way by the local gentry and nobility. So much for Lady Helen's assurances that her presence at Danville Hall would not meet with censure. Oh, God, she thought, if only I had not come here! She glanced into a wall mirror to reassure herself that her hair was still in place and then stood with her back to the wall, waiting for Lady Kettering to finish speaking to Miss Olivia Brandon. Miss Brandon was a local beauty of both fortune and rank who, she had heard, was a front-runner in the Lord Danville matrimonial stakes.

It was with great interest that she surveyed the raven-haired and white-skinned Miss Brandon, and her heart ached even more, for everything she saw only served to substantiate the rumor. She was tall and beautiful, with a low, musical speaking voice and, it appeared, a lively wit; for even now, the normally dour Lady Kettering was baring her large teeth in an unattractive smile at something Miss Brandon had said. Katrina's face grew warm as they looked in her direction, realizing that it was she who was the object of their amusement.

Well, she thought, lifting her chin defiantly, in for a penny, in for a pound! Whatever shred of reputation she might have had would be gone by the end of this evening, so she might as well make the best of it!

She was about to follow the Kettering ladies to the music room when a footman approached her in the upper gallery; he bowed and whispered a message to her.

"Eh? What was that?" cried Lady Kettering. "Speak up, man!"

"His lordship asks me to convey his compliments to Miss Vernon," responded the footman in a loud voice, "and would she do him the honor of joining his private party in the blue saloon."

"Pray excuse me, Lady Kettering; Miss Kettering." Katrina smiled sweetly and gave them the slightest of nods before following the footman. She was aware, with a sense of triumph, that no one in the vicinity, including Miss Olivia Brandon, could have failed to have heard the message. The unwitting thought that she was doing exactly what she had vowed not to do, drawing attention to herself and Lord Danville, failed to quell the surge of excitement, for she had won the first skirmish and was prepared to do battle with the gossips, whatever the cost.

She hesitated outside the doors of the blue saloon, wishing all at once that she had someone, even Lady Kettering, to hide behind, but there was no time to dwell on such hen-hearted thoughts. The footman flung open the doors and, before she knew it, she had been ushered into the perfumed atmosphere of the saloon which, true to its name, was decorated in blue with elegant furnishings of pale blue, sapphire and gold. At first the lights from a myriad candles in the ornate chandeliers dazzled her, and she stood alone, blinded and bewildered. Then she took a hesitant step forward to find Lord Danville before her, and she instinctively put out a hand to him. He bowed and carried it to his lips, holding it in his for a moment, while he said softly, "My dear, my very dear Miss Vernon. I am overcome by your beauty." He bestowed upon her such a look of warmth that even had she maintained the icy manner she had originally intended, it would have been instantly melted. Tucking her hand comfortably into the crook of his arm, he moved forward to present her to his guests, who numbered more than a dozen.

"Miss Katrina Vernon, who is to sing for us tonight," he announced, and then proceeded to introduce his friends to her, one by one.

It was only after the presentation, when she had time to think, that Katrina realized he had assembled in one room the leading musical figures of the day: Michael Kelly, the Irish singer who had been a friend of Mozart and appeared in the premiere of his *Marriage of Figaro* in Vienna, now an impresario and manager of the Opera House; Thomas Attwood, the prolific composer of opera and music teacher to Princess Caroline—he was another Irishman, but shy and diffident, the absolute antithesis of the extroverted Mr. Kelly; the overpowering Earl of Guildford, who was famous for his theatrical entertainments and concerts in his own private theater in Wroxton Abbey; Mr. Salomon, the leading violinist and concert impresario. . . .

The main guests of honor Lord Danville saved until the last. Katrina extended her hand to the elegant, smiling elderly gentleman who stood before her, and gasped as she registered his name.

"Signor Clementi, this is a signal honor," she said, and sank into a deep curtsy before the famous composer and pianist, and was then presented to his wife, who had just come into the room, a placid Englishwoman many years his junior.

"And now, Miss Vernon, I should like to present you to Madame Catalini. Angelica, my dear, this is Bartini's pupil, Miss Katrina Vernon, of whom I have spoken."

The tall, handsome woman nodded and smiled in the grand theatrical manner, and Katrina sank into another deep curtsy. The renowned prima donna was dressed in a stunning gown of white crepe in the classical style, with a half train and overdress of transparent gold silk, the neckline cut exceedingly low to display as much as possible of her ample bosom. Her dark hair was dressed high, with gold-spangled ostrich plumes to give it even more height. The effect was overwhelming, but the smile she bestowed upon Katrina was warm and gracious.

"Justin tells me you have a charming voice, my dear Miss Vernon. We are all most eager to hear it." She continued speaking in general terms about music in her attractive, resonant voice, her Italian accent more pronounced than Clementi's. But Katrina heard little of what she said. For a moment she wondered if this was Danville's current mistress, for she had used his first name and behaved toward him with an easy familiarity, but when she was introduced to Monsieur Paul Valabrègue, Madame Catalini's extremely handsome husband, she realized that whatever Madame Catalini and the Viscount might have been to each other in the past, they were now merely good friends, for the Valabrègues obviously adored each other.

Overwhelmed by such illustrious company, Katrina was torn with apprehension and determined to speak with the Viscount immediately. He was about to present her to another lady who had entered the room, but Katrina begged him in a low voice to allow her to speak to him in private. He raised his expressive eyebrows at this but led her to the window alcove.

"I am deeply flattered, my dear Miss Vernon, that you should request this cozy *tête-à-tête*, but is it not a trifle indiscreet?" His eyes danced with amusement, but so agitated was she that this only served to infuriate her all the more.

"How could you ask me to sing in such company!" she demanded. "Before such—such illuminaries as Angelica Catalini and the great Clementi! To make me look a fool before them! You must have lost your senses! Or is this yet another of your famous wagers?" She was so distraught that she came close to striking him when she saw that his gray eyes were still laughing at her.

"I did not tell you, my dear girl, because I knew that this would be your reaction. Can you seriously believe I would expose you to ridicule here, in my own house, by my own friends? It is you who must have lost your senses to think such a thing of me!" Now the amusement had gone from his eyes, to be replaced by an intensity that made her waver and look down as he continued. "Katrina, you must regain your self-confidence, or you will never again be able to sing in public. Believe me, I would not encourage you if I did not consider you perfectly able to perform most competently in such company."

"What is the matter, Justin?" demanded the rich voice of Madame Catalini.

Katrina started, realizing with embarrassment that she must have been overheard. The dark eyes flashed over her, and she turned away with a muffled, "Excuse me."

"Has this abominable man been upsetting you, Miss Vernon? If it were not his own house, we would instantly banish him."

"Should I take the hint and leave you two charming ladies alone together?"

"Not at all. I only ask what it is you have done to over-set the so charming Miss Vernon."

Katrina raised her eyes to meet the prima donna's penetrating but kindly gaze. "Madame Catalini, I consider my talents entirely inadequate for me to perform in such illustrious company. Had I but known, I should never have consented to do so. I was merely informing Lord Danville that I cannot, I will not, sing tonight."

"But, my dear Miss Vernon, you are among friends here. We shall not—*come si dice*—be *judging* your performance. We wish merely to hear the fresh new voice Justin has told us so much about."

"You are most kind," murmured Katrina, "but I cannot—"

Her words were interrupted by another voice, this time male, letting out a roar that surprised her and most of the other occupants of the room.

"Katy Vernon! Dashed if it ain't my dear little Katy!"

Only one other person besides her father and uncle had ever called her Katy. She whirled around with a gasp to greet the young man who had so unceremoniously burst into the room. He was impeccably attired in evening dress, but she would have known those unruly blond curls anywhere.

"There I was, taking a well-earned respite from blowing

away on the horn, when I heard someone mention your name and, deuce take it, they were right. It *was* you!''

"Oh, my dear Des, I cannot believe it! What are you doing here?" He had caught both her hands in his, as if he would embrace her, but checked himself in time, and now she looked up at him with unbridled delight.

The Duke of Branscombe's third and youngest son, Desmond, Lord Charrington, was a year younger than she and had been one of her dearest friends when she had been growing up in Dorset. From the time they were children, they had been like brother and sister, and later attended the same balls and parties and acted in amateur theatricals together. It was Des who had taught her to ride and to drive his high-perch phaeton. "Never tell me you have progressed so far on the horn that you can play in such distinguished company," she quizzed him, her own mortification quite forgotten in her joy at seeing him.

"Indeed I have, although I own I was not Danville's first choice. The other horn-puffer fell sick, and so I was sent for. But I can't say I blame you for thinking I won't come up to scratch, for it was you that had to listen to me practice when I was a mere novice."

Now she suddenly became aware of Madame Catalini and Lord Danville standing by with looks of extreme wonderment on their faces. "Oh, pray forgive us for being so uncivil, but I have not seen Lord Charrington for more than two years, and we were the closest of friends in Dorset when we were children together." She was about to make the introductions, quite forgetting in her confusion that the Viscount already knew Desmond!

"I had, of course, surmised that you must be acquainted with Lord Charrington, Miss Vernon, but had not realized you were such intimate friends." Lord Danville's tone was decidedly cool. "As a *close friend*, perhaps *you* can prevail upon Miss Vernon to sing for us tonight, Charrington?"

"Prevail upon her to sing? Indeed I can, for she's by far the best I've ever heard. Present company excepted, of course, madame," he added with a gallant bow in the prima donna's direction. "Never tell me you won't sing, Katy! Why ever not?"

Katrina gave him a speaking look. "Because I have not been singing for an age, Des. I could not."

"Could not? What a bag of moonshine! I've never known you to balk at a fence!"

She glared at him. "Of course not! But this is a different matter altogether."

"Fudge! Don't tell me you've turned chicken-hearted!"

"Not at all," snapped Katrina, her eyes flashing. "Oh, very well then, I shall sing—and place the blame upon you if I make a cake of myself." She almost wished Desmond had not come into the room.

"Wager a pony you won't! Well, I'd best get back," and, with a wide grin at her and a hasty bow to Madame Catalini, he departed, throwing over his shoulder a breezy: "See you later, Katy," before leaving the room.

"*Cielo!*" said Madame Catalini, with a twinkling laugh. "That young man is like *un ciclone,* a—a whirlwind. But he achieved more than we did, Justin. He persuaded Miss Vernon to sing."

"Indeed he did." The Viscount's tone was caustic, and he gave Katrina a look which she found impossible to fathom. "Come, our audience awaits us and must be growing restless. You shall sing first, Miss Vernon."

"I am afraid," she said, forgetting herself so far as to grasp his arm.

Immediately, the cool, withdrawn expression left his eyes, and for a fleeting moment he laid his hand upon hers. "There is no cause to be afraid. We are all friends here."

"Indeed we are," said the affable Michael Kelly, who was standing close by. "And will all be cheering you on."

Now they had all surrounded her, and the warmth of their concern and the knowledge that she was indeed in the company of friends renewed her confidence.

"But who is to play for you, Miss Vernon?" asked Clementi.

"Lord Danville," she replied, with a shy smile at the Viscount.

"Lord Danville!" The elderly composer looked greatly surprised at this, and went so far as to raise his eyeglass to survey the Viscount through it.

"Danville playing the accompaniment for you?" said Michael Kelly. "Never say so, Miss Vernon!" And he gave a great crack of laughter, which was taken up by most of the others in the room.

Katrina was seized with indignation at this incivility to their host. The Viscount might be a dilettante, a mere amateur, but he was deeply sincere about his music-making, and they had no right to hold him in ridicule. "I find him a most able accompanist!" she retorted in his defense.

"An able accompanist! Do you, do you indeed!" Mr. Kelly dissolved into laughter, quite overwhelmed by the thought.

How abominably rude of them, Katrina thought. She caught Lord Danville's eye and was at least relieved to see that he was taking the roasting in good part. As he saw her looking at him, he gave a slight shrug of his broad shoulders, his lips quirking into a wry smile. Now she was doubly determined to sing her very best, so that he would appear a most competent performer. Her own fears were set aside, and she gave him a radiant smile to reassure him that she took no part in this cruel funning.

When she entered the music room, she momentarily recoiled at the sight of the lines of chairs, most of them occupied, but once she herself was seated in the front row with the guests of honor, and heard the announcement of her own name, it was too late to do anything but walk serenely and confidently to the front of the pianoforte, wait for Lord Danville to be seated, smile graciously at him, and begin.

As soon as she had sung the first few bars, her nervousness departed, her breathing settled, and she knew that exhilarating feeling of being in control of both her voice and the audience. The enthusiastic applause that greeted her first song, Caldara's plaintive *"Sebben, crudele,"* reassured her that she had sung well, and thus she was able to abandon herself to the lively, joyous words of the *"Vittoria mio core,"* underscoring them with the expressive use of her eyes and countenance. This time the applause was even warmer and, smiling delightedly, she took her bows and was escorted back to her seat by Lord Danville.

She sat there glowing throughout the performance of a short symphony by Clementi, the maestro himself conducting the performance from the pianoforte, although she had heard him adamantly resist all attempts to persuade him to perform as a soloist. "I am a composer and teacher—and a man of business—now. I leave solo performance to my pupils," he said.

When the symphony was completed, Katrina was so busily engaged in graciously responding to the congratulations being offered her that it was not unitl the concert was almost ready to begin again that she realized she had not thanked Lord Danville for his part in her success.

"Have you seen Lord Danville?" she asked Desmond, who had procured her a glass of lemonade, after reminding her that he had won his wager. He had also told her that she was singing better than ever and was looking bang up to the nines.

"Danville? No. Daresay he's gone off somewhere to be alone. Always does before he plays."

"Oh, no, Des! Don't tell me he is going to perform as a soloist!" Remembering his own friends' gibes at his playing ability, she shrank from the thought of an exhibition of his shortcomings as a performer before this glittering assembly.

"By the bye," interpolated Lord Charrington, with a sudden frown. "What's Danville to you, Katy?"

"What do you mean?"

"Just what I said. Dashed attentive to you, ain't he? For all I like the man as a friend, he's a notorious rake, not at all the sort of man I like to see you cozing up with! And don't gammon me by saying he's merely playing the pianoforte for you, for I saw the way he was looking at you. You'd best take care, or he'll be offering you a *carte blanche*!"

"What a muttonhead you are, Des! Besides, at the ripe old age of more than two and twenty, I am perfectly capable of taking care of myself."

"Are you? Not so sure of that. 'Devil' Danville, they call him, you know. He's up to all the tricks in the book. And the marriage mart's not one of them, even if the fair Olivia is casting her line in that direction. So you'd best be on your guard!''

''Don't be concerning yourself, my dear Des,'' she retorted, with a harsh laugh. ''I'm not the green girl I used to be, you know!'' And she swept past him to her seat.

Although she had been stung by Desmond's words, she was now infinitely more concerned about Lord Danville's forthcoming debacle than the likelihood of his asking her to become his mistress. As the oboe sounded its plaintive note and the musicians tuned their instruments, she prayed that the Viscount would play something simple and brief. His competency was most certainly adequate to perform such a piece.

But to her utter dismay, it was announced that their host would perform a concerto for the pianoforte by Mozart, one of his later works, written in the key of E flat. She gripped her hands on her reticule, its clasp digging into her palms, as the Viscount, severely elegant in his black coat and knee breeches and ivory watered-silk waistcoat, seated himself at the pianoforte and adjusted the stool. He gave the signal to begin and himself conducted the orchestra most competently in the fanfarelike opening, but as the music moved toward the introduction of the pianoforte, Katrina's heart thudded in her breast. Please, God, assist him, she prayed. Even as the prayer ran through her mind, he had begun; and she knew instantly that she had either completely misunderstood his friends' mockery or they had deliberately misled her, for his long fingers executed the delicate, intricate, fiendishly difficult runs and roulades with an ease and perfection and beauty of tone which suspended her breath, until she was forced to release it and, with it, all the pent-up tension.

She sank back into her chair, allowing the music to flow over her, exulting in the exquisite pleasures of listening to and watching its performance. Lord Danville performed without affectation, with no mannerisms, and seemed unaware of his audience; his face registered only the excitement of the music itself, nothing more.

When the second movement began, its darkness took her by surprise. The poignant beauty of it was reflected in the

Viscount's face, and at times he closed his eyes in the intensity of his playing. The ineffable sadness of the music, the melancholy interpolations of the woodwind, his wondrous playing, all swept her away, so that she was at one with the music, at one with the man who interpreted it with such depth of feeling. She found it almost impossible to restrain tears at her realization that one who could interpret this music with such intensity had indeed a soul worth saving, and inwardly her heart cried out his name: *Justin!*

The final movement came as a shock, for it was as if the composer had shaken his head at his dark thoughts and laughed himself out of his despair, crying: "Away with melancholy!" Again Lord Danville's countenance reflected the music, for even as his fingers played the skipping theme, his face was lit by the quirky look Katrina knew so well.

As the concerto moved to its brilliant finale, she knew herself to be changed but could not bring herself to acknowledge in what way. Even when the music had ended and most members of the audience had risen to their feet with shouts of "Bravo!" she still sat, stunned by this revelation of Lord Danville as a man of intensity, of sensibility, of *soul*—a revelation which had been made possible only through the medium of music, and which she knew instinctively he would labor diligently to negate.

And she suddenly knew that, despite her concern that he would never be able to reveal this hidden aspect of himself other than through the medium of music, she loved him and would sacrifice everything—reputation, security, and, most especially, her pride—to grasp at whatever little happiness he was willing to give her.

"Why so pensive, Miss Vernon? Was my performance truly *that* distressing?"

She started, the blood rushing to her cheeks as she found him standing before her. To her great embarrassment, she saw that nearly everyone had left the music room to seek refreshment, and that the few who were left were watching her and Lord Danville intently.

"May I?" He sat down on the chair beside her. "What is

the matter, Katrina?'' he asked softly, for he could see that she was laboring under some great emotion.

"You were—'' She looked up into his face and bit her lip, but nothing could restrain the tears which now filled her eyes and threatened to run down her cheeks. She pressed one hand to her mouth while blindly searching in her reticule for her handkerchief, only to find that he was holding out his own to her. She took it and pressed it to her eyes. "What a ninny you will be thinking me, but . . . you were— I never thought— I believed—'' She was incoherent.

"Oh, Katrina, my dear sweet girl.'' He leaned over her, his eyes searching hers, a tender smile on his lips. "You were not to know. Besides, I *am* a deuced poor accompanist. My preference is to be the key performer, you see!'' He gave her a wry smile at his attempt at a pun, and then, glancing around, to see if they were being observed, reached for her hand and bore it to his lips, kissing it lingeringly.

"That is not what I meant,'' she said, allowing her hand to rest in his. "Your playing was— Oh, I cannot explain it, but it revealed to me an aspect of you I had not realized existed.''

"Did it indeed!'' He arched his winged eyebrows at her.

"No, do not turn it to mockery!'' she cried. "It is what you always do. You never permit me to come close to you!'' Even then she expected him to turn her words upon her and make a jest of them, but this time he did not.

His eyes darkened, and his breath came fast as he gripped her hands in his. "My darling Katrina, I *must* somehow contrive to speak with you alone this evening.''

But it was certainly too late to do so now, for his guests were returning for the third part of the concert and were casting speculative glances in their direction. More grist for the gossip mill, she thought.

She was assailed by both disappointment and relief to find that no opportunity arose for them to be alone together after the concert had finished. The Viscount escorted Madame Catalini into supper, she having given a brilliant performance in arias from Portogallo's *Semiramide* and from various Mozart operas, although she refused to give them a preview of *The Marriage of Figaro*. "You must all come to the Opera

House in June, when I shall be singing Susanna in the premiere performance in England," she told her adoring audience.

Katrina was escorted into supper by Desmond, which delighted her, for having extracted a promise from him that he would not bring up the subject of Lord Danville and her again, they spent the remainder of the evening talking over old times and arguing hotly and with much hilarity on every subject under the sun. She felt as if she were back in Dorset and the months in prison only a bad dream. As the evening drew to a close, she was reluctant to let Desmond go, wishing she could take him back to the parsonage with her, but he gave her his word that he would present himself there early the next afternoon, and with that she had to be content.

She was waiting in the great hall for Lady Kettering and her daughter when Mr. Kelly appeared before her. Having once again bestowed effusive congratulations upon her singing, he drew her aside. "Miss Vernon, I trust you will not think me presumptuous, but as I am not sure we shall meet again before I return to London, perhaps you will pardon me for asking you a rather impertinent question. Have you ever considered singing as a profession?"

"A profession? Why no, Mr. Kelly." The famous Mr. Kelly's countenance was a trifle pink beneath his modishly curled hair, but she did not think him foxed.

"I was amazed to learn just now that you are employed as a governess, and it was only that circumstance which prompted me to speak to you on the subject. If you would ever be comtemplating taking up the profession of singing, particularly opera, would you be so kind as to contact me?" He handed her his card.

She was considerably taken aback by the offer, but the suggestion was a fascinating one. "But would I be sufficiently competent, Mr. Kelly?"

"Yes, indeed! We are always interested in fresh voices, particularly when they are allied to such a *speaking* countenance as yours!" He kissed his fingers to her in a flamboyant gesture. "In truth, there is a small part in *The Marriage of Figaro* which you could play most adequately: the part of the little peasant girl, Barbarina. Not a starring role by any means, but it has a little arietta and would make a good start to your career. With your voice and appearance and those *expressive* eyes, you could become quite a go!''

She was not sure if she should be insulted or complimented by his offer, but decided, on looking into his earnest, shining face, that it was meant as the latter. ''Indeed, Mr. Kelly, you have quite overwhelmed me! I am most flattered—and honored—that you would consider me good enough to perform at the Opera.''

''Will you consider it, then, Miss Vernon? You will find me at the Opera House, King's Theater, Haymarket; or, failing that, at Drury Lane, where I am music director.'' He tapped the card in her hand, made her his theatrical bow once more, and then bade her his adieu.

How amazing! And how kindhearted he was! It had been a long time since she had felt quite so at home as she had tonight with Lord Danville's friends, and to discover that her dear Des was one of their number had made her happiness complete.

As she took her public and, therefore, of necessity, formal farewell of Lord Danville, she was about to mention Mr. Kelly's extraordinary offer when she had the sudden recollection that this might not be wise; and looking into the smiling but inscrutable eyes of the man she now knew she loved, she decided to keep Mr. Kelly's address card as a form of insurance against the uncertainties of the future. After all, there were far worse fates than that of becoming an opera singer!

Chapter Twelve

The revelation of Lord Danville's profound sensibility, and her discovery that she was not merely infatuated but deeply in love with him, was not at all conducive to sleep that night. For more than two hours she lay restless in bed, her mind whirling with images and snatches of music, trying desperately to come to terms with her own feelings and her present situation. She was able to reach only two conclusions: one, that she loved the Viscount and had probably been in love with him since their first encounter at Danville Hall; the other, that she was about to be offered a new position—as his mistress. Everything pointed to it: his embraces, the warm looks, the suggestion that he must meet with her alone as soon as possible. Until the concert she had been determined to refuse his offer of a *carte-blanche*, but now that she knew she loved him, her heart argued that it was surely better than no relationship at all.

Yet, while she tossed and turned, reliving his looks and words and the memory of his impassioned playing, another thought refused to be suppressed: if she became his mistress, she would be seriously deceiving him. She tried to thrust the thought away; after all, it was not as if he were asking her to marry him. But the reminder was sufficient for her to determine not to offer him any encouragement and to allow him to make all the advances. That way, perhaps, she would feel less guilt-ridden.

Hard on the heels of this unwelcome reminder of her past came its natural successor. How would she contend with the physical demands of being a mistress, for surely the primary duties of a *chère-amie* would be performed in bed? She had deliberately avoided such thoughts before, for whenever Lord Danville had embraced her, somehow all her fears had been forgotten in her fervent responses to him. Now they loomed like monsters in a nightmare in her overtaxed brain, and she succumbed to a fit of the sick shudders which had frequently assailed her since her father's death. She got up, teeth chattering, to take out some extra blankets from the wardrobe drawer and piled them on the bed, but nothing could warm her, and she lay there, her body shaking as if she had the ague, her eyes wide open, staring at the whitewashed ceiling.

Eventually she fell into a fitful sleep and awoke, a dull ache in her head, to find the sun shining in the window. She jumped out of bed and knelt on the window seat to look out. It was a beautiful day; the snow had not melted, and the dry, brown earth was brushed with pristine white. Sunlight sparkled on the silvery trunks of the beech trees and their frost-tipped branches. There would be no hunting today, the ground would be too hard, but Lord Danville's guests would probably go shooting. Desmond had told her that was to be the plan if the frost remained.

The beautiful day and the anticipation of seeing Desmond again banished all her dark thoughts, and she hurriedly put on her gray morning dress, prepared to answer Julia's barrage of questions about the concert.

While she was taking her breakfast in the nursery with her charge, Lady Helen entered, and Katrina was forced to repeat her history of the concert, but not in such detail. Lady Helen did not, for instance, demand to know what each lady had worn literally from top to toe, as Julia had. Once she had completed her résumé of the concert, she tentatively mentioned the subject of Lord Charrington's calling upon her that afternoon.

"I am mindful that it would mean a slight break in Julia's lessons," she said hesitantly. "And I have already taken far too much time away from my duties."

"Nonsense! I am delighted to hear that you have met an old friend. We shall invite Lord Charrington to take tea with us when he calls."

But when Desmond called at the parsonage and was seated in the parlor with the ladies, he politely declined Lady Helen's invitation to take tea with them, enthusiastically exclaiming: "It's such a *famous* day! Danville's got up a riding party, and Katy, I mean Miss Vernon, is invited to join us."

Katrina shook her head and frowned at this. "Oh, no, I could not possibly—"

"Danville's had a sprightly little gray filly saddled up for you. All it needs is Lady Helen's consent, and I'll have my groom bring it round."

"I haven't mounted a horse for more than a year, and besides, I have nothing to wear," Katrina said resolutely. "And you forget, Des, I am an employee here. I cannot neglect my duties."

Lord Charrington looked slightly abashed at this, but Lady Helen smiled. "I have yet to see you neglect your duties in any way, Miss Vernon. I shall give Julia a lesson in embroidery; not, you may recall, one of your assigned duties," she added with a twinkling look.

Lord Charrington gave a crack of laughter at this. "Still can't ply a needle, eh, Katy? I can remember when—"

"I have nothing suitable to wear for riding," Katrina hurriedly interposed, not sure with which story of torn petticoats or ripped stockings he was about to regale Lady Helen.

"I am sure we can quickly shorten the hem of one of my habits, if Lord Charrington is willing to wait," replied Lady Helen. "You look pale today; the fresh air will do you good," she added in a coaxing tone.

"Oh, do go, Miss Vernon," cried Julia. "I've never seen you ride a horse."

Realizing she was hopelessly outnumbered, Katrina acquiesced and was sent upstairs to prepare herself for the ride, while Lady Helen and Mrs. Bateman worked on the hem. Meanwhile, Lord Charrington, having sent off his groom to the Hall, engaged in a lively game of spillikins with Julia on the parlor floor.

Lady Helen's green velvet habit, although too large about the bodice, looked extremely fetching with Katrina's chestnut hair. The wide revers opened to display a fall of lace at her throat, and the outfit was topped off with a dashing velvet bonnet with an ostrich feather that curled down her cheek. Apart from the black leather gloves, there was not a hint of mourning about her attire. Looking into the mirror to adjust her hat, she was not sure which she was anticipating the more: spending time with Des, the ride itself, or seeing Lord Danville again. All three, most probably, were responsible for her glowing countenance, which quite belied Lady Helen's insistence that she needed fresh air to banish her pallor.

When she saw the lively little filly Lord Danville had provided for her, she hesitated for a moment, wondering if she could ride it.

"Told him you were a bang-up rider and not to give you any slugs," said Desmond. "Not that it's likely he has any in his stables. Wait till you see his black gelding. A real goer!"

It felt like old times to be tossed into the saddle by Des, and as she settled herself and took up the reins she felt completely at home, as if she had ridden only yesterday. They talked without ceasing until they passed through the main gates of Danville Hall. Then Desmond fell silent and, allowing his groom to move out of earshot, slowed his mount to a walk.

"Katy, what's between you and Danville? I know I gave my word not to talk of it last night, but I must know."

The expression on his normally cheerful countenance was so serious that Katrina bit back the hasty retort that he not concern himself with her business. "We are merely—friends." She gazed straight ahead of her, between the filly's ears, not wishing to meet Desmond's intense look.

"Friends? Ha! You must think me a sapskull to expect me

to believe that! You and I are friends, but I cannot believe that Danville and you have the same—''

''I do indeed look upon him as a friend, Des,'' she told him with great emphasis, avoiding his frank blue eyes. ''But I also love him.''

''Thought as much! What a gudgeon to fall for his line!''

''I'm not certain it is a line. I believe he has a *tendre* for me, although I cannot undersand how he could be attracted to such a little dab of female.''

''Course he is! Couldn't help it!'' He leaned across and squeezed her hand. ''But you're a ninnyhammer if you believe it's wedding bells he's got in mind, for it ain't!''

''Of course I don't think so! I'm not so green as you think me, Des. He might consider marriage with a woman of considerable wealth and rank like Olivia Brandon, but an impoverished governess? No.'' She averted her eyes from him again. ''I am not even certain he wants me for his mistress. I've been warned before that he tires of his women as soon as he's seduced them.''

''Yes, well, that's one of the many tales about him. He's never kept any of his birds of paradise for very long, but I've heard he's always exceeding generous in his leave-takings.''

''So, I could at least look forward to a few jewels and perhaps a cash settlement for my pains!'' Her tone was bitter.

''This is a devilish stupid conversation! We both know you'll not accept his *carte-blanche*, however much you think you love him. You never were one to flout convention, Katy. Besides, you've too much Vernon pride to become Danville's plaything.''

''Perhaps I've changed.''

''Farradiddle! You haven't changed one whit!''

''Let's speak on another subject, Des,'' she begged. ''I have been so looking forward to this, and you are quite spoiling it.''

He pulled up his horse and took her reins, drawing her to a standstill beside him. ''Marry me, Katy,'' he said bluntly.

She stared at him, open-mouthed with atonishment. ''Marry *you*!'' She was about to go into whoops of laughter, but the flush of his cheeks stopped her.

"Marry me, and then you won't have to work as a governess or become the mistress of a notorious rake. We'd deal famously together."

"Oh, Des." Tears rushed to her eyes at his kindness. "My dearest Des. You know how I love you, but not at all in the way a wife should feel for her husband. It would be like— like incest. You know it! I am quite overcome with gratitude for your offer, but I must refuse it."

Although he tried hard to hide it, she could see he was relieved at her answer. "Then allow me to take you back to Dorset. You could stay with Caroline; not your style, I know, but better than being employed as a governess."

"Caroline!" The thought of living with Desmond's older, married sister was not an appealing one. She was indolent to the point of sloth and kept dozens of dogs, which were allowed the run of the house. "What a ramshackle idea! Why, just the *thought* of the smell in her house makes me nauseated! No, no, Des. Allow me to arrange my own affairs. I give you my word I'll come to you if I'm in a fix."

"Just as your father came to mine when he was in queer street," he said sarcastically.

Her heart skipped a beat at the thought of her father. If only she had been able to persuade him to appeal to Desmond's father, how different things might have been. "My father had more pride than sense," she said in a small voice. Then she rallied, determined not to dwell on the past. "I am very happy with Lady Helen; I am treated as one of the family there. As for Lord Danville, I am well able to handle him, and I assure you he will not force me into anything against my will. Now, let us see if I can still gallop without falling off!" Before he could say any more, she spurred her horse, racing ahead of him down the long avenue.

When they reached the Hall, they were informed that the riding party had already set off and would have reached the east wood by now. They caught up with them in the densest part of the wood, where the deep carpet of fallen beech leaves slowed them to a walking pace. The party consisted of only five others: Lord Danville, Mr. Kelly, the Earl and Countess of Guildford, and Miss Brandon, the latter acknowledging

Katrina with a glacial stare and the slightest inclination of the head. She looked magnificent in a military-style habit and matching hat of magenta velvet. Katrina, who had thought her own costume quite dashing, felt completely overshadowed.

As soon as she met Lord Danville's eyes, she knew that he was in one of his difficult moods. His lips curled into a semblance of a smile, and his eyes were full of mockery as he bowed his head to acknowledge her. "Ah, Miss Vernon. So Lord Charrington was eventually able to persuade you to join us."

The blood rushed to her cheeks at the sarcastic tone of his voice. "Forgive me for keeping you waiting, my lord, but I had no riding dress and had to borrow Lady Helen's." She spoke in a quiet, level voice, which, she hoped, did not betray her anger at his implied criticism of her tardiness, but at the same time she flashed him a withering glance—and was immediately sorry for it, for the hard look had gone from his eyes, and he was obviously regretting having given her a public set-down.

"I beg your pardon, Miss Vernon,' he said quietly, almost humbly. "It was not my intention to chide you for keeping us waiting." He eased his mount away from Olivia Brandon to ride beside her, and Katrina saw that the lady's dark eyes narrowed at this. "How do you like the mount I chose for you, Miss Vernon?"

"She is beautiful! You could not have chosen better. I feel as if I had been riding her for years; as if she were my very own."

"Then," he replied in a low voice, giving her one of his intense looks, "so she shall be!"

She colored and shook her head in warning to him, not daring to reply with Olivia Brandon's eyes boring into them, for she had now moved to ride on the other side of Lord Danville.

"Trapped, by God!" said Desmond, laughing. "How do you do it, Danville? Flanked by two beauties, leaving the rest of us out in the cold."

"Observe my methods, my dear Charrington, but I doubt you have the necessary style!"

His superior tone and the challenging look he flung at Desmond so vexed Katrina that she smiled and said sweetly: "Pray excuse me, my lord. Desmond and I have much news to catch up on, and I am sure you wish to return to your *tête-à-tête*." She gave the Honorable Miss Brandon a look of wide-eyed innocence and was rewarded with a smile of pure disdain.

Aware that she had been guilty of a breach of conduct, she did not dare glance in Lord Danville's direction as she fell back to ride beside Desmond, but she felt a coldness around her heart as she watched the aristocratic, well-matched pair ride ahead, darkly handsome as they engaged in animated conversation. She felt a pain like a stab of a knife when she saw the warm expression in the Viscount's eyes as they rested on Olivia Brandon's beautiful face, but she had no desire to ride with them, to be put in the shade by Miss Brandon's extreme beauty and even more extreme sense of superiority. And Lord Danville was doubtless both greatly flattered and amused by this juxtaposition of two females—one his intended wife, the other his intended mistress!

Steeled by this thought, Katrina laughed and rattled on, even going so far as to flirt with Desmond, not realizing she was doing so until he said, with a frown: "Doing it a little too brown, Katy. Making a cake of yourself!" And she flushed with embarrassment and turned her face away from him.

A tearing gallop across the common did much to restore her good humor, although when she and Desmond returned she realized from Miss Brandon's raised eyebrows and even more disdainful expression that she must look a sight, with her bonnet askew and her hair all blown about her face. Lord Danville was silent, his lips set into a thin line, until he opened them to suggest they return to the Hall for refreshment, as it was growing chilly.

Not half so chilly, thought Katrina, as is the atmosphere herebouts!

As she sat in a remote corner of the library, pretended to be immersed in a book of Piranesi's etchings, Katrina watched the Viscount take up his customary arrogant pose by the fireside. She could not help contrasting it with the last time she had been in the library with him. The memory of his passionate kisses and tenderness swept over her so that she had to dig her nails into her palms to stop tears from welling up in her eyes. She had no idea why he was acting so coldly toward her, but she recognized only too well his swift changes of mood. Yet it was only last night that he had so fervently stated that he must see her alone. He was, as he had always been, inscrutable, quite impossible to fathom.

Because she was immersed in her thoughts, she had not realized that, apart from Madame Catalini, who was studying a score at the far end of the library, everyone else had left the room. She was about to approach the fire, for she was beginning to feel cold, when the door opened and Lord Danville walked in again.

She halted, confused by his sudden reappearance. "Oh where are the others?" she asked him.

"Miss Brandon has gone to change. The gentlemen are in the gun room examining my collection. Have no fear, I shall return your *dear Des* to you in due course!"

Surely he could not be jealous of Desmond! Yet the curl of his lips and the inflection of his voice suggested it. Her heart leaped at the thought that it could be jealousy of Desmond that was responsible for his coldness toward her. She gave him a little half-smile. "I was coming to sit nearer the fire, as it is a trifle cold by the window."

He drew back and gestured toward the chair nearest the fire, but his face still bore a look of cold hauteur. For a moment it appeared that he was about to quit the room, but then he took up his position by the fire, one foot on the rail, swinging his eyeglass to and fro on its black riband. The only sounds to be heard were the crackle of logs and a low humming from Madame Catalini.

Unnerved by the silence between them, Katrina was the first to speak. "Would Madame Catalini not prefer to work in the music room?"

A sardonic smile twisted his mouth. "Why, my dear Miss Vernon, you are surely not suggesting we should be left alone together?"

She gritted her teeth, but was determined to keep her

temper. "Not at all, my lord; although it would not be for the first time, would it? I was merely wondering why she would prefer to study here."

"For the very simple reason that she finds it warmer here than in the music room."

Further silence. Aware that he was studying her intently through his quizzing glass, she refused to be disconcerted by his rudeness and picked up a book from the oval table beside her, pretending to read it. But after two or three minutes she threw it down on the table, unable to contain herself any longer.

"Oh, do sit down and stop staring at me through that ridiculous glass!" she ordered him.

He looked amused at her outburst, as if he felt he had won the round, but obeyed the order, seating himself on the chair across from her. "What is Charrington to you?" he demanded boldly.

She had to restrain a smile at this, for it was said in much the same vein as Desmond's question about him had been, albeit more ferociously. "Desmond?" She tilted her head questioningly at him.

"Yes. *Dear* Desmond," he replied between his teeth. "What is he to you?"

"I might as well ask in reply, what is the Honorable Miss Brandon to you, my lord?"

"Olivia?"

"Yes, your *dear* Olivia."

"What the devil has that to do with you?"

"Exceedingly well put, my lord! The very words I should have chosen had I been a man, not a delicately nurtured female."

His face paled with anger. "The circumstances are entirely different."

"Oh, indeed? I cannot think why. But before we carry this rather nonsensical conversation any further, allow me to set your mind at rest. Desmond is a dear friend, like a brother to me; and I strongly resent your having given him a public set-down, especially when he is supposedly a friend of yours, because of some idiotish quirk of jealousy on your part."

"Jealousy! My dear Miss Vernon, you flatter yourself."

Her cheeks burned at his acid tone, and her body tensed with anger. "My dear Lord Danville," she replied, her tone matching his, "I would remind you, as you once reminded me, that my affairs are none of your concern."

"Exceedingly well put, Miss Vernon. 'Affairs' is a good word to use!"

"I am so glad it meets with your approval, my lord. Nevertheless, pray recollect that I am not in any way responsible to you for my actions, and I therefore resent the implication that I should be."

He sprang up at this and strode to her side with such a grim expression on his face that she shrank back in the chair. Leaning over her, he gripped her wrists and hauled her to her feet. She knew it was useless to struggle against him, but said in a low voice, "Let me go, my lord. Madame Catalini will see us. Release me immediately!"

"Not until you can assure me there is nothing more than friendship between you and Charrington."

"I will do no such thing. You do not own me!"

"Not literally, no; but nevertheless you are mine. Although you resist me, even now you are afire with longing for me to take you into my arms, are you not? Come, look into my eyes and deny it."

She closed her eyes, unable to deny it, for it was devastatingly true. Her body ached with the desire to press close to him, to feel his lips on hers, to become one with him.

"Oh, Katrina," he breathed. "For God's sake, stop fighting me, for you can never win."

For one breathless moment, she thought he would kiss her, but a descreet clearing of the throat from Madame Catalini brought them to their senses, and he released her with a heavy sigh and retreated to his chair and sat down, leaving her shaken by her reaction to him. What a weak fool he must think her, she thought as she seated herself, that he need only suggest taking her into his arms to have her subjugated to his will. She was about to inform him that he need not think her so easily seduced into submission when he disarmed her by giving her his rare, unaffected smile, to which it was impossible not to respond. Immediately, the tension between them ebbed away, and when he spoke again it was as if nothing else had passed between them.

"You will be glad to hear, Miss Vernon, that my agent, Carlton, has at last finished with my business in town and is returning to Danville tonight. I mean to discuss the Danville estate with him this evening. Tomorrow I shall take a tour of the entire estate with him, and I have asked Edward Standish to accompany us to Pudsey Lane in the afternoon. It was your suggestion, you will recollect, to shield myself from harm by taking Mr. Standish with me. You see how I cater to your demands!"

She smiled warmly at him, ignoring the last remark. "Oh, I am so glad, for this cold weather is causing the cottagers a great deal of hardship, and Meg Foster is failing fast. I had not liked to mention it again, for I felt sure it was our visitors that had put it out of your mind."

"Not at all. I had not forgotten but decided that despite your insistence on haste, it would be best to wait until Carlton had returned. Although, as I told you, I am convinced he has been neglecting many of his duties during my long absences from Danville, he knows more about the management of the estate than I. I do assure you that although it is more than a fortnight since you first made your request, it will be dealt with very soon."

She tried to hide a smile, but was evidently not entirely successful.

"Have I said something to amuse you, Miss Vernon?"

"Not really. I was merely thinking that my first discussion with you on the subject of your tenants could hardly be termed a *request*!"

He chuckled good-humoredly and was about to reply when the door opened to admit a group of his guests, led by Miss Brandon, who shot a sharp glance in Katrina's direction

"A game of billiards has been proposed, and we have come to carry you away to the games room, Justin."

Assuming the air of languid hauteur Katrina had first seen at the Merriot ball, he stood and made her a slight bow and, glancing in Madame Catalini's direction, merely said: "I leave you in good company, Miss Vernon," before strolling away to join his friends. As the door closed and the sounds of voices retreated, Katrina sat staring at the place where he had been.

"Superb, is he not?"

She started and looked up to see Madame Catalini's tall, graceful figure before her. "I often tell my dear friend Justino that he should be on the stage." The prima donna sat down on the sofa, arranging her flowing draperies around her.

"I have heard others say the same thing," replied Katrina. She looked up to meet the dark, liquid eyes of the singer and immediately felt that here was another woman who had seen behind Danville's façade. Madame Catalini leaned forward and took her hand.

"He is a dangerous man," she said, tapping her knuckles with her ivory fan, "and you are very young. *Perdonate*— forgive me for talking thus to you, but I could now allow you to leave without first speaking to you. It is too late, I know, to tell you not to love him, but I must warn you that if you proceed any further, you take the chance of having your heart broken by him. He is forever revenging himself upon us poor women for what he suffered at the hands of females in his youth. *Povero Justino!* His music and his books are the only mistresses he is faithful to, for they cannot cause him pain. Yet such poor fools as we cannot help hoping that we will be his savior, his one redeeming love." She gave a throaty laugh. *"Cielo!* It would make a perfect libretto for an opera, would it not? My advice to you, *cara* Signorina Vernon, is to run very quickly from this place and never return. Marry yourself to some young boy like Lord Charrington and forget 'Diavolo' Danville." She released Katrina's hand but continued to look intently at her, the dark eyes glowing. "But I see in your eyes that it is too late even for that, and so I can only wish you *bella fortuna*!"

She rose with a flutter of draperies and bent over Katrina, lifting her chin with a perfumed hand. "I deeply pity you, *cara* Signorina, but I tell you something: for as long as it lasts, being loved by him is heaven on earth!''

With these bittersweet words, the singer swept from the room, leaving Katrina even further torn by doubts and misgivings than she had been before.

Chapter Thirteen

It was not until the following evening, after dinner, that Katrina heard the outcome of the Viscount's visitation of Pudsey Lane. She wished with all her heart that she could have been a member of the expedition. She would have given the world to see the elegant Lord Danville treading through the mucky gutter of Pudsey Lane, his haughty nostrils offended by the stench. But she had to be content with the description Edward Standish gave, which, although fairly matter-of-fact, was sufficiently illustrated with snippets of conversation and little asides to give her a reasonably satisfactory picture.

"In summation," said Mr. Standish, stretching his legs out to the parlor fire with a sigh of contentment, "Lord Danville was appalled at the general state of the cottages and at once gave orders for their immediate repair. He is even considering having them torn down eventually and building new, sanitary homes for his tenants. So, my dear Miss Vernon, we have a great deal for which to thank you." He gave her his engaging smile. "Without you, all this would never have been achieved."

She shook her head. "Oh, no, sir. I am convinced it only needed Lord Danville to see Pudsey Lane for himself. Once that objective was achieved, I was certain he would not stand by and do nothing. I do not think him *uncaring*," she added, her face growing warm. "It is only that he has never been taught to consider the welfare of those less fortunate than himself. It needed only for it to be drawn to his attention."

"I believe you overestimate Lord Danville's humanity and underestimate your own ability to persuade him, but whatever it needed, it is you who are responsible, and you must allow us to express our gratitude."

"Yes, indeed," said Lady Helen, looking up from darning one of Julia's stockings. "only *you* could have approached Lord Danville." Her eyes were fixed on Katrina's with such a compelling expression that she was forced to look away.

"I fear Mr. Carlton will not be feeling quite so grateful for your intervention," said Mr. Standish. "Lord Danville made mention that it was Miss Vernon who had been the instigator of these inquiries into the management of his estate."

"Oh, dear," exclaimed Katrina. "I must remember to avoid Mr. Carlton."

"Oh, dear me, no. You have no cause for concern. He merely looked greatly surprised and then said, in a laughing manner, 'Miss Vernon? Ah, I must note the name of the chief informant against me!' But although he is not a favorite with the lower class of the tenantry—I do not know of many bailiffs or stewards or agents who are!—he is a pleasant, well-bred gentleman, generally well liked by everyone in the neighborhood, and always a welcome guest at a party or ball. He is far too affable a gentleman to make mention of it to you."

"I am glad of it, but I wonder that so affable a gentleman would have so callously neglected the management of Lord Danville's estate."

"Yes, I, too, have been wondering at that," said Lady Helen. "Perhaps it is because he spends so much time in London; and ever since the Viscount's father died—for Carlton was engaged by him, you know—he has, of course, been virtually his own master here, for Lord Danville comes down but once or twice a year to hunt or to spend time working in his library."

"I am surprised Lord Danville is able to leave his magnificent music room for so long."

"Oh, but he has a similar music room in each of his houses and takes his favorite scores and musical instruments with him wherever he goes; even his pianofortes!"

The conversation moved to other topics, but Katrina reflected, as she marked Julia's French exercise book, that they had never before conversed for so long on the subject of Lord Danville. She often had the feeling that the prolonged presence of the Viscount at the Hall was an acute embarrassment to Lady Helen and Mr. Standish, and that they would infinitely prefer it if he reverted to his old ways and rarely visited Danville. She had a burning desire to solve the mystery of what had happened between them, but every time she considered her theory that Lord Danville had attempted to seduce Lady Helen at some time in the past, she came up against the inescapable fact that Mr. Standish's living was on the Danville estate; and she could not envisage any man, least of all the upright Mr. Standish, residing on the estate of his wife's seducer. It was a great puzzle and probably one that would remain unsolved, for it certainly was not something about which she could make open inquiries.

She returned her thoughts to Julia's rather erratic employment of the verb *avoir*, until Mrs. Bateman carried in the light supper of hot chocolate and toasted muffins which heralded the end of another day.

When she went to her room, she found the little fire, which Sally had lit, glowing in the fireplace. After more than a year of dressing and undressing beneath the bedclothes for warmth, she still considered a fire in her bedroom the height of luxury and, as she drew on her pale blue flannel nightgown and nightcap, she reflected for the hundredth time on her good fortune to have been employed by Lady Helen. She pulled on her fleecy dressing down and, taking up the quilt, wrapped it around her and curled up in the window seat, her favorite spot in the room.

She opened the curtains a little and looked out the window. It was a clear, bright night, and from this point she could just see in the distance a corner of Danville Hall. No doubt the

Viscount's guests would be up for many hours yet, making music and dancing and playing cards and billiards, undoubtedly well entertained by their host; and she experienced a deep pang of longing to be by his side, instead of the sable-eyed Miss Brandon. Her thoughts moved to Madame Catalini, and she wondered when and for how long the famous opera singer had been Lord Danville's mistress. She had evidently not been prostrated by a broken heart recently, for her affection for her husband was unmistakably warm. Yet there had been a sense of regret in her voice, an unspoken wish that *she* could have been the one to capture Lord Danville's heart forever; but, she had implied, no woman on earth had the power to do so.

Katrina closed her eyes and hugged the quilt around her, but it was a frustrating substitute for the strength and warmth of the Viscount's arms. She was convinced he cared for her; his jealousy of Desmond had been genuine, she was certain of that. But then, when she thought of his consummate acting skill, her assurance left her, and she wondered if his expressions of jealousy had been merely a plot to make her feel more secure in his affections. Dear God, the man was impossible to fathom! So frequently had she been warned not to trust him by people who knew him well—Lady Bainbridge, Desmond, Madame Catalini—that she no longer knew if she were capable of coming to her own conclusions about him without the intrusive influence of others' opinions.

One thing was certain: Whatever his motive, he had carried out his promise to investigate conditions on his estate for himself, and for that she was deeply grateful; for although her feelings for him had occasionally clouded her resolution, she had never entirely forgotten her vow to press him on the subject of his cottagers' sorry plight.

On the very next afternoon, she was able to see, to her amazement, that he was indeed a man of his word, for when she accompanied Lady Helen and Sally to Pudsey Lane to visit Meg Foster and a woman who had given birth to a stillborn child, they found the Lane a hive of activity. The thatcher was already at work on the decrepit roofs, and laborers were digging up the road and the gutter running down it.

"Oh, Katrina, I cannot believe it!" Lady Helen grasped her hand, and they smiled warmly at each other, both pairs of eyes damp at the sight. Sally, too, seemed strangely elated, for her cheeks glowed, the color considerably enhancing her elfin face, before she was sent on ahead to tidy up the cottage of the unfortunate woman whom Lady Helen was to visit.

To Katrina's surprise, she was now included in the warmth of the cottagers' affection and singled out to receive many a murmured "G'day, Miss Vernon," as she made her way behind Lady Helen to the Fosters' cottage.

It was Dick who provided her with an explanation for this, after he had handed her a mug of over-sweet tea, made from the tea and sugar Lady Helen had provided. "His lordship called us all out into the lane and told us what he'd do for us, and he said it was all on account of Miss Vernon. Said she'd been the one who'd brung it to his notice and pressed him to do summat about it." He drained down his tea and took out his knife to work with great dexterity at fashioning a belt from a piece of hide.

"Oh, Dick, I cannot believe it! To announce it to everyone! I vow I shall be unable to face any of you here again. There was no need for him to announce such a thing publicly."

"Publicly or not, we all knew it for a fact. For whatever Parson and his lady did for us, they never got Danville to do owt. It was you as did it, and we all knew it, afore he said a word."

"It was good of him to acknowledge my part, although I must own I did very little."

"Whatever you did, miss, 'twere enough. But you should've seen that swine, Carlton—begging your pardon for the language, miss. His smarmy face were as black as a thundercloud. If he'd had his way, he'd have put a torch to the cottages, with us in 'em! He stood beside his lordship, and you could tell he'd like to've struck him down right there. He must have got a right set-down for him to look that way."

Katrina gripped her hands together. "Oh, dear, I do hope I

won't have to meet Mr. Carlton at any time. With all this publicity I have been receiving, he will be even more inclined to lay the blame at my door.''

"Not him! He's too clever by half to let the nobs see him in his true colors. It's only us common folk he don't bother to put on the dog for. You'll not have any bother from Carlton, miss. And if you do, you just let me know and I'll see to him. It'd be a pleasure!'' His work-roughened hands tightened on his knife, and she caught the dangerous glint in his eyes.

"Oh, Dick, I beg you not to do anything rash. You mother needs you. You must behave yourself for her sake, if not for your own.''

He scraped back the bench and bent to stir a pot that hung in the caldron above the fire. "She won't last much longer,'' he said quietly, his back to her. "His lordship sent the doctor this morning. Said it were only a matter of weeks, mebbe days. So all the repairs and such have come too late for her.''

Her heart went out to him, as she saw his shoulders quivering. She got up and stood behind him and said softly, "Dick, I intend to speak to his lordship on the subject of employment for you, so please try to stay out of mischief.''

He turned his ungainly body and looked at her, his face stained with tears. "Thank'ee, Miss Vernon. I'll not forget your kindness. If ever I can do aught to repay you, you've but to ask.''

His face had turned brick-red with embarrassment, and she hastily changed the subject. "Will you be at the servants' party at the Hall on Boxing Day, Dick?'' she asked brightly.

"Doubt it. Depends on me ma.''

"Yes, of course it does. But it would do you good to get out and enjoy yourself for a change.''

"Can't dance.'' His laconic tone was belied by another flush of embarrassment on his cheeks.

"You don't have to. Many people don't, including me. There will be much in the way of feasting and entertainment to compensate.''

"Will you and Lady Helen's household be there?''

She tried to avoid the eager look in his eyes, strongly suspecting the boy had an infatuation for her. "Oh, yes,'' she replied. "I heard Lady Helen say distinctly that they would all be attending the servants' party."

"Then I'll come. So long as there's someone to stay with me ma. I won't leave her on her own."

"I'm sure there will be someone who is not going to the party who would be happy to stay with her." She ventured to touch his hand, hoping he wouldn't think it encouragement on her part. "I am so sorry your mother is failing, Dick. I had hoped that perhaps if the cottage were repaired and she received good medical attention—"

He flung himself away. "It all came too late," he said bitterly. "If it'd come sooner— But I swear I'll get that swine Carlton for it one day." He turned on her, his eyes burning.

She laid a finger on her lips and shook her head, glancing in the direction of his mother, who was being fed by Lady Helen. "You must banish all such thoughts, Dick." His breathing came heavily, and so tense was he that his neck muscles were knotted. She grasped his arm and forced him to sit down again. "I give you my word I will speak to Lord Danville about you as soon as possible, but in return you must promise me that you will behave yourself."

He looked up at her, and she felt the tension easing from him and released his arm. "If only we'd had another steward."

"Well, you didn't, and even if you had, your mother might still have become ill. You cannot blame it all on Lord Danville or his agent."

"I blame 'em both for their neglect. But Danville I blame less 'cause he didn't know. It's Carlton who knew and treated us like dogs and made our women feared of him and had us beaten and jailed for nowt!"

"Put it all out of your mind. I intend to do all I can to have the man dismissed, but you must understand that my influence with his lordship is not that great."

He gave her a sly grin. "That's not what I hear, miss."

Katrina was exceedingly glad Sally chose that moment to enter the cottage to announce that Mrs. Green was ready for Lady Helen's visit.

"Do you know Dick Foster, Sally?" she asked the little

maidservant and, to her great surprise, the girl's face turned bright red as she nodded wordlessly.

When she saw that Dick's face was not much paler than Sally's, she realized that she had made a ludicrous mistake in thinking Dick was infatuated with *her*. She had before her the unmistakable signs of two young people in love, or at least strongly attracted to each other.

"Dick's teaching me to read an' write," muttered Sally.

"Oh, I see. How very kind of you, Dick."

Before Katrina could say any more, Lady Helen joined them to discuss his mother's care and the doctor's visit with Dick. Katrina took Sally's arm and led her across the lane to the door of Mrs. Green's cottage. "Is there something between you and Dick Foster?" she asked bluntly.

Sally's eyes filled with tears. "I love him, miss, and he loves me, but me pa would flay me alive if he knew I so much as looked at Dick. He says he's a no-good, rascally troublemaker, with no work and too much lip on him. *And* he calls him Satan's kin on account of his limp and him being a bastard." The girl's hands clasped and unclasped in her indignation as she poured out her troubles to Katrina, who had to strain to catch all she said, with the noise of the workmen's hammering and shouting in the background. She marveled at the power of love, that it could make a girl who normally spoke no more than two or three words at a time so voluble.

"Dry your eyes, Sally. I don't think Dick a rascal, but he must be made to realize that he cannot always thwart authority the way he does. I intend to speak with Lord Danville about him, but he must behave or nothing can be done for him." She smiled encouragingly at the girl. "You, in turn, must obey your father and not be creeping down to meet Dick, as I opine you have been doing. Once Dick is gainfully employed, I am sure your father will be prepared to change his mind about him."

The problem of Dick and Sally was yet another complication in her already overcomplicated life. It was a distinct relief to return to the nursery and spend the rest of the day helping Julia with the picture in watercolors she was painting as a surprise for her mother for Christmas. And later that evening, Dick Foster's problems were forgotten in preparation for the Danville ball, which was only two days away.

As she had told Dick, the household of Mr. Standish would be attending the Danville servant's party, but, as she had guessed, Lady Helen and her husband would not be going to the ball. "It is our *duty* to attend the party for the servants and tenantry," Edward Standish had said. Had Katrina not known otherwise, she would have thought the statement a pompous one, but she realized that even the servents' party would be dreaded by her employers. In a way, she was curious to see them both together in Lord Danville's company, but her memory of Lady Helen's acute discomposure at their unexpected meeting at the Hall convinced Katrina that it would be an exceedingly embarrassing meeting for all parties, even Lord Danville, who was such an expert at hiding his feelings.

As for the Danville ball, Lady Helen had made no excuse for declining the Viscount's invitation, merely stating that they would not be attending, but that they had accepted on Katrina's behalf.

When the subject of the ball was again broached that evening, Katrina hesitantly voiced her concern about one particular aspect of her attendance. "Forgive me, but if I must accompany Lady Kettering and her daughter, I should infinitely prefer to stay at home!"

Lady Helen smiled at this. "I cannot say I blame you. I always feel as if I have a smut on my nose or my bonnet's askew when I'm in Lady Kettering's company! Have no fear, Katrina. I have asked the Hamiltons if they would be so kind as to take you, and they said they would be delighted to do so."

"Oh, how very kind of them! I particularly like Captain Hamilton and will at least not have to make any conversation during the journey!"

"Yes, Mrs. Hamilton does like to talk, does she not? But she has the kindest heart. Now, Katrina, what of your evening dress? Did you purchase the new ribbons for it yet?"

The remainder of the evening was spent on discussing her

costume for the ball. Despite the addition of the new ribbons of silver lace, Katrina had already decided that she could not hope to compete with the Honorable Miss Brandon while dressed in a comparatively modest gray gown, but nothing, not even her anxiety as to what Lord Danville's mood might be this time, could dampen her anticipation of seeing him again.

Chapter Fourteen

The Viscount was evidently keeping country hours, for the invitation stated seven o'clock, an unfashionably early hour for a ball in town. But to Katrina, who had spent the entire day either torn by anxiety or elated with excitement—sometimes, it seemed, a mixture of both—to have to wait until seven o'clock was ordeal enough. By the time the Hamiltons' carriage arrived, she had gone through various scenes in her mind, all of them involving the Viscount: Lord Danville amorous, Lord Danville mocking, Lord Danville tender, Lord Danville inscrutable, and, worst of all, Lord Danville aloof.

When they arrived at the Hall and were ushered into the magnificent ballroom, it was to find so many people in the vast, mirror-lined room that she was not certain that any of the scenes she had played out in her imagination would apply; for with upward of two hundred guests to attend to, the Viscount would be hard put to even greet her, let alone spare her a few minutes of his time.

She resigned herself to listening to Mrs. Hamilton's chit-chat for the next hour or so, but as soon as she had sat down, Desmond sauntered up to them and, having been presented to the Hamiltons and listened politely to Mrs. Hamilton for the best part of ten minutes, at the first sign of a break in the one-sided conversation he made his apologies and bore Katrina away to a small anteroom. There she found a group of Lord Danville's musical friends, including Madame Catalini and her husband and Michael Kelly, all of whom greeted her with warmth and drew her into their circle as if she were an old friend of many years' standing.

"I have a performance in less than a fortnight and cannot risk exposing myself to crowds," said Madame Catalini, "so we have chosen this little room, where it is cooler and less noisy. We thought as you will not be dancing, Miss Vernon, that you might prefer to spend a little time with us here. Ah, and here at last is our host."

Katrina turned quickly as Lord Danville entered the room. He was elegance personified as he paused to survey them all through his quizzing glass; the severity of his black coat and silk knee breeches and the contrasting snowy whiteness of his cravat admirably set off his dark good looks. Having greeted his friends, he advanced toward Katrina. She had thought he would merely shake the hand she proffered him, but, bending his dark head, he carried her hand to his lips, looking up at her with such a tender expression in his eyes that her heart turned in her breast. She knew a fleeting pang that her rival, Miss Brandon, was not in the room to see it, but nothing could spoil this moment, not even Desmond's frown as he watched them.

"You are not dancing, Justin?" asked Madame Catalini. "I am most chagrined that you have not as yet signed my card."

"My dear Angelica, although I am besieged by fair ladies wishing me to sign their cards, yours will be the very first, although it goes entirely against protocol, you know."

"Perhaps it is you should have a dance card, Devil!" said Mr. Kelly, laughing.

"My dear Mic, what a suggestion! You must think me quite overbearingly conceited to say such a thing!"

They all joined in the laughter at this, Katrina with them. How warm a feeling it gave her to be accepted as one of them! For a moment she wondered whether they would as warmly welcome her if she were Danville's mistress and decided almost at the same time that they would, for as theatrical and musical performers, they lived by a less strict code than did the ton, and as she infinitely preferred their company to that of members of society, she would be perfectly happy. She stood beside the Viscount, content to be silent, while the lighthearted banter continued. Her entire being glowed at his proximity, and she wished that this could always be her place—by his side.

He turned to look down at her. "You are exceedingly silent, Miss Vernon. Have you nothing to add to this abuse of me?" He raised his winged eyebrows quizzically.

"No, my lord. Nothing.'

"Well, well, that will make a change; for I must tell you," he said, addressing his friends, "that when we are alone, Miss Vernon outdoes you all in her censure of me. She considers me a hopeless reprobate and an incompetent and callous landlord. She has even gone so far as to inform me that it is decadents such as I who will cause a revolution in England!"

"My lord," Katrina protested hotly, "you have no right to repeat what was spoken privately between us!"

He smiled delightedly at this. "My dear Miss Vernon, I do so merely to demonstrate to my friends how good you are for me! Your dear Desmond himself saw me walking down that abominable Pudsey Lane, and I swear he relished every splash of mud on my polished boots!"

Desmond grinned. "Coming it a bit strong, Devil! Should have seen him, Katy, doing the nice with his cottagers, and they all sullen and wishing him in Hades. But would you believe it, by the time he'd done his rounds they were 'Yes, m'lording' and 'No, m'lording' him, and one fellow even went so far as to cheer as he left."

A small chuckle escaped the Viscount. "There you are. An eyewitness account! You see before you a reformed man, thanks to Miss Vernon. And therefore I wish you in all seriousness to join me in a toast." He nodded to the footman, who carried forward a tray of long-stemmed glasses filled with champagne. Katrina frowned a protest at the Viscount, but he responded with a dancing smile and such a glowing look in his eye that she was struck dumb. "I give you all a toast: To Miss Katrina Vernon, who has opened my eyes to my own inadequacies and my heart to her beauty and goodness."

"Miss Vernon!" came the unified response, as she stood before them, speechless and blushing. He could not have come closer to a public declaration of his feelings for her if he had tried!

"Come, we are putting poor Miss Vernon to the blush," said the kindly Mr. Kelly. "But Justin is quite serious about his appreciation, Miss Vernon, for he told me himself yesterday evening that he intends to make inquries into *all* his estates after what he has found at Danville."

"And a pretty penny it will cost me, too. From being a wealthy but woefully uncaring landlord, I shall become an impoverished but much-loved lord of the manor. But enough of this! You have promised me your hand in a dance, Angelica; what is it to be?"

"Are you certain you wish to bestow such an honor upon me, Justino?" She cast a laughing glance in Katrina's direction.

"Indeed I am, my dear madame, for otherwise I shall be overwhelmed with pleading looks and possibly even outright requests from less fortunate ladies."

"You are a terrible man!" She laughed and rapped him on the arm with her fan. "*Non disperare*, Miss Vernon. I shall return him to you very soon."

The Viscount favored Katrina with a smile and a small shrug signifying resignation to his fate, and the two sailed from the anteroom, pausing in the doorway before the prima donna made her grand entrance into the ballroom on Lord Danville's arm.

Immediately, Desmond drew Katrina aside, obviously burning to speak with her. "What the deuce do you mean by it, Katy?"

"By what?" she asked, bewildered at his outburst.

"By not telling me that matters had gone this far between you and Danville. He might as well have proposed to you before us all!"

She threw her head up in astonishment to meet Desmond's blue eyes, and her breathing quickened. *"Propose?"*

"Aye, devil take it; propose. That's what I said."

"Do you mean a proposal of *marriage*?"

"Of course I do, you goose-cap! What else could I mean? That he was presenting you with a *carte-blanche* before us ʾall? Of all the harebrained ideas! You must think me a complete muttonhead if you think I meant that!"

"You must be foxed, Des!"

"Well, I ain't. You must be touched in your upper works not to see what's going on! Do you truly think that a man in Danville's position would publicly announce that his heart has been won by your beauty and goodness, and offer a toast to you, if he were about to make you his *chère-amie*? You must be completely hen-witted to think it, or else so green you should be growing in a garden!"

She was utterly bewildered by Desmond's words; although she heard what he said, their meaning evaded her. Marriage? How could the Viscount be considering marriage to her, a governess, the daughter of a bankrupt with whom she had spent several months in a debtors' prison until his ignominious death. It was Olivia Brandon whom Lord Danville was considering as a wife, not her. And yet . . .

She clutched Desmond's arm, desperately wanting to believe what he was saying was true, but convinced that he had misconstrued the Viscount's intentions. Perhaps Desmond was too much the greenhorn to appreciate the niceties of Society. Perhaps it was acceptable among the theatrical set to publicly hint at a liaison. The more she thought about it, the more her head spun, until she was certain she would faint if she did not sit down immediately.

"You don't look quite the thing, Katy," said Desmond. "Can I get you anything?"

"No. I need only to sit down for a moment." When he had led her to a chair and pulled one up beside her, she took his hand in hers. "Oh, Des, do you truly think—Are you certain?" she whispered.

"If 'Devil' Danville ain't about to propose marriage to you, I'm a monkey's uncle. That's how certain I am!"

"Oh, Des. What on earth shall I say to him?"

"What shall you say to him! Well, of all the—How the deuce should I know what you should say to him?"

"It's just that—I have no one else to advise me."

The indignant look fled from his face, and he took her hands in his and squeezed them. "Course you don't. Stupid of me. Do you love him, Katy? I mean, he's exceeding warm in the pocket, worth more than a hundred thou, a year, you know, but he could be a devilish difficult man to live with, unless he truly is reformed; but I've never known a man of the town of Danville's age to reform." He caught her eye and flinched at the indignant look she gave him. "Devil take it, Katy. There's no point in my saying any more, is there? If you love him that much, nothing I can say will put you off, will it?"

"No, Des. It won't."

"Then why the deuce did you ask me in the first place, you pea-goose!" He grinned at her and then leaned forward and hugged her. "I want to be the first to wish you happy, so be sure to let me know as soon as he pops the question."

"I will, you can be sure of that. But, Des, how nonsensical this will all seem if he doesn't propose to me at all. And how embarrassed I shall be!"

"Gammon! For if he don't propose, no one will know it but you and I, and what he said earlier to you will soon be forgotten by everyone else."

"I do hope so, for I should be mortified if they were all waiting for him to come up to scratch and he never did!"

"Don't you worry your head on that score. If he don't, you're not responsible for his lack of conduct. Stubble it! Here he comes."

The Viscount entered the room in earnest conversation with the man of medium height who walked beside him. Something that had been said made them both look toward her, and in that instant the smile she was giving Lord Danville across the room froze into a rictal grin upon her face and her body turned to stone.

"Who is that man?" she managed to ask Desmond through clenched teeth.

"What man?" asked Desmond. "Oh, you mean Carlton. That's Danville's agent, Marcus Carlton."

Marcus Carlton! She forced back a hysterical laugh at this

blow fate had struck just when she thought happiness was within her grasp. How could she have been so stupid as to forget the chief reason she could not marry Lord Danville—or, for that matter, *any* man? Well, there was no chance of her forgetting it now! Oh, God, they were approaching. Where could she run? How could she hide from them? Legs trembling, she stood up, feeling for the back of the chair to steady her. Please, God, let me get through the introductions without breaking down, she prayed; let him not have *that* satisfaction. Through a haze, she watched Lord Danville presenting the smiling Marcus Carlton to his guests.

Now they were before her, and Lord Danville was presenting Mr. Carlton to her. She mechanically extended her hand to the man whose name she had never learned—until now; the man who had forced himself upon her in prison; the man she held responsible for her father's death. She heard herself go through the motions of the introduction. "Mr. Carlton," she said with a small nod and a flickering smile. It was almost over now. Only a moment or so more and she could flee this house, this village, this *world*.

He knew her, of course, but then he had been forewarned, and only a widening of his eyes and a glitter therein betrayed him as he murmured, "Your servant, ma'am." He spoke a few trite pleasantries to her, which she, standing immobile before him, did not hear.

Although she did not dare look at Lord Danville, she could sense his concern, and he suddenly said: "Excuse me, Carlton," and, taking her arm, drew her aside to ask her, "Are you not well, Katrina? You are extremely pale."

Still she could not meet his eyes, but fixed hers on the mother-of-pearl buttons on his silk waistcoat. "I am feeling a trifle faint, my lord. If I could perhaps retire to a quiet room—"

"Of course. I will send for Mrs. Hamilton immediately."

"No, no. I should prefer to be alone." Her eyes flew to his face and then away again.

"Good God, Katrina. What is the matter?"

"Nothing, it is nothing. Oh, please, my lord, let me go. I must be alone." A weight was pressing so hard on her chest she was finding it difficult to breathe, and cold panic began to creep upon her. She knew that she must remove herself immediately, or she would become completely irrational.

He pressed her hand into the crook of his arm and led her out of the room. So gentle was he with her, she was strongly tempted to pour out the truth to him. But what would that avail her? Either way their relationship was at an end. Her one desire was to remove from Buckinghamshire as soon as possible, and hope that he would never discover the truth about her and Carlton. She had been a fool ever to think that the past would not one day catch up with her!

She could not stifle the small sob that welled up inside her, and he halted as they were crossing the hall and looked at her with such concern that she felt a pain through her heart. "Katrina, will you not tell me what has over-set you so? I cannot bear to see you like this."

She averted her face from his searching look. "I assure you, my lord, it is nothing at all. I have the headache, that is all, and it needs but a darkened room for me to be recovered from it."

He led her down a short flight of stairs and then opened the door to a small sitting room, which was cozily furnished with chintz-covered chairs. "I am taking the liberty of placing you in Mrs. Talbot's sitting room, where you will not be disturbed. I shall ask her to attend you here immediately."

"No, no. I beg of you," she cried. "All I wish is to be left alone."

He lit the oil lamp on the small, revolving bookstand and helped her to a chaise longue, upon which she lay down and closed her eyes. As he bent over to cover her with a paisley coverlet, she opened her eyes again, and he knelt on one knee beside her and ran his hand gently down her cheek. "Try to sleep, my darling." With exquisite tenderness, he kissed her eyelids and then, feather-light, her mouth.

Only when she heard the latch close did she allow the pent-up tears to flow unchecked down her cheeks. They came so fast that they ran into her ears and down her neck, soaking the cushion upon which her head lay. She made no attempt to dry her eyes or to turn on her side, but lay in a cocoon of despair, unable to think of one redeeming factor to alleviate her misery.

She must have eventually fallen into a doze, for the creak of the slowly opening door awoke her. For a moment she thought Lord Danville had entered, or perhaps Mrs. Talbot, but to her horror she saw that it was Marcus Carlton who was treading across the floor toward her.

She started up and regarded him with horror, aware that he stood between her and the door. The recollection of his strength and ruthlessness pounded in her brain, and she knew that her nightmares were once more reality. She could smell again the dust on the floor of the large closet into which he had thrust her and, as he drew nearer, the memory of the pain and horror of that time overwhelmed her, so that she was terrified she would become insensible and thus incapable of fighting him off, as had happened before.

"Do not look so fearful, Miss Vernon. I mean you no harm."

Dear God, how she loathed the very sound of his voice; the pleasant, well-bred tones sounded even more disgusting when she knew what evil they masked. She flung back the cover and swung her legs onto the floor. "If you advance but one step, I shall scream and scream until everyone in this house hears me," she declared, trying to steady the tremor in her voice.

"Oh, I think not, my dear Miss Vernon," he said in silken tones. "May I?" He sat close beside her on the chaise longue and detained her from rising with one firm hand. "You would regret it if you did so, I can assure you. I have no intention of harming you, my dear Katrina, although I have much cause to do so. You are the sole person responsible for my possible dismissal from the lucrative and eminent position I have held for the past dozen or so years. Until you came here, I managed the Danville estate without any interference whatsoever. Then I discover not only that a snip of a girl whom Danville lusts after has set him against me, but also that this is the very same girl who *used* me."

"I used *you*! Why you—you fiend! You led me to believe you were a man of honor who wished only to lend assistance to an unfortunate girl and her ailing father, and then you—you—" She could not continue.

"My dear girl! I cannot believe you expected me to provide costly medicines and food and wine and fruits out of season without any recompense. Surely you were not as green as all that? You cannot tell me you were, else why did you permit me to kiss you—frequently, you may remember?"

She averted her face, sickened by the knowledge that what he said was true. "I was dazzled by your acts of seeming kindness in that dreadful place," she whispered. "I thought myself in love with you; even your refusal to tell me your name gave you an aura of romantic mystery in my eyes. Your weekly visits were the one brightness in my dismal life. But you, you monster, knowing how much I cared for my father, took gross advantage of my innocence."

"And devilish exciting I found you, too, my fair Katrina. You are like a tiger cat when aroused. Curbing you gave me the greatest pleasure." His eyes glittered, and he took her face in one strong hand, forcing her to look into those strangely opaque eyes. She recoiled in horror at his intention, but he gripped her face so hard that his fingers bruised her jaw, and she felt his mouth clamping down on hers, forcing her lips apart. Her fingers formed into claws, but to fight him was useless, as she had learned before, to her cost. Despite his lack of height, his body was hard and strong as whipcord.

He released her abruptly and, without turning from him, she scrubbed at her mouth to remove the stain of his kiss. He smiled at this. "Although your kisses arouse my desire for you once more, I shall not trouble you this time, Miss Vernon. But we must quickly come to some understanding before we are discovered here together. That could be certain to sully your spotless reputation, would it not?"

"The only understanding I have is that you are a rapist and a murderer!" she spat at him.

"Oh, come now. Such harsh words from so charming a lady! A rapist? When you had permitted me to kiss you countless times and had accepted costly gifts from me? And a murderer, because I defended myself against the attack of an aged maniac wielding a knife? I can assure you that a court of law would find it impossible to convict me on such evidence, my dear Miss Vernon. But let us waste no more time. Understand this: I have no desire to be turned off from such a highly lucrative sinecure as I have held at Danville, without even a recommendation. Unless you undertake to plead my cause with Danville and have me reinstated, I shall be forced to inform him that you were my willing mistress during your stay in the debtors' prison and that we were lovers in the full physical sense. You understand me, Miss Vernon? I take it that Danville has not yet received any such favors from you or, knowing our Viscount, he would no longer be buzzing around you like a bee around a honey pot. So it would come as a severe disappointment to him if he were to discover that his innocent Katrina was not quite as innocent as he thought, would it not?''

"You are—*vile*!"

He smiled as if he found the epithet pleasing. "Let us quickly come to some agreement on the matter. You are close to snaring Danville. I wish to maintain my position here. I give you my word not to betray our former relationship to Danville if I am retained as his agent. Surely that cannot be too difficult for you to arrange, considering you have attained a great deal more for his flea-ridden cottagers?''

She was trapped, for even though she intended to quit the village of Danville and her position as governess, she could not bear the thought of Carlton besmirching her name with lies. "I cannot think," she said uncertainly. "You must allow me time to think.''

"I shall give you until the night of the servants' party on Boxing Day. That is four days from now. I shall expect your answer then. Meanwhile, I bid you farewell, sweet Katrina, and wish you all the blessings of Christmas.'' He smiled, bowed, and left the room.

She sat shivering on the edge of the chaise longue, frozen with misery, no longer afraid, for she was beyond fear now. Yet, despite her own abject despair, her heart ached even more for Lord Danville. If ever he discovered her relationship with Carlton, his disillusionment with the female sex would be complete. "He loves only his music and books," Madame

Catalini had said, "for only they cannot hurt him." Whatever he had suffered in his youth was nothing in comparison with her own duplicity: holding herself out to be an innocent girl when she had in fact sold herself, albeit unwittingly, to a man whose name she had not even known. And although she had done so for the sake of her beloved father, she knew this could not excuse her. All the old feelings of self-loathing she thought she had conquered rose up again, and she wished she were dead.

Chapter Fifteen

A knock came at the door, and it opened again, this time to admit Mrs. Talbot, followed by a footman bearing a tray. Mrs. Talbot came forward and said in a coaxing tone: "I thought you might be liking some tea, Miss Vernon. A good cup of tea is a powerful steadier of the nerves and—"

"Thank you, Mrs. Talbot, but I should prefer to go home right away. Thank you also for allowing me the use of your room; I trust it did not cause you any inconvenience." Katrina spoke in a monotone, as if repeating words she had learned by rote, and as she spoke she folded the paisley cover into a neat square and then laid it on the back of the chaise longue, smoothing out the creases with the flat of her hand.

Now Lord Danville came to the door to inquire after her health. As he came forward, she felt an unbearable longing to cast herself into his arms and beg him to take her away, anywhere, so long as they could be alone together, able to shut out the world; but she remained mute, looking into his face as if she were trying to imprint it upon her memory.

He took her hand, and she gave him a pitiful little smile. "I fear you are not feeling any better," he said softly. "May I bring Dr. Merivale to you?"

"No, no. I thank you. I wish only to be taken home."

"I shall order the carriage immediately and will myself accompany you to the parsonage."

"No, there is no need for you to leave your guests," she cried, terrified to be alone with him. She could not bear the thought of perhaps receiving a proposal from him tonight.

But he would not listen to her, and within one half hour she found herself alone with him in the luxuriously appointed chaise, carried at a slow pace down the driveway. He sat opposite her, his anxious eyes fixed on her face.

"Have I said anything to upset you, my dearest? Please tell me if it is so, for as you know, I have a wicked tongue."

She hated to see him so humble, so concerned, when he was not the cause of her anguish. "No, my lord. You have been nothing but kindness itself to me." She bit her lip to hold back tears, as her heart cried out to him: Oh, Justin, my love, if only I could tell you!

"It occurred to me that it might have been the meeting with Carlton that upset you."

She stiffened at this, but shook her head vehemently. "Oh, no. Of course not."

"I thought perhaps you were concerned that he would be vexed with you because of your complaints of his misman-agement. Was that it?"

"No, not at all." She summoned up a false smile. "I found Mr. Carlton most pleasant." The die was cast. She had lost the opportunity to tell him all.

He leaned across and took her cold hand in his. "I had meant to speak to you on an extremely important subject tonight, but this is neither the place nor the time, with you so unwell. I can only reiterate if there is anything I can do to make you more comfortable you have but to name it, and it shall be done. For, as I believe you already know, Katrina, I love you."

She would have done anything in her power to have avoided this declaration of love at such a time, and she could not bring herself to respond, although inwardly she cried out, And I love you, my darling Justin, and always shall.

He released her hand and gave her a rueful little half-smile, obviously disappointed by her lack of response, and then settled back against the cushions, observing her through half-closed eyes until the carriage drew up outside the parsonage. He sprang down and himself let down the steps and assisted her to descend. Waiting only to see her inside, and with a curt bow and a good-night to her and Mr. Standish, who had opened the door, he returned to the chaise and climbed up on the box, taking the ribbons from the coachman, and drove away.

Murmuring, in response to Edward Standish's kindly inquiries, that she was tired and suffered the headache, and declining his suggestion that he send Sally up to her, she hurriedly bade him good night and climbed the stairs to her room. Once there, she put down her candle and began to undress. Finding it impossible to undo all the tiny buttons down the back of her dress, she dragged it over her head, uncaring that the buttons popped off and rolled across the floor. Her shoes and stockings and slip were disarded in the center of the room. Pausing only to drag on a nightgown, she climbed into bed and lay there, shivering and dry eyed, her hands clutching the softness of the woolen blanket for comfort.

Although her initial instinct had been to flee this place immediately, calm reflection made her realize the impracticality of this plan. It lacked only two days to Christmas; how could she leave the family who had been so good to her at such a time? And if she did intend to accept Mr. Kelly's offer of employment—if, that is, he was serious—she would have to wait until he returned to London before she could approach him. Most importantly, she must see Carlton again to assure his silence. The thought of having to meet with the smiling villain once more cramped her stomach, but face him she must. This necessitated having to go to the servants' party, for there would be no other opportunity to see him.

The hardest thing to bear would be another meeting with Lord Danville. I must not even think of him, she told herself, but the memory of his expression as he told her he loved her swung into her mind. "Justin, my love," she whispered, permitting the luxury of using his Christian name now that she knew she had lost him forever; and now the tears came, and she turned her face into her pillow.

She awoke the next morning with red, swollen eyes and aching muscles from having lain in a cramped position all night. She dreaded having to face Lady Helen, but briskly telling herself "the sooner the better," she washed and dressed, even though she felt more like burrowing back beneath the covers.

Mrs. Bateman gave her a sharp glance as she bade her good morning in the hallway. Katrina's heart sank when she was told she was to take breakfast with Lady Helen and Julia in the dining parlor. She dreaded the necessity of inventing a convincing explanation for her woeful appearance.

It was Julia, not Lady Helen, who drew attention to it. "Why are your eyes all red, Miss Vernon?" she demanded. "Have you been crying?"

"Hush, Julia," said her mother. "How many times must I tell you not to ask personal questions?"

Katrina gave her a wan smile. "I had a bad headache at the ball last night, Julia, and it made me feel unwell. That is all."

"Oh. Are you better today? I do hope so, for you promised to tell me all about the ball, remember?"

"We shall see." Katrina bent her eyes to the task at hand, eating a boiled egg which she did not want. Every mouthful seemed to stick in her throat until, unable to swallow any more, she laid down the tiny silver spoon, leaving the egg half finished in the egg cup, and stared into space. The sound of Lady Helen's voice brought her back to reality, although she still felt as if there were a wall of glass between her and the real world.

"Julia, I wish you to go and start your work or practice your pianoforte pieces on your own, whilst I speak with Miss Vernon. Do not return until I send for you."

"Yes, Mama."

As soon as Julia had left the room, Lady Helen rose and looked across the table at Katrina. "Let us go into the parlor and sit by the fire for a few minutes, Katrina."

Katrina obediently followed her employer, content to be told what to do in her state of semiconsciousness. Once they were settled by the glowing, banked-up fire, Lady Helen leaned forward.

"Although I hesitate to pry into your personal affairs, Katrina, I cannot bear to see you so desperately unhappy. Is there anything we can do to help you?"

Katrina looked down at her lap, picking at the fringe on her shawl. "No," she whispered. "But I thank you for your concern."

"Forgive me for asking this, but did something happen between you and Lord Danville to upset you in some way last night?"

Katrina shook her head, unable to speak, and at that very moment Mrs. Bateman burst into the room and announced in a highly agitated manner that Lord Danville was at the door, and what should she do with him.

"Oh, no," breathed Katrina.

Lady Helen hurriedly rose and clasped her hands together at her waist. "Pray show Lord Danville in, Mrs. Bateman, and would you then be so kind as to make some coffee?"

Both ladies were on their feet when Lord Danville was ushered in by a distinctly flustered Mrs. Bateman. His height and presence made the small parlor seem even smaller as he strode forward to greet Lady Helen and shake the hand she proffered him. "Forgive this lamentable intrusion at such an early hour, but I felt impelled to come and inquire after Miss Vernon's health."

Katrina, watching them together, saw that flags of color flew in both their faces and there was, as before, a great deal of tension between them.

"Pray be seated, my lord, and you too, Miss Vernon. Mrs. Bateman will be bringing in fresh coffee in a moment."

When they were all seated, Lady Helen looked at Katrina, waiting perhaps for her to speak, but the younger woman could not think of anything to say.

It was Lord Danville who broke the awkward silence. "I trust you are feeling more the thing today, Miss Vernon?"

"I am very much recovered, I thank you, my lord. My headache is almost gone. I believe it must have been some sort of megrim."

She knew he was not in any way convinced that it had been only a headache that had caused her strange behavior, but he smiled politely and murmured suitable words in reply. Only his gray eyes betrayed his concern. She dreaded seeing this concern turn to deep hurt and then cold fury, a natural consequence of the pain she would be inflicting upon him in the near future, by leaving him without any explanation.

He and Lady Helen made desultory conversation while they sipped their coffee, with Katrina contributing only when directly addressed. She longed to get away. Every moment spent in the Viscount's company was painful to her now. As she feasted her eyes on his dark, shining hair and his elegant, masculine figure in the exquisitely cut riding clothes, she reflected that in a few weeks it might be difficult to conjure up even his face in her mind's eye. The thought was such a melancholy one that she gave an involuntary gasp, which drew their attention to her.

To her consternation, Lady Helen rose from her chair. "I must leave you for a short while to attend Julia. No, Miss Vernon, please remain here in the warmth. I shall be but a few minutes." She went from the room, leaving behind two people who silently eyed one another.

Katrina's hands fluttered nervously about her face. "I wish she had not left. It is I who should be seeing to Julia," she said distractedly. She pressed her fingers to her mouth and looked across at him.

The sudden severity of his expression and the manner in which his lips were compressed in a thin line made her even more nervous. "It is patently obvious that you do not welcome my presence here, Miss Vernon," he said harshly.

"Oh, no, my lord. Indeed it is not—" She came to a halt, unable to continue.

His face softened a little, and he extended a hand to her. "Will you not tell me what is the matter? I give you my word that whatever it is I shall understand. You cannot think me such an ogre, Katrina, that you are afraid to share your concerns with me. I beg you to tell me what happened last night to trouble you so profoundly."

Now was the time to tell him the truth, but she could not do so. "Nothing, my lord. I keep telling you that nothing whatsoever happened. I had a severe headache, that is all."

"Very well. There is nothing more to say but to wish you well, Miss Vernon." He rose slowly from his seat and, drawing himself to his full height, looked down at her. "I apprehend that we shall not be meeting at the servants' party?"

She had risen when he did and met his haughty look steadfastly. "I believe I am to accompany Lady Helen and Mr. Standish there."

"Ah, so you do not go so far as to eschew my company forever, then, Miss Vernon?"

"I was unwell, my lord," she protestly feebly, looking away from him.

"Ah, yes. Unwell. So unwell that you deemed it necessary to entertain a certain gentleman in Mrs. Talbot's room?"

She started at this, her eyes drawn to his. "My lord?"

"Yes, my dear," he drawled. "Pray let us have no more lies on the subject." His lips curled into a sardonic smile. "I was informed by Jarvis, when I returned from accompanying you home, that one of the footmen had seen Carlton go into Mrs. Talbot's room while you were there, and that he came out more than ten minutes later, looking decidedly pleased with himself. My servants at least are loyal, Miss Vernon, even if my women are not!" He grasped her wrists so tightly she thought her bones would be crushed. "I could see that you had met Marcus Carlton before, sweet deceiver," he hissed. "But I never realized quite how well you had known him."

"You do not understand, my lord. You cannot—"

Still gripping her wrists, he gave her a little shake. "Little fool! Do you not see that if you had welcomed me here this morning, I should have thought nothing of it? You have much to learn about men, my dear. All that was necessary was to tell me why Carlton was with you last night and display your usual warmth toward me and I should have succumbed, but your coldness and lack of any explanation leave me with no alternative but to believe that you have grossly deceived me."

Releasing her, he stepped back, his eyes riveting hers. "I shall not ask what this man is to you, Katrina. The fact that you will not volunteer the information is explanation enough."

He took her face between his hands, forcing her to look at him unwaveringly. "By God, if we were in any place but this I would drag it from you, but here, at least, you are safe from my wrath!"

He released her as they heard Lady Helen's step outside the door. "We shall meet again, Miss Vernon, at the servants' party on Boxing Day. Meanwhile, I wish you a joyous Christmastide!" He bowed ironically, his hard mouth twisting into a derisive smile, and left the room.

She heard him speak abruptly to Lady Helen and then the sound of the front door opening and shutting, and the clatter of hooves as he rode away with his groom. Well, at least Marcus Carlton had created one shortcut for her: she no longer had to face an amorous lover eager to propose marriage to her. She hurried past Lady Helen in the hall, avoiding her inquiring look, and went into the nursery to set Julia to copying some of Bewick's bird sketches. Then, on the pretext of fetching another book from her room, she ran upstairs and sat in the window seat, staring blindly out the window.

There was still Christmas to get through, and then the ordeal of the party on Boxing Day. Her heart gave a sudden jolt, as she realized that she was facing an even greater problem: How could she plead Carlton's cause with the Viscount now that she was alienated from him? Dear God! She must harness her thoughts and work out a way to win Lord Danville over again. She shrank from further deception, but once she had fled there would be no need for him to discover the true reason for it. She must devise a plan to make him love her again, so that she could plead on Carlton's behalf, telling the Viscount that he was a friend who had assisted her and her father in prison, and that she had hesitated to tell him for fear he would be jealous.

Oh, she would out-act the great Danville himself! And, having won him around, she would quit him forever!

Chapter Sixteen

Christmas Day passed in the usual bustle of activity attendant upon a rector's household: Holy Communion, Christmas breakfast, Sung Matins, Christmas dinner, and then a quiet evensong which brought Katrina closer to tranquillity than had any other time during the Christmas week. The gentle strength of the message Edward Standish gave in his firm voice renewed her faith, assuring her she would not be alone during the trial that was to come.

In contrast with the elegance of the ball before Christmas, the noise and exuberance in the servants' hall on Boxing Day was indescribable—and so was the smell. But all the nobility and gentry took it in good part, joining in the rustic dances with such enthusiasm that it might have been thought it was a relief for them to put off for one evening the airs they affected during the rest of the year.

To one person, entering the hall with the rector and his lady wife, there was no sense of relief whatsoever. The noise and heat and smell only served to intensify the headache Katrina was suffering, this time genuinely.

Lady Helen, giving her a sharp look, said, "We shall not have to remain in the servants' hall all evening, Katrina. One or two dances and some mingling will suffice to start, then we can take a respite for a while before we return."

Katrina gave her a wan smile and squared her shoulders, realizing that she must rally herself if she was to achieve her objective tonight. Flagging spirits and pale looks would not entice Lord Danville back to her side. She summoned up a smile as she saw Dick Foster limping toward them, looking spruce in a suit of dark homespun and a clean white shirt. Although he bowed most correctly to Lady Helen and Katrina, it was Sally his eyes were upon, and she colored up and giggled when he turned and made her a bow as well.

"I'm powerful sorry I can't dance with you, Sal, but will you take a walk with me instead?" He offered her his arm and she, having looked for and received Lady Helen's approving nod, put her hand in it and walked away beside him with a glowing, defiant look.

"Her father will be furious with me," said Lady Helen. "But it is a rule at the servants' ball that no one can refuse a dance. Besides, Sally is a good influence on Dick. He becomes a different person in her company. I cannot therefore think ill of their occasionally meeting."

"If only Dick had some sort of employment," sighed Katrina, guiltily recollecting that she had promised to speak on his behalf to Lord Danville. But even if she did speak to him about Dick this evening, what good would his promise on the matter be, once she had fled? She must put it out of her mind and concentrate on the immediate problem.

A local farmer in heavy boots approached Lady Helen and, with a face as red as a beetroot, asked for her hand in the next dance. As she watched poor Lady Helen desperately trying to avoid having her toes crushed, Katrina was glad she had an excuse not to dance, although it must be said that the participants did seem to be thoroughly enjoying themselves. The scrape of a country fiddle set her feet tapping, and she sat back in her hard wooden chair, content to watch, but ever on the lookout for Lord Danville.

He had greeted them in the great hall, giving Lady Helen an inscrutable, almost challenging look as he took her hand. She had avoided looking at him at all. Katrina he had greeted frostily, merely touching her fingers when she instinctively offered her hand to him. She knew then that in trying to win him around she had set herself an uphill task.

She was relieved now to see Desmond bearing down on her, he having returned to her seat a buxom girl dressed in dimity whom Katrina recognized as Mrs. Hamilton's kitchen maid.

"Save me!" he said to Katrina. "By God, these country wenches come on strong! I came near to being ravished on the dance floor!"

"Oh, Des." She laughed up at him. "Serves you right! Just think of all those poor housemaids you were always trying to kiss at home."

"That's different! Good God! Look what she's done to my neckcloth!"

Indeed the folds of starched white muslin were sadly limp and mauled about. "Deuce take the girl! I'll never get it set to rights."

"What a coxcomb! As if it matters at a do like this! Come upstairs where there is a mirror, and I shall straighten it for you. Or perhaps you could ask Lord Danville's man to help you?"

"Lord Danville's man! Don't be so bird-witted! Do you really think I would ask that nose-in-the-air Rawlings to assist me with my necktie? I knew I should bring Croft with me, but Martin would insist that as he was older he had first call on him!" The fact that he had to share a valet with his older brother irked Desmond greatly.

Laughing, Katrina drew him out of the room, only too glad to have an excuse to remove herself from it, for her head was pounding harder then ever. There was a small anteroom off the great hall, where the overflow of coats and cloaks were hanging. She ordered Desmond to sit on the brocade-covered bench, as otherwise she could not reach him, and proceeded to undo his neckcloth and retie it, a task she had performed for him many times before.

"Lord, you're a pretty girl, Kath," Desmond declared, grinning up at her, and then kissed her.

Katrina's laughing retort froze on her lips as she perceived

Lord Danville's tall figure poised in the doorway. He bowed coldly as he saw her looking up at him, and the blazing look in his eyes turned to icy contempt.

"Get on with it, Katy!" said Desmond impatiently, unaware of Danville's presence, as his back was to him.

Katrina immediately rallied and continued her work with shaking fingers, while saying to Lord Danville, who had turned to leave, "This is a task at which you would be infinitely superior, my lord."

Desmond cast her a wrathful glance and sprang to his feet to face the Viscount, his face flushed. His lordship raised his quizzing glass to survey alternately the ruined neckcloth and Katrina's countenance. "Not even I could rescue that disaster, Charrington," he drawled. "Order a footman to fetch Rawlings and have him fix it for you."

"Not Rawlings, Danville," pleaded Desmond. "Dash it all, he'll look down that long nose of his as if I were something that crawled out of the cheese."

"If he does, you have my permission to give him a thorough dressing-down. Now, allow me to bear Miss Vernon away for a few minutes before I return to dance a schottische with my cookmaid. By the bye, whose idea was it to have this cursed servants' party?" he demanded, with a darkling look at Katrina.

"Why yours, of course, my lord," she replied, all innocence. Thank heaven, he appeared to be in a malleable mood. It had been a close thing when he had seen Desmond kiss her, but by brushing it off as if it were utterly unimportant—as it had been—she had managed temporarily to reassure him.

He led her upstairs to the music room, where they found only Maestro Clementi playing the pianoforte. They entered quietly so as not to disturb him, and Lord Danville seated Katrina in one of the gold-striped, satin-covered chairs beside the Adam fireplace, while he remained standing.

"Although, no doubt, you will remind me it is none of my business, permit me to suggest that you should not allow Charrington to kiss you."

"He was only funning, my lord," she said in a coaxing

tone. "You must believe me when I tell you we really are like brother and sister. He is but a boy to me."

He looked as if he wished to believe her, but his better judgment would not allow him to do so. She took a deep breath, recognizing that this might be her only opportunity to restore herself in his eyes.

"Would you be so kind as to be seated, my lord?" she asked softly. "You forget how tall you are and that it makes a person's neck ache to be always looking up at you." She smiled up at him, and had an unbearable urge to take his hand and kiss it. Recollecting that this was not the time to resist such instinctive urges, she did so, holding his hand first to her lips and then her cheek.

"Do not do that," he said harshly, drawing his hand away, but he did at least sit down. For a minute or so he sat tensely watching her, saying nothing. Then he spoke. "I cannot fathom you, Katrina. You are a strange amalgam of the highest respectability and the basest impropriety. You appear at a society ball dressed in purple satin when you are in mourning for your father, and accompanied by the most vulgar of your relations; yet when I address you I discover a woman of quality and sensibility. Your cousin Letty is the *on-dit* of the town—not, I admit, that you bear any responsibility for that, but she is your uncle's daughter, and therefore of your blood. You accept my embraces with most improper abandonment and, I must say, at times with a suggesion of experience; yet you seem conscious of convention and what is correct. In addition to all this, you entertain my estate agent in a private room, where you are resting because you 'had the headache'; and tonight I discover the man I consider my friend kissing you, only to be told, with the greatest sincerity, that he is like a brother to you. Either I am the greatest dupe alive and will shortly confirm this to my cost, and be laughed out of town, or else I have at last discovered a women who is truly unfathomable."

"If I am, my lord, we make a good pair!"

Their eyes met and locked, hers willing his to soften. She was rewarded with a hint of a smile from him.

"I came here this evening determined to break with you

forever, Katrina. Yet here I am willing, nay, longing, to hear a logical explanation from you regarding your conduct with Carlton. Am I a fool, or is there actually one woman in this world who is not 'practicing to deceive'?''

Her heart constricted in her breast at the knowledge that she was about to do that very thing. But I do it only to save you further pain, my love, she cried silently. Although she meant to leave him, at least she would depart with her honor intact, in his eyes; and in the letter she intended to write him, she would assure him she had gone away only because her pride forbade her to become his mistress, and she did not deem herself to be of sufficient rank or fortune to become his wife.

She stood up and walked toward the golden harp that stood against the wall, and then turned to face him, holding out her hand to him. He rose and came to stand before her, taking her hands in his, a questioning look in his eyes. Having said a silent prayer that neither her expression nor her voice would falter when she lied to him, she immediately started into her tale.

"As I have told you before, my lord, my father was an exceedingly proud man, so proud that he chose to languish in prison rather than allow me to appeal to our friends—all of whom, as I have since learned, would have willingly come to his aid. Even my Uncle William, who offered us what little he had, was refused. Therefore, by the time my father became so ill that he could no longer even read in prison, everyone who might have assisted us had been rebuffed, and I was left alone to care for him. He needed medicines and food which I was unable to give him. Imagine my gratitude, therefore, when a gentleman who was visiting a young man in prison offered me his assistance." She swallowed a lump in her throat and gave him a bright smile to cover it. "He was kindness itself, and although he brought us many gifts of food and wine and physic, and came to our aid when my father was—was attacked, he steadfastly refused to divulge his name. It was only when he walked into the room on the night of the ball that I realized that your agent, Mr. Carlton, and our—our benefactor were one and the same. That is why

I permitted him to speak to me privately in Mrs. Talbot's room. I wished to express my deepest gratitude for his kindness.''

She could see that he was almost convinced, but there was still a shadow of doubt in his mind.

"But if you were so glad to see Carlton, why then did you react so strangely to him?"

"It must have been that the sight of him recalled all the unhappy memories of the prison and my father's untimely death." She drew her hands away from his and turned her face away from him, her grief genuine enough, for she was torn by the angish of having to shield her seducer and the man responsible for her father's death.

"Do not torment yourself, my darling," His hands were gentle on her shoulders, turning her to face him. Afraid to look into his eyes, she buried her face against his chest, pierced by memories of his tenderness when they first met, and her heart cried out at the thought of having to part from him. He tilted her chin and ran his fingers over her lips before crushing her to him. His mouth found hers and, knowing that this was to be their last time together, she responded without restraint. She opened her lips to his searching mouth and pressed herself against his hard, lean body, feeling its heat despite the layers of clothing between them, breathing in the subtle fragrance he always wore.

He lifted his mouth from hers to catch his breath, saying only, "Katrina, my sweet love," in a desire-roughened voice. He pulled her even closer, running his hands down her back to press her to his body. If they had been alone and in another situation, she was certain she would have given herself to him. One tiny part of her brain stood aloof, marveling at this relaxation of her fear of the physical side of love. But then, all she had ever known at his hands was tenderness and controlled passion and ecstasy. No wonder she did not fear the ultimate act of love with him!

The sudden realization that this was something she would never experience doused her ardor as if she had been immersed in an icy pool, and she drew away from him, shivering, her hands restlessly tidying her hair and touching her mouth, which was tender from his passionate kisses.

"You are right, my love," he said with a rueful smile. "A few minutes more and I fear I should have lost all control."

"Whatever will Maestro Clementi be thinking of us?" she whispered, using the composer as an excuse to have ended their embrace.

"The maestro? Why, nothing; for my esteemed teacher is entirely ignorant of our very presence, as he always is when he is playing. You need not concern yourself with him. Indeed, there is no necessity for concern at all, for even in the most regulated cirlces it is deemed proper for a gentleman to be alone with the lady to whom he is intending to propose marriage."

She raised startled eyes to his face. "Oh, no, my lord," said said in an agitated manner. "Please do not."

He took her nervous hands in his. "Can you love me, Katrina? Enough to be my wife? For I am not the easiest man to deal with, as you well know. But from the very first time I met you, at the Merriot ball, I have loved you. Do not ask me why. Perhaps it began with sympathy for your circumstances, coupled with shame for my own despicable conduct, but it soon changed to admiration for your unaffected manner, your quick wit, and your gentle beauty. You were the first woman for many a year who did not flatter and flirt and cajole me. It was, although a blow to my pride, exceedingly refreshing!"

She longed to respond in kind, to list all the things she loved about him, but to do so now would be rank hypocrisy. She met his gaze frankly and said: "I love you with all my heart, my lord—"

"Not 'my lord,' dearest. Give me my name."

With a little sob, she said it: "Justin. I love you, Justin. I am most deeply honored by your proposal of marriage, but beg for just a little time to consider it. My uncle—"

"How formal you make it sound. I thought we had dispensed with all formality between us. And if you were about to say that I must first apply to your uncle for leave to pay court to you, I have already done so."

"Oh!" She closed her eyes, reeling at this further complication.

"He was very happy to give his consent, and said he would be writing to you, or might even call on you in the near future. Do you still need time for consideration?"

"Just a very little time," she whispered.

"Very well, my love. But just a little time, for I am all impatience for your answer."

"You shall have it by tomorrow, my—I mean, Justin. But you must return to your guests, or they will be wondering at your absence."

"I had hoped to make a public announcement of our engagement tonight, but—"

"Oh, no, my lord. Not tonight!"

"Well, well. Do not look so troubled. I shall not press you any further." He looked very much disappointed at her reluctance to give him an answer, but it would have been wanting in conduct to force a decision from her.

"Before we leave here, my lord, may I beg one favor from you?" Her heart beat sickeningly fast at this, the culmination of her scheming.

"Not if you continue to address me as 'my lord'!"

"Very well—Justin, may I ask one thing of you?"

"Name it!"

"That you restore Mr. Carlton to his former position as your trusted agent, in gratitude for his kindness to me and my father. I am certain that now you have evinced interest in your estate, he will insure that it is managed correctly."

"Very well, my love. You see, I can refuse you nothing. I also give you my permission to inform Carlton this very night that he is restored by your good offices on his behalf. You shall tell him so yourself, and I shall not envy him his time alone with you, providing it is a very little time!"

Lightheaded at this unexpectedly easy capitulation, she permitted him to kiss her again, before escorting her back to the servants' hall. Having seated her in a quiet corner, he reluctantly left her for his promised dance with the plump cookmaid.

Having received Lord Danville's permission to speak to

Carlton in private, she steeled herself to face the approaching encounter.

Marcus Carlton was presently engaged in a boisterous game of blindman's buff nearby, and, as she watched, she saw him catch little Sally and, having torn off her blindfold, kiss her full on the mouth; then, taking her hand, he drew her to the other end of the hall, to the fury of Dick, whose hands clenched into fists at the sight.

Immediately, Katrina caught a footman's attention and sent him after Carlton with the message that Miss Vernon wished to speak with him. The footman returned with the reply that Mr. Carlton would be pleased to wait upon her in fifteen minutes. Her teeth clenched at the hidden insolence in the message, and by the time he presented himself to her, pleasant-faced and smiling and saying all that was correct, she was at screaming point.

"It is so warm in here, Mr. Carlton, let us withdraw to the conservatory," she said, and suffered him to draw her hand through his arm, trying not to shudder when he surreptitiously squeezed her hand. Only by telling herself that the ordeal would soon be at an end and that it was for Lord Danville's sake could she even bear to be near him. The sight of the dark hair on the backs of his hands nauseated her, as did the ever-pleasant smile.

The conservatory was empty but for a couple in a far dark corner behind a large tropical plant, who were too much occupied to overhear them. She set a space between herself and Carlton and waited for him to initiate the conversation.

"Well, my dear Miss Vernon, you have news for me?"

"Yes, Mr. Carlton. I have been able to persuade Lord Danville to retain you as his agent." The bald statement was sufficient. There was no need for explanations.

But Carlton appeared to think otherwise. "I would dearly like to know how you persuaded him, my dear lady." He came a step closer to her. "Come, tell me how you managed it." His voice dropped to a conspiratorial whisper. "Never tell me you offered him your sweet, virginal body in exchange for my security! That would be a poor bargain, would it not?"

She wanted to strike his smiling face, but forced herself to remain calm despite his insults. "It is enough for you to know that your position is secure, sir." She was afraid to antagonize him by saying more.

His smile broadened. "Why, I do believe our foolish Viscount asked for your hand in marriage! Am I correct?"

Her lack of response was confirmation enough.

"Well, well, well! I wonder how his lordship would react if I were to tell him—"

"You will tell him nothing" she cried. "That was our bargain, you remember?"

"Why, so it was, my sweet Katrina. But *you* may remember that we were not then talking of marriage between you and the Viscount. I shall feel it necessary to exact further payment if I am to remain silent whilst watching my esteemed and excessively wealthy employer marry my former mistress."

"I was never your mistress!"

"Oh, but my dear lady, you were! If only for one ecstatic encounter. Can I stand by and allow a peer of the realm to marry a woman he believes to be a pillar of virtue, when in fact she has been possessed by me? No, as a man of honor I could not!"

"A man of honor!" she cried, half crazed with fear of him and of what he might do. The hot and humid atmosphere in the conservatory pressed upon her, making her feel lightheaded.

"Not so loud, my dear. Do you wish all the world to know of our relationship?"

"There is no relationship, as you well know, sir." Her eyes blazed with fury, but she quailed before his smile.

"Ah, but there shall be, there shall be. I see no reason why we should not continue to be *friends* after your marriage, do you? After all, it is a matter of common knowledge that the Vernon females are women of easy virtue."

"What do you mean, sir?" she demanded.

"Why, don't tell me you haven't heard about your cousin Letty. She has kept two gentlemen vying for her favors these past weeks, but has now naturally chosen the wealthier, but very much older—eight and fifty, to be exact—Earl of Swinton, and is now snugly established in his expensive town house in Grosvenor Square.''

So that was what Lord Danville had meant when he had said Letty was the *on-dit* of the town. ''Oh, my poor uncle!'' she exclaimed involuntarily.

''Just so.'' He took her wrist and drew her closer. ''So you see, my dear—'' To her surprise, he suddenly released her, his eyes widening as he looked past her to the entrance into the conservatory. ''What the devil—''

Katrina spun around to see Dick Foster standing in the doorway, holding the left hand of a disheveled Sally, who was shaken with violent sobs. Her right hand held together the ripped bodice of her once pretty blue and white sprigged muslin dress.

''Sally, what on earth has happened to you? Dick—'' She had been about to demand an explanation from the lad, when she saw that he was looking past her at Carlton with such murderous intent in his eyes that she instinctively stepped in front of the man.

''Get away from him, miss.'' Dick's voice was raw with passion. He slammed the door shut behind him, without taking his eyes from Carlton's face.

''No, Dick, don't!'' cried Sally, between sobs.

''You keep your mouth shut, Sal, and stand out of the way.'' He released her, and she ran to Katrina's side.

''Oh, Miss Vernon, what'll we do?'' She raised her tear-stained face to Katrina's in supplication.

''What in the devil's name is this all about?'' demanded Carlton, advancing toward Dick.

''You know durned well what it's about, curse you!'' growled Dick ''You made Sally kiss you, but that weren't enough for you, oh, no! You tried to do more, and when you found she weren't willing you tore her dress and would've gone further if she hadn't escaped and run to me.''

Carlton gave a light laugh. ''What a pack of lies! You're a troublemaker, Dick Foster, and will end up on the gallows at Danville Cross if you're not more careful.''

''Well, if I do, I'll make durned sure it's worth it!'' Breathing heavily, Dick launched himself so suddenly at

Carlton that he was able to knock him down. Sitting astride
his chest, he pounded Carlton's face, yelling at the top of his
voice that he was going to kill him.

Both Katrina and Sally tried to drag him away, but it was
impossible to get near him for his flailing fists. Katrina was
about to call for help, when two burly footmen burst in and
dragged Dick from Carlton, who scrambled to his feet to face
an incredulous Lord Danville. "What in God's name is
happening here? You could be heard all the way downstairs.
Perhaps someone will supply me with an explanation." His
voice was frigid, his eyes hard as he surveyed the scene.

Carlton's nose was bleeding profusely down his shirt and
waistcoat, and he was trying to mop at it with his handkerchief. There were cuts on his cheekbones, and his lip was
also bleeding. Katrina knew a thrill of triumph as she watched
him, wishing *she* had been the one to inflict the injuries upon
him, knowing exactly how Dick had felt. She opened her
mouth to explain, but Dick had already begun an incoherent
tirade against Carlton, interspersed with much yelling and
cursing.

"That is enough, Foster!" Lord Danville spoke in a au-
thoritative voice. "One more word from you, and I shall
order a whipping to cool you down!"

"You'll have to kill me first! That's the nobs' answer to
everything, aren't it? A whipping! You don't even give me no
chance to tell you what he did to Sally." The boy was visibly
shaking as he vented his rage on the disdainful Viscount.
"You're swine, the lot of you!" he roared and, throwing off
his captors, he flung himself at Danville, his knife glinting in
his hand.

Sally began screaming, but Katrina went ice-cold. Oh, no,
Dick, no! She knew the lad had no intention of harming the
Viscount, for even now he was standing before him hesitantly,
shivering and close to tears.

"Give me the knife, Dick," Lord Danville said quietly,
holding out his hand, and Dick dropped the knife at his feet
and covered his eyes with his arm. Immediately, the two
footmen closed in on him, pinning his arms behind him so
that he grimaced with pain.

"Fetch a rope," ordered Carlton, taking over from one of the footmen and giving Dick's arm a further twist, which elicited a groan.

Nothing more was said until Dick was trussed up like a capon. Then, "Explain, Carlton," demanded Lord Danville, ignoring Sally's sobs and Katrina's pleading looks.

His lordship's agent launched into a story of how the little housemaid had been only kissed by him in the game, and that it had been not he, but Foster who had torn her bodice. Then, dreading her father's wrath, they had concocted this farradiddling tale as a coverup.

"You're a cursed liar!" yelled Dick, struggling desperately against his bonds. "You tell him, Miss Vernon. You knowed I was telling the truth!"

Carlton strode to the boy and quite deliberately hit him hard across the mouth.

"Dammed villain!" cried Katrina, unable to restrain her violent indignation any longer. The Viscount's eyes narrowed as he looked toward her. She shrank from the expression in their dark depths.

"Bring the girl here, if you please, Miss Vernon. Now, cease your weeping, child, and tell me exactly what happened. The truth, mind."

"Please, your honor, it were like Dick said. Mr. Carlton wouldn't let me alone. He kept trying to kiss me and—and touch me, and—oh sir—" She broke into a wailing, and Katrina put an arm about her to calm her.

"Hush, Sally, don't upset yourself. Just tell his lordship the truth."

She sniffed loudly and with gulping sobs continued her disjointed tale. "When I begged him to stop, he put his hand over my mouth, and then he tore my new dress. Then he said he had to leave, but he'd be back, and I didn't know what to do, but Dick came and found me."

Lord Danville gave the distraught girl a searching look through his quizzing glass and then let it fall. "So, here we have two stories: one from an hysterical housemaid coupled with a ruffian who pulls a knife on his lord, the other from a gentleman of honor. Which am I to believe?"

He directed his gaze at Katrina, as if demanding that she decide; and she knew all at once that, although it meant the destruction of her scheme to shield him from further pain, she could not defend Carlton against these two young people who had been most bitterly wronged. Nor could she abandon the people of Danville to the mercies of such a heartless tyrant as Carlton. That, at least, she owed them, in return for her few weeks of happiness in their midst.

She released Sally and lifted her chin, meeting Lord Danville's eyes without flinching. "Send Dick and Sally *and* Mr. Carlton away, my lord. I must speak with you privately." Her voice was calm, a sense of peace descending upon her at the thought of no longer having to lie to him.

"I will be heard," yelled Dick. "I've a right to be heard!"

"You shall be heard—in a court of law, Foster," replied Lord Danville. "When you stand trial for attempted murder!" He nodded to the footmen, and they dragged Dick out, the sound of his shouts and Sally's hysterical weeping echoing through the great hall.

As soon as the conservatory door had been closed again, Katrina spoke. "I wish to speak with you, my lord, but not while that man is present." She cast a look of intense hatred in Carlton's direction.

Lord Danville lifted his eyebrows inquiringly at her. "He must remain, Miss Vernon, in order that he may make answer to whatever it is you have to say."

"I have only one thing to say, my lord, and that is Mr. Carlton cannot be trusted. He is not a man of honor—indeed, far from it!"

"But you yourself begged me but one half hour ago to restore him as my agent because of his kindness to you and your father, Miss Vernon. Now you tell me he is not the honorable man you thought him. What has happened to change your mind in such a short time?" His gray eyes were cold and hard as marble as they met hers.

"Nothing has happened to change her mind, my lord," interjected Carlton, "but that she—"

"I beg you, my lord, do not allow that man to speak until I have finished," she cried. "He will—"

But Carlton would not be shouted down. "What Miss Vernon does not wish you to know, my lord, is that she became my mistress in the debtors' prison when I was visiting John Harrison there."

"It is a lie!" she cried out, gripping Lord Danville's arm, willing him to hear her. "Justin, you must not believe this man. He—"

He stepped back from her, drawing his arm from her grasp as if contact with her sickened him. "Miss Vernon, did you or did you not have some sort of relationship with this man while you were in the debtors' prison?"

"No, my lord! That is to say—yes, my lord, but if you would only allow me to—"

"That is enough, Miss Vernon. I prefer not to hear any of the sordid details." His voice was infinitely weary. "First you tell me that Carlton is your dear friend, then you tell me he is a scoundrel; and he informs me that you were, or are—it really does not matter which—his mistress. I prefer not to hear any more from either of you."

"I beg you, my lord, hear me out," she pleaded. "He is lying—"

"Miss Vernon did not wish you to know the truth about her involvement with me, my lord," interposed Carlton, "because she hoped to continue it, married or not."

"Oh, infamous monster!" Katrina started toward him, her bosom heaving, but Danville's drawing voice stopped her.

"I had not realized you were quite so insatiable, madam!"

She turned and gave him a long, stricken look. Laughter and strains of music filtered through from the servants' hall, and a canary in the gilded cage nearby sang its sweet song. "I should like to go home now, if you please, sir," Katrina whispered.

"Leave us, Carlton," the Viscount ordered peremptorily. "I shall speak to you later."

"Do not be believing anything—"

"I said, leave us!"

She saw the meaning look Carlton threw her but paid no heed to it. Her head was swimming, and the floor felt as if it were shifting beneath her feet. She passed her tongue over her dry lips.

Lord Danville made no move toward her, and when he spoke he was looking down at his watch, seemingly more involved in the winding of it than in what he said. "I think it would be best in the circumstances if we did not disturb Lady Helen or Mr. Standish. I shall ask Charrington to take you home."

"Oh, no, not Desmond. Please, not Desmond." she looked wildly about her, like a trapped animal, so totally over-set that she knew if she did not escape soon she was in danger of breaking down.

"Why not Desmond?" he demanded.

She shook her head, unable to reply.

"Oh, I believe I comprehend. You do not wish the friend of your childhood to discover your true nature, is that it?"

She met his sardonic expression and the cynical twist of his lips with a pleading look, wishing only to be taken home.

"Very well, madam. It will suffice for a woman of your reputation to have as escort the girl who has served as the catalyst in this Cheltenham tragedy. I shall order my carriage to take you home immediately. I am leaving for town the day after tomorrow. As we shall not be meeting again, I shall bid you adieu and take the liberty of wishing you well in *all* your endeavors, madam."

His voice came to her as from a great distance, and she could not see him distinctly through the haze of tears. When he was gone, she groped for a chair and sat down, overcome with nausea and fatigue. Sally was brought to her almost immediately and, within half an hour, they had been returned to the parsonage.

For the remainder of that evening she was so occupied with calming the little housemaid's frenzied anguish over Dick's fate that she had little time to consider her own; and later, when she lay in bed, she was too emotionally exhausted even to think, and soon fell into the blessed oblivion of sleep.

Chapter Seventeen

"We should be very much obliged if you would provide us with an explanation of what happened at Danville Hall last night, Miss Vernon." Edward Standish's face was set in its seldom seen, most forbidding expression. "All we have heard are the most outrageous rumors, and we are hoping you will be able to furnish us with the truth."

Katrina had been summoned from the nursery to face her employers immediately after breakfast the following morning. She felt extremely unwell, sick and faint, and desperately wished they would ask her to be seated. But Mr. Standish remained posted behind Lady Helen's high-backed chair, and she could only clutch at the edge of the dresser next to her, for support.

"I do not know what you have heard," she began.

"We should prefer to hear your version first," said Lady Helen, who was seated stiffly upright, her hands clasped tightly in her lap, her feet on a tapestry-worked footstool.

Katrina hesitated, her mind spinning, not knowing what to say, but she knew inexorably that only the bald truth would satisfy them. Yet to tell them everything was out of the question.

"It seems that Mr. Carlton assaulted Sally. Dick Foster

attacked him, for Dick loves Sally and she him, you see, and then—and then Lord Danville entered and Dick came at him with his knife; but I know he had no intention of using it. Dick was arrested and is likely to be charged with attempted murder. I brought Sally home and was eventually compelled to give her a few drops of laudanum to calm her." The recital was disjointed, but she was too weary to give it any form.

Lady Helen appeared shocked. "But, Katrina, what did Mr. Carlton have to say to all this? What explanation did he give?"

"He vowed it was Dick and not he who had assaulted Sally."

"And did Lord Danville believe Mr. Carlton's version of the episode?"

"I do not know. All I do know is that he did not appear to believe any of us," replied Katrina, praying they would go no further in their interrogation.

"Forgive me, Miss Vernon, but I must pursue this matter further," pressed Mr. Standish. "Two members of my household have been involved in what I must term a decidedly unsavory incident. It is therefore my responsibility to discover the truth of the matter. I must tell you, Miss Vernon, that I was informed last night by Lord Danville that he intended to reinstate Carlton at your request. Yet later that same evening, after this contretemps with Mr. Carlton and Sally, he announced that he was leaving for London and that Carlton had been dismissed. And upon my asking about his intended marriage, he told me there would be no marriages for him—ever!"

"Oh, pray do not speak any further on the matter, sir!" Katrina begged him, her hands twisting together in her agitation.

"Yes, pray do not, Edward." Lady Helen sprang up to put her arm around Katrina's waist. "Sit down at once; you are as pale as a ghost." She cast a warning glance at her husband.

But Katrina moved from her encircling arm and resolutely faced them both. "I regret that I must give you my notice to quit, due to—circumstances beyond my control. For your sake and for my own, I should prefer to leave as soon as possible, but shall naturally understand if you wish me to remain until you have found a replacement.''

"Oh, Katrina, is there nothing we can do to help you?"

"No, I thank you, my lady. Nothing. You have been more than kind to me. I regret very much—It is—'' Her voice broke, and she turned away blindly, saying, "Pray excuse me," and hurriedly left the room.

But when she reached her bedroom, it was to find no peace for her there either, for Sally was lying in wait, and as soon as she entered, cast herself upon her, crying that Dick was to be charged and would stand trial for attempted murder. It was Mrs. Bateman who had relayed this news to Sally, after hearing it from the dairyman who had delivered the milk that morning.

"Oh, miss, they'll hang him for sure for drawing a knife on his lordship, or leastways transport him to that dreadful place 'cross the world. I'll kill myself if they do!'' And with this dire threat, she threw herself on the floor and was about to go into a fit of hysterics.

"Oh, poor Dick! Stop that at once, Sally! How can I possibly think with you making all that noise! If you want to help Dick, go to your room at once, lie down, and do not come near me again this morning!"

Sally was so surprised by this unusual outburst from Miss Vernon that she picked herself up from the floor, dried her eyes on her apron, and scuttled from the room.

With a sigh of relief, Katrina sank into the little tub chair by the fireplace, which had been neither cleaned out nor laid that morning. Her brain was seething, overwrought with the confusion of the past twelve hours. She blamed herself for what had happened. Had she warned Lord Danville about Carlton, told him the truth when she had first encountered Carlton at the Hall, all this would never have come about. The fact that she had withheld the information to avoid causing him pain was now immaterial. Because she had lied to him about Carlton, an innocent boy might die, a young girl's heart be broken; and Lord Danville had still not been protected from disillusionment.

She knew what she must do, but shrank from it. The thought of facing him again, of foisting herself upon him, seared her pride, but it must be done. She could not allow Dick Foster to be sacrificed because of her own folly. But what if he refused to see her? She would insist. She had no reputation left to lose. By now, the story—or, at least, Carlton's version of it—of her liaison with Lord Danville's agent would be known to everyone, even Desmond! She flinched at the thought, and only hoped that her fallen reputation would not prevent Michael Kelly from substantiating his offer to establish her as a singer at the Opera, for she intended to apply to him in London as soon as possible.

Half an hour later, pale but resolute, she confronted Lady Helen. "I beg leave to take the gig, my lady. I wish to drive to the Hall to speak to Lord Danville about Dick, and time is of the essence."

"No, Miss Vernon. I cannot allow you to go. You would lay yourself open to all manner of—"

"Oh, don't you see? *Nothing* can hurt me now. My reputation is already torn to shreds. I have lost Justin. What else have I to lose?" She impulsively caught hold of Lady Helen's hand. "If I have even the slightest influence left with him, I *must* use it to save Dick!"

Their eyes met in a long look, and then Lady Helen nodded. "Yes, I understand. Very well. Take the gig, and John to drive you, and God be with you in your endeavor."

When she arrived at the Hall, she told John to return to the parsonage with the gig. It might be useful to have an excuse for not being able to leave as soon as she was admitted. *If* she was admitted!

It was a frosty-faced Jarvis who met her in the entrance hall and informed her that his lordship was not at home to any visitors. It particularly hurt her that the elderly butler whom she had considered an ally would look upon her with such haughty coldness, but she realized that this would now be the general reaction of all the Viscount's servants and friends, and she must become inured to it.

"I must insist upon seeing him, Jarvis. It is imperative. If you refuse to tell him that I am here, I shall be forced to seek him out myself. Has he risen yet? Where is he? In the library? The music room? You may as well tell him I am here, for I shall not quit this place until I have spoken with him!''

"Miss Vernon, I have strict orders that he is not receiving anyone today. I cannot believe you would—''

"Oh, yes, you can, Jarvis! You have already heard so many ugly tales you would believe anything of me, is that not so?''

His rigid frame unbent a little. "Miss Vernon, I beg you not to insist upon seeing him." He gave her a pitying look. "It will do no good.''

"It is not for me, you know," she said lightly, "but for Dick Foster. Tell me where he is, and I shall say I pushed past you. He, too, would believe anything of me!''

"He is in the library, Miss Vernon, but—''

"Thank you, Jarvis.''

She sped across the tiled floor and, brushing past the protesting footman, pushed open one of the heavy doors to the library and then closed it softly behind her, praying that the Viscount would be alone. One swift glance around assured her that was the case. Lord Danville was seated by the fire, a decanter of brandy at his elbow. His coat was thrown across the sofa and he sat in his shirt-sleeves, slumped down in the chair with his long legs stretched out and his feet on the fire rail. It appeared as if he had slept all night in the chair, if he had slept at all, and as she came closer she saw that he had not been shaved.

He glanced up as she approached, and exclaimed, "What the devil are you doing here!" without attempting to rise, his very posture an insult.

The decanter was still half full, so he had evidently not been drinking all night. Even if he had been, he was definitely not foxed, but perhaps a little castaway, for his eyes glittered strangely as they met hers. The slow, raking perusal of her from head to toe was also insulting, but although she felt her face grow warm, she folded her hands calmly before her to still their shaking.

"My lord. I came to beg you not to press charges against

Dick Foster. You know he did not intend to harm you and that he had suffered much provocation.''

He ran his fingers slowly down the black riband around his neck to raise the quizzing glass and regard her through it, knowing full well how she hated the habit! She drew in a deep breath, vowing not to lose her temper with him.

"Ah, yes, madam," he drawled. "It was, I collect, your lover who had offered Foster the provocation of which you speak." His lips quirked into a sardonic smile while his eyes continued to express contempt.

"I refuse to be drawn into an exchange of verbal fisticuffs with you when that boy's life is at stake, my lord."

"What is a crippled by-blow to you? Don't tell me he is another of your—"

She advanced toward him, hands clenched at her sides. "You have said enough, sir!" she warned him, breathing hard. "Do not push me too far!" She stood beside his chair, looking down at him.

He slowly drew in his legs and rose to his feet, towering over her. She stepped back only to collide with the sofa behind her. His proximity made her breathless. "I came here to beg you to save Dick, because he is worth saving. Despite his innate intelligence, he has all his life been beaten down by his betters, because of both his parentage—or lack of it—and his deformity. With just a few words you could undo all the wrongs that have been perpetrated against him throughout his short life."

His lips parted in a wolfish smile, and he moved so close to her she could smell the fumes of brandy on his breath. Recognizing that he intended to do everything in his power to insult her, she tried not to shrink from him. Her usual delight at being near him had been replaced by a heart-hammering fear of what he might do to her in his present state of mind.

"What are you prepared to offer in return for Foster's life, my dear Miss Vernon, eh?" His hand reached out to draw her close, and she stiffened at his touch.

"My lord," she protested, her breath coming painfully fast.

"Come, come, my dear girl. It means nothing to you to

offer a liberal reward in return for favors, does it? Mr. Carlton received most generous bounty merely for food and wine and physic. Should I then receive less for a boy's life?''

"Justin, I beg you—'' Blindly, she put out a hand to ward him off, but he dragged her to him, bending her back against his arms, crushing his mouth on hers. She found herself being borne inexorably backward, until she felt the sofa beneath her and his weight upon her. Terror overwhelmed her as she felt his hands dragging at her cloak and then roughly carressing her body. She opened her mouth to scream, but he clamped his hand over it, his eyes glaring down at her with a blazing fury.

"Oh, no, Justin, not like this. Please, no!'' she cried out against his hand. Despite the strength terror gave her, she was no match for him.

Suddenly he released her and stood above her, his chest rising and falling rapidly, his face ashen. "You see what you have brought me to,'' he flung at her through clamped teeth. "Turned me into no better than an animal. Now get up and get out, before it is too late, and never let me see you again!''

He lurched to the fireplace and kicked at a vast log, sending up a shower of sparks; then, placing both hands on the mantelshelf, he leaned his head on his arms in a gesture of weariness and despair.

With trembling fingers, she straightened her bodice and, striving to conquer her fear of him, came to stand behind him. "Don't you see, Justin, my dearest love? That is exactly what *he* did. He forced me, as you would have done had you been him. I was never his mistress. Oh, I was so very grateful for his kindness and thought myself in love with him for it—a foolish girl's love for a nameless knight in a fairy-tale romance. But he was not a chivalrous knight!'' She was trying to breathe evenly as she spoke, striving to control the tears that coursed down her cheeks. "Carlton was the man of whom I told you when I first met you, the man who assaulted me and was the cause of my father's death.''

He slowly turned his ravaged face to look at her, and she gave him a piteous smile. "What hurt me most, my dearest Justin, was that you would believe his words above mine.

How could you have thought it of me? I know I should have told you the truth as soon as I encountered Carlton here, but it was you I wished to protect, not myself. I knew how much you had been hurt by women in your youth. First your mother abandoned you, and then some other woman hurt you. I would have done anything in this world to have saved you from further pain and disillusionment. But I failed, did I not? Just when I thought I had succeeded, everything fell apart.'' She ventured to touch his arm, and he grasped her hand so tightly that she winced.

"Carlton forced you against your will? He ravished you?'' It was as if he had understood nothing but this.

"Yes,'' she whispered.

His glaring eyes devoured her face as if he were trying to brand it on his very soul, but when she thought he was about to speak, he flung himself away from her, stumbling against the satinwood side table, which crashed to the floor, shattering the crystal vase of dried flowers that stood upon it. Paying no heed, he strode to the door and left the room.

She stood, bewildered, wondering if he would return, but when the door opened again it was to admit Jarvis, who stared at her with puzzlement in his eyes.

"His lordship asked me to convey his apologies for leaving you so abruptly, and upon his orders the carriage will return you to the parsonage.''

So he was gone, gone without even a word. He'd fled to some refuge until she had quit the Hall. Her quest to have Dick released had been a failure. She had achieved nothing but further humiliation at his hands.

She was waiting in the entrance hall for the carriage when, to her dismay, Desmond came out of the breakfast parlor and upon seeing her ran across the hall. "What the deuce is going on between you and Danville?'' he demanded, gripping her arm. "I swear I shall do something violent if I don't soon have an explanation from you. I'm damned if I know whether it's Carlton or Danville I have to call out, but I'll drill them both full of holes if I have to!'' His bright blue eyes blazed with indignation.

"Hush, Desmond, there is no need to be calling anyone

out," she said in agony. "The kindest thing you can do for me now is to be quiet and let me alone. If you say one word more, I shall be quite undone and shall break down here, before all the servants, which is what I wish to avoid above all things. I beg you, Des; please go away and let me be." She turned from him and addressed Jarvis, who was hovering nearby, pretending to ignore them. "Is the carriage here yet, Jarvis?"

"Not yet, Miss Vernon. I shall advise you the moment it arrives. Would you prefer to wait somewhere more private?" He gave Desmond a frowning look.

"No, no. So long as it will be here soon."

"Katrina! Will you answer me!" demanded Desmond.

She drew him out of Jarvis's hearing and the gave him a loving smile. "If you really care for me, Des, you will not press me for an answer at this time. Believe me, I have done nothing dishonorable in God's eyes, only in the eyes of society. I have told Lord Danville, but he is much too hurt to forgive me. If I do not have your support, your friendship, I am utterly alone."

He put his arm around her and hugged her to him. "Of course you have it," he said roughly. "What made you think otherwise, you silly goose?" His lightness of tone was belied by the depth of feeling in his eyes. "I shall take you home to Dorset, and we'll work something out."

"No, my dear, dear Des. I must be responsible for my own life, but I thank you for your faith in me. I think I am about to become an opera singer, if Mr. Kelly will still have me." She hoped her bright smile would help to relieve his anxiety.

"But what about Carlton? Curse him! I've been itching to get my hands on that scoundrel ever since I heard—"

"Pray say no more, Des." She turned from him for a moment, taking a few agitated steps toward the doorway. Then, striving to calm the rapid beating of her heart, she returned to him and looked up into his troubled countenance. "Mr. Standish told me this morning that he—Mr. Carlton—has been dismissed. That is all I care about, that he will no longer be the agent at Danville. I beg you to forget him, as I soon hope to do."

"I shall call on you tomorrow, when you have had time to rest."

"I had rather you did not, Des. Allow me time to myself to gather my thoughts. You shall call on me when I am again settled in London."

A footman spoke to Jarvis, who approached with a little cough, to announce that the carriage was at the door. She kissed Desmond and hugged him close, not caring what the servants thought. "I shall write and send you my new direction," she told him.

She turned at the doorway and raised her hand; the memory of his anxious expression remained with her throughout the brief drive to the parsonage.

Lady Helen greeted her at the door, but Katrina could only shake her head in response to her inquiries. "You did all you could, my dear. Come, you are frozen. I insist that you go to bed and rest before you collapse. I have had two hot bricks in it ever since you left, and the fire has been lit."

She allowed Lady Helen to lead her upstairs and to undress her and put her to bed. The last thing Katrina remembered was Lady Helen's cool hand smoothing back her hair from her damp forehead.

Chapter Eighteen

She awoke to almost total darkness, bar the faint glow from the few coals still burning in the fireplace. Taking up her candle, she felt her way across the room to the hearth and then bent to ignite a spill to light the candle. Shadows rose and dipped on the walls as she held it up to look at the clock on the mantelshelf. Twenty minutes to eight o'clock. She had slept for more than seven hours! And despite the dull ache of misery deep within her, she felt not only rested, but also, in a strange way, relieved. The sword of Damocles that had hung above her for so long had done its worst, and she knew she would now have to set everything behind her and think only of the future. Perhaps one day she would even be capable of being as sanguine as Madame Catalini about her love for Lord Danville. Meanwhile, she must apply herself earnestly in endeavoring to forget him and everyone else in the village of Danville. She still had Desmond and would renew their friendship once she was firmly established in London again.

So resolute was her mood that she also came to the realization that she was ravenously hungry. Perhaps it would be possible to creep down to the kitchen and procure some bread and cheese without disturbing anyone. She pulled on her dressing gown and took up the candle, but when she opened her door she saw that the oil lamp had already been placed on the landing table. Blowing out her candle, she set it down beside the lamp and then trod carefully down the stairs.

She was safely past the dining room door and almost at the head of the short stairway to the kitchen when the parlor door opened and Mr. Standish came out. He started when he saw her, and called out: "Is that you, Miss Vernon?"

She stepped back into the shadows, vexed at being discovered in her dressing gown, but he came toward her and said in an urgent tone; "Please come into the parlor."

"I am not dressed, Mr. Standish," she protested. "I was about to go to the kitchen for—"

"Never mind. Pray come into the parlor immediately. We had not wished to waken you when Jarvis came down from the Hall with the news, but—"

"Jarvis! Oh, God, something has happened to Justin!"

"No, no, I assure you. Apart from a few bruises, Lord Danville is perfectly well. Pray come in where it is warm. We cannot be standing out here."

She followed him into the parlor to find Lady Helen there in earnest conversation with Dr. Merivale, the elderly physician who cared for rich and poor alike in Danville. Lady Helen hurried forward and grasped her hands to draw her to the fire. "Oh, my dear Katrina, we did not wish to disturb you, but there have been such happenings!"

Katrina had never seen the usually calm Lady Helen quite so agitated. "Pray forgive my attire, but Mr. Standish said— What has happened to Lord Danville? Will someone please tell me?" she pleaded, anxiously scanning each of their faces.

"Ring for Mrs. Bateman, Edward. Miss Vernon has not eaten. Sit down, Katrina."

"I do not wish to sit down, nor do I wish to eat. I wish only to hear what has happened to Lord Danville!" Katrina felt she would go into a fit of strong hysterics if someone did not immediately answer her.

It was Dr. Merivale who at last took pity on her. "It is not a tale for ladies' ears, Miss Vernon, but as you seem determined to hear it . . . But first I must insist that you be seated.''

Obediently, Katrina sat down on the sofa, allowing Lady Helen to wrap a soft kerseymere shawl about her shoulders to shield her from a nonexistent draft. Only then did Dr. Merivale, without any further preamble, launch into his narrative.

''I received an urgent call to Danville Lodge around noon, Miss Vernon, and arrived there to discover Mr. Carlton in a sorry state: bleeding profusely from numerous cuts on his face and hands and half throttled, his throat extensively bruised. From the rather incoherent tale told me by Mr. Carlton's man, it appears that Lord Danville had burst into the house a short while before and set about Carlton with his whip, then went on to complete the assault with his bare hands. He was like a maniac, apparently, cursing and shouting that he would rid the world of Carlton, and that he was not enough of a gentleman even to be called out. At first the servants were at a standstill, not knowing what to do, but they soon came to the realization that if they did not subdue Lord Danville, he would murder Mr. Carlton before their very eyes. Eventually, with the assistance of Lord Danville's groom, who had followed him to the lodge, they wrestled him away from Carlton and managed to calm him. Shortly thereafter, he was persuaded to return to the Hall.''

''Oh, dear God!'' Katrina whispered, totally unnerved by this tale of violence.

The physician shifted his small, rotund form a trifle to peer at her over the top of his spectacles, and then continued. ''After I had treated Mr. Carlton and insured that he was as comfortable as could be expected under the circumstances, I went directly to the Hall, where all Lord Danville's guests were engaged in departing—most precipitately, I should imagine! There I found their host shut away in the library, behind a locked door. It took much persuasion on my part to gain an entrance, but once he opened the door to me I realized he would do very nicely, for he cursed me roundly for my interference and said he trusted I had done nothing to prolong the life of that blackguard, Carlton. I informed him that Mr.

Carlton was not seriously hurt, but he replied only that he was sorry to hear it, and regretted that he had not, as he put it, done a more thorough job on him."

The doctor's history, although recounted in a pedantic manner, gave sufficient information for Katrina to realize two things: the Viscount had attacked Carlton because of what she had told him, which meant that he had believed her; and that he was not seriously injured himself.

"Oh, I must go to him," she said distractedly. "I must! But, of course, I cannot. Please help me," she appealed to Lady Helen. "What shall I do?"

"If you will take my advice," said Dr. Merivale, "you will all keep away from Danville Hall at present. Even you, Mr. Standish. I know you may feel it is your duty to carry out a professional visitation, but I would advise against it. Lord Danville is not in a very pleasant state of mind at the moment."

"You mean he is drinking?" demanded Katrina.

Dr. Merivale's bushy gray eyebrows came together at this rather unseemly remark, but he nodded. "He was when I left him, Miss Vernon, and as that was many hours ago I do not think he will be in a fit state to receive visitors, particularly of the female variety. I advised him against travel tomorrow, but he insists he is closing up the Hall and leaving for town first thing in the morning. And speaking of leaving, I must be getting home myself." He pulled himself out of the deep chair and gathered up his stout cane. "I thank you for the magnificent dinner, my lady. Good night to you both." He stumped out into the hall with Mr. Standish, who closed the door behind them.

Katrina sat, stunned by the physician's story, yet at the same time warmed by the knowledge that Lord Danville had been moved to commit such an act of violence on her behalf. It demonstrated a lack of complete indifference to her, a suggestion of caring that gave her a glimmer of hope.

"If only I might go to him," she uttered again. "But it would be useless now. I am convinced it was his pride that impelled him to attack Carlton." She spoke disjointedly, thinking aloud. "He would not wish to see me."

Lady Helen came to sit beside her on the sofa, wafting the faint scent of the lavender water she always used. "I believe you are wrong. I think that when he is fully recovered, Lord Danville will indeed wish to see you."

"Oh, no, no. You do not understand. I cannot—"

"Do not say any more, Katrina. I know you are determined to leave here as soon as possible, but I beg you to wait, at least until Lord Danville recovers."

"I hate to think of him locked away by himself," murmured Katrina, "with no one to attend to him."

"And so do I. That is why I am asking, no, *begging* you to wait another few days."

Katrina gave her a ghost of a smile. "It is of no use. You heard Dr. Merivale say that he is leaving for town in the morning."

"Yes, of course. I had forgotten." Now it was Lady Helen's turn to appear distracted. She paced across the room and back again and then paused before Katrina.

"Oh, if only I had never seen him!" cried Katrina.

"Never say that! You have been so good for him." An expression of intensity glowed in Lady Helen's lovely eyes. "Never has he loved anyone as much as he loved you; with such an unselfish love. His pride perhaps has been hurt, but that will not last. His love for you will endure, I am sure of it."

"How can you say that? What do *you* know of him?" cried Katrina, and then recollecting her suspicions about Lord Danville's relationship with Lady Helen, she exclaimed, "Forgive me. I should not have said that! I am distraught."

"I understand." Lady Helen seemed to hesitate for a moment and then sat down again beside her. She seemed strangely restless, twisting her plain gold wedding band about her finger. "Katrina, the time has come for me to make a confession that will prove excessively painful, but it must be done. You have long labored under the illusion that it was Lady Bainbridge who recommended you to me for the position of governess. If you cast your mind back to the day of our first meeting, you will remember it was you who rather hastily reached that conclusion and, by saying nothing, I reinforced your deduction. In truth, it was Lord Danville who recommended you to me!''

"Lord Danville! But—why? I do not understand!"

Lady Helen ran her hand distractedly through her golden hair. "He came to me—it had been many years since—he came to me directly after he had visited your uncle's bookshop to beg a favor of me." She put a hand to the pearls about her white throat. "He asked if I would immediately reply to your advertisement in the *Morning Post* and, if you met with my approval, take you into my household, as he deemed you in dire need of protection."

Katrina was struck with astonishment by this revelation. "But why did he do this?"

"Why?" Lady Helen gave her a fleeting smile and then took her hand. "Because, he informed me, he had fallen deeply in love with you and intended to marry you, if you would have him."

"Impossible!" gasped Katrina. "He had met with me but twice and both times under the most unpropitious of circumstances!"

"So I believe! Nevertheless, that is what he told me. His intention was to wait until you were settled here with us and then to come down to Danville and apply himself to wooing and winning you."

"Pardon me for saying so, my lady," said Katrina in a soft voice, "but did you not consider that he might have been deceiving you, that in truth it was as his mistress that he envisioned me?"

Lady Helen smiled. "No, my dear Katrina, I did not. Do stop selling yourself short! His intention from the very beginning was marriage. 'Devil' Danville he may be called, but you surely cannot believe him such a son of Beelzebub as to enlist the aid of a clergyman and his wife in seducing you!"

"How can you be so sure? Even I cannot always fathom him."

"Ah, I was afraid you would put me to the test, and I would have to reveal all. Katrina, you have been so torn with doubts about your own worthiness, that you have failed to consider how unworthy others might be."

"Others? You surely do not mean yourself, Lady Helen. I cannot conceive of anyone more worthy!"

"Well, you may remove me from the pedestal," Lady Helen said wryly, "for I do not belong there!"

Now Katrina recollected that Letty had said something about an elopement and a scandal, but surely to elope with a curate was not so excessively scandalous, except perhaps in the narrow confines of London Society. "Do you mean because you eloped with Mr. Standish? Surely that was because your family disapproved of your marriage to a lowly curate, was it not?"

A flush of red mantled Lady Helen's cheeks, "No, it was not only that. I eloped with Edward on the very eve of my marriage to another man."

"Oh!"

"Oh, indeed!" Lady Helen fixed her eyes on Katrina in a compelling fashion.

"Oh, dear Lord!" Katrina released her breath slowly, at last realizing the truth. "Justin!"

"Exactly so. Justin. On the very eve of my marriage to Lord Danville, I ran away with Edward. Oh, it was all most decorous; you cannot imagine it being any other way with Edward, can you? He took me to his aunt and waited until the scandal had died down before marrying me, but you can imagine what was said—particularly when I presented Edward with our first child a scant nine months later!"

"Oh, poor Justin!"

"Poor Justin indeed. It was a contemptible thing to do to him, particularly as he was deeply in love with me; although, I fancy, as he was only twenty-three at the time and I but sixteen, it was perhaps not a love that would have lasted."

"But did you not wish to marry him? Did you not love him?" It was beyond Katrina's comprehension that she could prefer the stolid Edward Standish to the Viscount.

"At first I thought I did. I suppose I was flattered by his loving me, for he was the most sought-after of all the eligible suitors of the day, being both exceedingly wealthy and handsome. But—but his passionate nature made me afraid of him." She looked frankly into Katrina's eyes. "Although his conduct was always that of a gentleman, I sensed that beneath his cool exterior there seethed a—a sensuality that gave me cause to fear him. I began to feel that we would be disastrously ill-matched, for mine was not a fiery nature. I dreaded even being left alone with him! Even then I had no intention of reneging, but shortly after the engagement was announced, I met Edward and we immediately fell in love. The rest you know.''

"I still cannot imagine either of you eloping in any circumstances!''

"Ah, but Edward can be most determined when he is moved to be so, and he was not only very much in love with me, but he also saw himself as a St. George rescuing a maiden from the dragon. Unfortunately, no one else saw it in quite that light, least of all our respective families.''

"What I still do not understand is how you come to be living at Danville, especially in such circumstances.''

Lady Helen placed the palms of her hands together and rubbed them in her habitual gesture of nervousness. "Yes, well— To put it shortly, we were cast off by our families. Edward could not procure a living, for the story of our elopement was well-known; he could not find employment of any kind. In desperation, and six months with child, I applied to Lord Danville, citing his past love—''

Katrina sprang from the sofa. "I cannot believe it!'' she cried, confronting the still-seated Lady Helen. "Forgive me, but how could you face him and beg for his aid after what you had done to him?''

"It was not easy. But I had my child to think of.''

Katrina would have scrubbed floors or plowed fields rather than apply for assistance to a man she had so heartlessly jilted, but she left the words unsaid, for she could see that Lady Helen was exceedingly distraught.

"He gave Edward the living at Danville,'' she continued, her hands rubbing nervously on the brocade of the sofa. "He said, in that sardonic way of his, to think of it as his belated wedding gift.''

Katrina stared at her. "And Edward was willing to take it? To accept a living at the hands of the man he had so deeply wronged?'' She turned and walked to the window bay and back again, unable to remain still in her agitation.

''Oh, Katrina! Do not think we haven't lived with the guilt of it ever since! But we were desperate! There was no one else to whom we could turn.''

''No wonder he so rarely visited Danville Hall!''

''Yes, that, too, we feel overwhelmingly responsible for, and not a day has passed that we have not joined together in prayer, begging God to show us a way to help Justin and absolve us for the wrong we have done him. Perhaps now you will appreciate why we were so eager to carry out his wishes regarding you, why we encouraged you to meet with him when at times it was not at all correct for you to do so. You must have wondered at it!''

''Indeed I did! But I thought that as you continually assured me it was acceptable conduct, I had nothing to fear!''

''We were so wishful to see him happily wed, for only then could we find total peace and contentment in our own marriage.''

''Well! Of all the— I cannot imagine how you could have done such a thing! Oh, the elopement, yes; for you would have been far too cool for Justin's taste. He has, as you said, an exceedingly passionate nature. But to accept a living from him and sit nice and tight on his estate all these years as if you were the best of friends! No wonder there was such restraint between you whenever you met. And here was I all the time thinking he had attempted to seduce you!''

''To seduce me! Oh, Katrina, you have such a vivid imagination!''

''Oh, no, I have not, for try as I might I cannot possibly imagine anything quite so incredible as that which you and Edward did to him. Did you ever consider what a laughing-stock you must have made of him? Not only to jilt him on his wedding eve, but also to settle down and raise a family on the estate of his family seat! It's a wonder he was ever able to show his face in Society again! Just think what it must have done to his pride, and he so young! No wonder he has mistrusted the female sex ever since!'' Her face, her entire body, burned with indignation.

"Oh, Katrina, I know it. Do not berate me." Lady Helen appeared close to tears, but Katrina could feel no sympathy toward her. "I am well aware of the wrong we did him. Every time we heard of a new *on-dit* concerning him or a new mistress, you can imagine how responsible for it we felt."

"I must go to him."

"No, no. You cannot."

Katrina lifted her chin and gave Lady Helen a little half-smile. "I most certainly can. I am not sure he will want me, but he can have me on his terms and do whatever he pleases with me. If he can demean his sense of pride so far as to have the woman who jilted him and the man she married live on his own estate, then I can easily pocket my pride and offer myself to him!"

Lady Helen rose abruptly and came to her. "Do not be so rash, I beg you. You heard what Dr. Merivale said. He may be in an even more violent rage by now and do you harm."

"Nonsense! Will you let me have the gig, or must I walk?"

"At this time of night? Katrina, be sensible! Oh, I wish I hadn't told you!"

"I am glad you did. It has cleared up a great many misconceptions in my mind." Katrina's voice softened, and she gave Lady Helen a trembling smile. "Forgive me for flaring up at you in such a manner, but I love him, you see." Tears rushing to her eyes, she ran from the room and up the stairs. Once in her bedroom, she scrambled into her warmest dress and shawl and pulled on her half-boots.

Ten minutes later, she ran downstairs again, to be confronted by Edward Standish in the entrance hall.

"Miss Vernon, I forbid you to go to Danville Hall at this time of night!"

"Mr. Standish, you cannot stop me! If you refuse me the gig, I shall walk." As she spoke, she tied on her hood and jerked the strings of her warm cloak more tightly about her neck.

"Allow me at least to accompany you. I cannot permit you to go there alone."

"No, no, Mr. Standish. Your presence would merely infu

riate him. I have given you my notice, so you need no longer feel responsible for me.''

Fire flashed in his light brown eyes, and she began to see how attractive this man could be when stirred from his usual sobriety. "Good God, Miss Vernon! Of course we still feel responsible for you. We *care* about you!"

"Forgive me, I know you care about me. But I *must* do this. Surely you can understand that. Remember, you, too, were capable of acting rashly when you felt it was essential to do so!"

He had the grace to redden at this, and with a wry smile laid his hand over his heart in a gesture of surrender. "Touché, Miss Vernon."

"That was unpardonable of me," she said. "Pray forgive me. I am overwrought."

"Not at all. I do understand, you know. But you must realize that our chief concern is for your welfare, not for what the gossips might say."

"Yes, indeed," said Lady Helen, at his elbow. "We hold you in deep affection, Katrina, and not only because of our hopes for you and Lord Danville. I am come to tell you that the gig is at the door, but will you not even take John with you?"

Katrina was in no mood for the old servant's plodding pace tonight. "There is no need. It is but a short drive, and I am certain no one in Danville would seek to harm me."

"Of course not. Oh, I had forgotten the one most important matter that Dr. Merivale omitted from his narrative; news that will make you extremely happy."

"What is it?"

"Apparently, when Dr. Merivale was about to leave the Hall, Lord Danville thrust into his hands a letter which he asked him to be sure to deliver to Mr. Gregg, the magistrate. Dr. Merivale did so, and Mr. Gregg read the letter in his presence. It was a request that arrangements be made to release Dick Foster from the roundhouse, as Lord Danville did not intend to press charges. Dick was home with his mother by the midafternoon!''

"Oh, thank God!" Katrina grasped Lady Helen's hands

and turned from her to Mr. Standish. "Surely now you must understand how I can love such a man. To be thinking of Dick even in the depths of his fury and anguish! I must go to him immediately!" she cried distractedly.

Lady Helen embraced her, and Edward Standish took her hand in his and held it for a moment. "God go with you in your quest. I admit we have a personal interest in the outcome, but we also pray for your happiness."

"Be sure to send word if you need any assistance, and Edward will be there directly," cried Lady Helen, as they opened the front door.

Katrina allowed herself a small inward chuckle at the thought of Edward Standish riding to her rescue. St. George and the dragon once again!

Mr. Standish helped her into the gig and handed her the little cob's reins. Having just caught his "God bless you," she was off, moving at a reasonable pace down the lane and through the High Street, and then driving along at a brisk trot until she reached the gatehouse of the Hall. She was not obliged to get down, for Will Smith came out, displaying great surprise at seeing her alone at such a time, but he pulled at his cap and ran to open the gates.

"Would you be wanting me to drive you up to the Hall, miss?" he asked.

"No, I thank you, Will. You get back into the warm. It is too cold to be standing outside."

As she moved off, she thought to herself, with a smile, that he was most likely wondering if she would be returning that night. She had been wondering the same thing herself!

She was moving at a brisk pace down the center of the avenue, the two side lamps providing sufficient light to enable her to keep clear of the grass verges, when suddenly a figure darted from behind the trees and sprang in front of her, forcing her to rein in the cob sharply.

"What on earth—" Fear caught at her throat, silencing her, for she saw in the lantern's light the swollen and bruised countenance of Marcus Carlton. She cast a frenzied glance backward in the hope that Will might have followed her, but all was darkness behind her. Ahead of her shone the lights of the Hall, tantalizingly close. Panic rose in her breast, and she swayed.

"Well met, Miss Vernon." Carlton approached the gig and dragged the reins from her lax fingers. "On your way to a rendezvous with your love?" So swollen were his lips, his speech came thick and slurred, but she realized from the smell of liquor on his breath that he had also been drinking. "Get down!" he commanded.

"Never! Give me back the reins, sir, and go your way. If Lord Danville catches you, he will complete the task he set out to perform!"

"Ah, so you have heard about it already, my dear Katrina, and this is why you are come. You thought that once you had me out of the way your new lover would be prepared to overlook our former relationship. Well, as you can see, I am not so easily got rid of. Get down!"

He grasped her wrist and made to drag her down. His touch sent a shock like a jolt of lightning through her body; his hand was hot and dry and she realized, as she met his glittering eyes, that he was burning with fever.

"Why do you not go home, Mr. Carlton?" she said in a coaxing tone. "You are not well. You should not be out on such a cold night."

What a vacuous, nonsensical thing to be saying to a man who was most demonstrably unstable, both physically and mentally, but her brain was numb with terror of him and unable to think.

He dragged her down from the gig, not caring that he hurt her; she felt the sharp edge of the step graze her legs and heard the rip of her skirt hem, but nothing mattered now but self-preservation. He pinioned her wrists, drawing her near enough for her to feel his body shaking, yet not near enough to actually touch him. Her eyes locked with his, widening at the insane light she saw there, and she gave an involuntary gasp of terror.

"Yes, my dear lady, you are realizing, are you not, that I have positively nothing to lose now? You do well to fear me."

He dragged her close against him, pressing her body to his,

but did not kiss her. Her heart beat wildly, but she kept her body rigid and unyielding against the loathsomeness of his.

He laughed. "Regrettably I have to postpone the revival of our first coupling for a short while, but do not be vexed, my love; it will be soon, very soon."

He pushed her away from him so unexpectedly that she staggered and almost fell against the wheel of the gig. He caught her up haphazardly and threw her onto the seat of the gig, grunting with pain as he did so. Scrambling up beside her, he turned the gig and drove it off the avenue and through the row of poplars, into the thicket.

"Oh, God!" she cried. "What are you going to do?"

"Calm yourself, my heart, and have patience. I am about to make a brief visit to my erstwhile employer and shall then return to you." He smiled a grotesque grimace and winced in pain. "I am in his debt and must repay him with interest. For years I have been no better than a hired servant, treated with contempt by a man who cares nothing for his estates, his lands, and yet I am descended from a family equally as good as his. And you, too, shall pay, my sweet Katrina, I promise you, when I return!"

He jumped down and began to tie the cob to the trunk of the nearest tree.

"You will not get anywhere near Lord Danville," she said scornfully.

"Oh, I have no intention of attempting to do so," he replied.

"And do you anticipate that I shall sit here and wait whilst you do whatever it is you intend to do?"

"Alas, no. I am certain you would raise the alarm as soon as I left you; and so, regrettably, I must do *this*!"

Too late she saw the short, thick branch in his hand. Before she could move, he sprang up into the gig and brought it crashing down on the side of her head, and she swirled into blackness.

Chapter Nineteen

"Wake up, miss. Wake up!"

An urgent voice was calling her; someone had need of her, but she had no desire to drag herself out of the warm darkness into cold light.

"Oh, please, miss. Open your eyes!"

She stirred, and groaned at the violent throbbing in her head.

"That's the way, miss. You'll soon be right as a trivet. You wake up now, miss, so's I can get you in the warm afore you freeze."

She opened her eyes to find not light, but darkness, bar the glow from the lantern held by a person whose anxious face was bent close to hers. "Dick!"

"Aye, Dick it is, miss." He grinned, evidently glad that she should be able to recognize him. "Do you think you could stand up, Miss Vernon?"

She ran her hand over the place where she lay, to discover that she was stretched out on a carriage rug on a bed of damp leaves on the hard ground. There was something she had to remember, something of the utmost importance. She tried hard to concentrate, striving to drag the elusive memory to the surface, but her brain was a jumble and nothing came.

She clutched Dick's arm as he knelt beside her. "Dick, I—"
But trying to remember only made her head ache the more.

Dick slowly stood up, drawing her up with him, only his
stocky strength saving her from falling. She stood, holding on
to him, nauseated and dizzy.

"Can you walk, do you think, miss? The gig's but a few
paces away."

"The gig?" she echoed stupidly.

"Aye. It were the gig as I seed first. The lantern caught the
shine of the metal. Then I found you. Proper fright you given
me. Thought you was dead, miss. Who done it, d'you
remember?" Slowly they moved toward the gig, which she
could now see ahead of them.

"I wish I could, but my brain refuses to function. How
came you here, Dick? Not poaching, I trust!"

"Poaching? Me, miss? Not after what his lordship done for
me. I was just on my way now to thank him for having me
released!"

His lordship! She stopped and gripped Dick's arm. "Dear
God! Carlton! It was Carlton who struck me down, Dick. He
was going to do some mischief to Justin, I mean, Lord
Danville. Oh, you must stop him! Go now! Oh, God, it may
already be too late!"

Dick was immediately galvanized by the news. "That
swine! I should've knowed it'd be him!" he muttered. "Pardon me, miss, but I'm going to take you back to the
gatehouse, then I'll drive the gig to the Hall and give them
the warning to be on the lookout for Carlton. I wonder what
made him leave the gig here? Mebbe didn't want to be heard
when he got near the Hall."

He caught her up awkwardly and carried her to the gig,
lifting her with difficulty onto the seat. She sat, clinging to
the rail, assailed by nausea from the rough handling.

"Drive direct to the Hall, Dick. Save time," she gasped.
"I have no idea how long it is since he left me."

The gig was already moving off across the wide grass verge
and then onto the avenue.

"Can't have been that long, miss, or you'd have been
frozen stiff. Nay, begging your pardon, I'm taking you back

to the gatehouse, 'tis nearer than the Hall. That way, too, we'll make sure Will Smith's on the lookout for Carlton.''

She endured the drive to the gatehouse with great fortitude; she was not only frantic with anxiety for Lord Danville's safety, but she also felt so sick that she had to steel herself not to succumb to the waves of nausea that swept over her. But although it seemed far longer, it was only a matter of minutes before Dick pulled up the gig and shouted, ''Hi, Will! Come out, quick!''

''Just leave me here, Dick!'' she cried. ''You must make haste, or it may be too late.''

''Don't you fret, miss. I'm off as soon as I can get you out. I'll tell them up at the Hall that you're safe.''

She heard voices and felt herself being lifted from the gig, but by this time she had used up all her reserve of strength; and as soon as she was laid on something soft and felt a rough but cool hand upon her brow, she again lost consciousness.

She awoke to the sounds of a crackling fire and a loudly ticking clock, and opened her eyes to find she was lying on a cushioned settle close by the fire in a snug parlor. Her eyes fastened upon the domestic clutter on the mantelshelf and roamed around the room until they lighted on a plump, middle-aged woman in a mobcap, who sat knitting in a nearby chair. Gingerly, she lifted her head and found to her relief that the sickening throbbing had dwindled to a dull ache.

''Is that you awake at last, Miss Vernon?'' said the woman, whom Katrina now recognized as Mrs. Smith.

She sat up abruptly and swung her legs onto the floor. ''Has Dick returned yet, Mrs. Smith? Is there any news of Mr. Carlton?''

''Now, don't you go fretting yourself. Just you sit still whilst I make you a good strong cup of tea.'' Mrs. Smith rolled up her ball of wool with painstaking precision and set the knitting down on the chair.

''Mrs. Smith,'' insisted Katrina. ''Will you please tell me two things: Has Dick returned, and is everything all right up at the Hall?''

''I'll be making that cup of tea first, and then we'll talk.''

The woman's eyes darted everywhere except in her direction. Katrina's heart pounded. Dear God, something *had* happened, she was certain of it. She slowly got to her feet, clutching at the arm of the settle to steady her.

"Mrs. Smith. If you do not answer me this instant I shall be exceedingly vexed! What has happened at the Hall? Something has, so do not be denying it!"

"Very well, miss. I'll tell you, but I didn't want to be troubling you with it till you were feeling a mite better. There's been a fire up at the Hall, a bad one, and that's as much as I know."

Katrina's hand flew to her throat. "Oh, God!"

"Most of the village has been up there afighting it. My Will went up more'n an hour ago."

"How long have I been here?" demanded Katrina.

"Oh, two hours at the least, for it's nigh on midnight now."

Two hours! Please, God, let Justin be safe, she prayed.

"But don't you be fretting, miss. It must be out by now, for you could see the flames leaping up afore, and now there's nothing but the smell of smoke left."

Katrina took a hasty step toward her. "Have you any form of transportation, Mrs. Smith? Anything!"

"Lord, miss, you can't be meaning to go out!"

"I certainly can! I am going immediately to the Hall, even if it means having to walk! Answer me, if you please. Is there a horse and cart here?"

"Nay, Miss Vernon. Will took them with him. There's only the old nag that's been put out to pasture. She's out back."

"Is your lad still here?"

"Aye, Tom's here. Will wanted for him to stay, in case—"

"Have him saddle up the nag this instant, if you please."

"But you can't ride that old beast in your present state, miss!"

"I am certain the old nag will suit me better in my present state than would some slap-up thoroughbred! Will you please see to it, Mrs. Smith. Pardon me if I appear abrupt, but I must see for myself what has happened at the Hall."

Muttering to herself, Mrs. Smith shuffled from the room at

a pace that made Katrina feel like screaming with frustration. The thought that Justin might even now be lying dead, perhaps charred beyond recognition, seared her brain, but she pushed it away, determined not to think the worst, for she needed to rally all her strength to get to the Hall.

The nag was a sorry beast indeed, with a shaggy hide and spavined legs, but it was better by far than walking the mile to the Hall. She refused to take even one cup of tea, despite Mrs. Smith's protests, but she did accept her offer to have the lad, Tom, ride the horse and take her up behind him, for Mrs. Smith had been horrified at the idea of her having to ride astride, with her skirts all hoisted up. Unbeknownst to Mrs. Smith, it was not modesty that made Katrina take Tom; her head was still spinning, and it would not do to be falling off the horse en route.

The acrid stench of smoke hung in the air, stinging their eyes as they drew near the Hall; its pall hung over the house and surrounding park, but at least the house still stood. She banished the thought that it might be only the shell of the house she was seeing, and, clinging to Tom's sturdy leather belt, she shut her eyes in another desperate prayer that Justin remained unharmed.

Her heart hammered so hard in her breast as they rode up to the flight of steps at the front of the house, that her entire body seemed to vibrate. "Go round to the back and see what you can do to help," she told Tom when she had dismounted. She paused for a moment, looking up at the house. From the exterior it appeared that the fire had been confined to the east wing, for only there were the timbers and window frames charred black and the walls smoke stained. She took a shuddering breath and, gathering up her skirts, mounted the steps.

Neither porter nor footman stood at the open door, and the scene in the great hall was chaotic, with hordes of servants and villagers mopping up the pools of water that puddled the marble-tiled floor. The sodden Axminster carpet was rolled up and laid along the row of blackened Corinthian columns by the wall. To her right were piled charred beams that were still smoking. The choking pall of smoke hung everywhere, catching at everyone's throat, so that above the noise of shouts and hammering was the continuous sound of coughing.

She caught sight of Jarvis, leaning against the wall, looking lost and bewildered, and she hurried up to him. "Jarvis! Lord Danville! Is he safe?"

"Oh, Miss Vernon, such a night, such a dreadful night!" The old man was close to tears and near to collapsing with fatigue. "Poor Master Justin."

She caught hold of his arm. "Please tell me, Jarvis," she cried. "His lordship—" Horror gripped her throat as her roving eyes caught sight of a cloth-draped figure laid out in an alcove. "Who is that, Jarvis?" she whispered in a hoarse voice, pointing to the figure.

"That's Carlton, Miss Vernon. That—that villain! He tried to burn down the Hall and all of us in it." His rheumy eyes were glazed with shock. "He was crushed by a falling beam, and I cannot feel sorry for it."

She released her breath in a long sigh. "No, indeed, Jarvis." She, too, could experience nothing but gratitude and relief at the news of Carlton's death. "Thank God," she whispered, feeling as if a great weight had been lifted from her. "You must rest, Jarvis," she said gently. "But first, please, I beg of you, tell me if Lord Danville is safe."

"Yes, Miss Vernon, he is. But my poor master; he is heartbroken at the loss of almost half his library. All those books he loved so dearly, gone!" Now the butler's eyes filled with tears, and he averted his face, embarrassed by this unseemly display of emotion.

"Oh, Jarvis! Where is he? Tell me where he is! I must go to him!"

"Oh, no, miss. You cannot! He is— He has been—"

"Drinking? Yes, I know. I am not afraid of him, Jarvis, and he needs me. Tell me where he is!"

"He's in his study upstairs. He went there almost an hour ago, once he knew the fire was safely out. Exhausted he was from working himself harder than any other man, trying to save his precious books. I would advise you to wait until tomorrow to see him."

"Of course you would, Jarvis, and have now done your

duty by doing so," she said softly. "Now you have but to direct me to his study, and I shall then leave you in peace."

Slowly shaking his head, he beckoned to a footman in smoke-blackened green livery. "Show Miss Vernon to his lordship's study," he told him. Then he turned back to Katrina. "God bless you, Miss Vernon. It's been a bad night, a bad night for us all, but most of all for him. Will you be sure to ring for me if you are in need of anything? I shall answer it *personally*," he said with great emphasis, and she caught his meaning immediately.

"Do not worry, Jarvis." She gave him a gentle smile. "I am in no danger from him."

"I hope not, miss. I sincerely hope not."

"Will you kindly do me one favor: have word sent to the parsonage that I am safe, for they must be wondering what has happened to me?"

"It shall be done, Miss Vernon."

"Now please do as I ask, Jarvis, and get some rest."

She pushed through the crowd of workers, dodging men with ladders and grappling irons, and followed the footman up the staircase and along the picture gallery and then through a small anteroom. The footman pointed to a door. "That's his lordship's study, miss."

"Thank you. You may go now."

As he went out into the gallery, he cast a backward glance at her, obviously not certain that he should desert her. She knocked lightly on the door, but on receiving no response, opened it and went in. For a moment she thought the room was empty, for it was dark but for the glimmer of the one candle that stood on a small table and the glow of the embers in the fireplace. Then someone stirred in the winged armchair and, her eyes now growing accustomed to the darkness, she saw Lord Danville there, his legs stretched out across the hearth.

She closed the door quietly behind her and moved into the room. She heard the clink of glass and the sound of pouring liquid, the candlelight catching the gleam of glass as he raised his hand.

"My lord."

"What the devil—" The glass was set down hard on the table. "I gave orders that I was not to be disturbed. Get out, whoever you are!"

Carefully, she felt her way around chairs and tables and across the dark room, and then stepped out in front of him. He was slumped in the chair, his long legs encased in buff breeches which were blackened with soot and water-stained. His shirt, which had once been white, was open almost to the waist, revealing his broad, dark chest. He looked up as she came into view, and his eyes narrowed. "Why, Miss Vernon, is it you?"

She was not encouraged by the sarcastic inflection in his voice. "Yes, my lord, it is I," she replied simply.

He thrust his hands into the pockets of his breeches and leaned his head back to look up at her. "You see what you have brought upon me, Miss Vernon? Are you satisfied with the results? Have you come to gloat and to tell me it is God's punishment for my past behavior?" His speech was slightly slurred, but it was impossible to tell how much he was affected by drink.

His bitterness was understandable under the circumstances, but she had expected that he would at least inquire after her health, perhaps question her about Carlton's attack on her. But she was determined not to add fuel to his torment, and replied calmly, "I do not comprehend your meaning, my lord."

A nerve jumped in his cheek. "But for you, Miss Vernon, all this would never have happened."

"Explain yourself, my lord."

"Explain myself?" She caught the dangerous glint in his eyes. "Why should I explain myself to you?"

"May I sit down? I am rather fatigued." In actuality, she was near to falling down with exhaustion, and her head was throbbing again.

"Do as you please," he said with a shrug, and took up his glass again.

She sat on the chair opposite him, her hands folded in her lap, while he scrutinized her from head to foot, an insulting half-smile on his lips. She reflected that it was at least an improvement on using his quizzing glass to look at her.

"So, Miss Vernon. Carlton is dead."

She flung him a startled look. "So I believe, and I thank God for it." She spoke quietly, trying not to display her agitation.

"And I would to God I had never met you!" he raged. "Had I not, my library would be intact, not burned and blackened, my treasures nothing but charred dust!"

"I am truly sorry!"

"You are truly sorry!" His eyes glittered in the candlelight, and she flinched at the venom in their depths. "You do not seem to comprehend what I am saying. That you, curse you, are responsible!" He raised his glass in a mock salute and suddenly his arm swung in an arc as he flung the glass and its contents into the fire. She started back as the glass shattered against the grate, and the spirit hissed and flared in the fire. Jarvis had been right; he was in a dangerous mood.

He rose and strode across the hearth to stand menacingly over her. "You seem strangely calm, Miss Vernon. Surely it was most foolhardy of you to come to me on such a night! Stand up!" He took her elbows and hauled her to her feet. "I have lost hundreds of precious volumes tonight: books that were collected by my father and his father before him; irreplaceable manuscripts. And had you not come here to Danville, had I never seen you at the cursed Merriot ball, this would never have happened!"

"I know it," she whispered, longing to put her arms around him. He was like a child who had suffered a bitter disappointment, lashing out at the person he loved. "But at least you are alive, and the Hall is standing, and the main part of your library has been saved."

"Damn you, with your platitudes and 'at leasts'! What is all that to me?" His grip tightened on her arms, and he dragged her to him, his mouth coming down on hers, brutal and hard as iron, bruising her lips. Her head was swimming, and she was still weak from the effects of the blow. She stood passively, too weary to struggle, until he lifted his mouth from hers and took her face between his hands. "Why did you come here, curse you!" he whispered harshly.

She tried to move away, wishing to set a distance between them until he was calm, but he would not release her. "Did you come to torment me? Well, you are succeeding!" His steely gray eyes glared into hers as if they would penetrate her very soul.

"I was on my way here to come to you when Carlton struck me down," she told him, meeting his piercing gaze unflinchingly.

"Struck you down?" He released her face and ran his hands down her arms to take her hands in a painful grip.

"Yes. He accosted me in the avenue. That was more than two hours ago. I have been unconscious most of the time since then. But for Dick I might have been frozen to death by now. Did Dick not tell you?"

"Dick?" He seemed bewildered by all that she was saying, and she realized that he was overcome more by shock and fatigue than by liquor.

"Dick found me, and it was I who sent him to warn you."

"Yes, I seem to recollect— Of course! Had it not been for Foster, the entire Hall would have gone up in flames. Carlton had already set the fire by the time Dick arrived. In the confusion he must have neglected to mention you. Perhaps he told someone else. You say Carlton—"

"Is he safe?"

"Dick? Oh, yes, yes. He was overcome by smoke for a while, and his lungs are a trifle raw, that is all. But you, you say you were coming to me?" He shook his head, his eyes glazing with his effort to comprehend. "Why would you come to me? I was certain you would never wish to see me again after the way I behaved toward you!"

"And I was certain you would never wish to see me again after—after learning about my—my involvment with Carlton. But never mind that now, it can wait. I am more concerned about you. You look so weary, my love."

He summoned up a sardonic grin. "The tenor of our conversation appears to have mysteriously changed, ma'am! Perhaps I should venture to ask you to be seated, for if I look weary, you look positively exhausted." He drew her to the sofa before the fire and sat down beside her, looking down at her hands, which he still held in his. "I regret I am not at all myself tonight, Katrina. I am not only damnably weary but also damnably cast away. You must forgive me."

"Of course I do. It is entirely understandable."

"Is it? Not many women would say so after the manner in which I have treated you. But then I am forgetting you are not like other women." He put his arm around her, and she leaned her head on his shoulder. "Pah! I must reek disgustingly of soot and smoke. I have not washed since the damned fire."

She lifted her head to look up at him and smiled at the black streaks on his face. Drawing her closer, he ran his fingers over her lips. "Did I hurt you, my love? Forgive me!"

She shook her head and, with a little sob, flung her arm around his neck and drew his head down. This time he was infinitely tender, his lips gentle upon hers, and she opened them to him. "Katrina," he groaned, his tongue probing the softness of her mouth. She closed her eyes, allowing herself to relax entirely against him, too weary to respond to his kisses as passionately as she would have liked, but conscious enough to be gloriously aroused by his touch. His hands caressed first the contours of her face and then her neck, where he could no doubt feel her lifeblood pulsing fast against his fingers. His mouth followed the same route, trailing kisses down her throat, and at the same time his hands circled her breasts, cupping and caressing them, and she moaned in ecstasy against his mouth. Now his hands were fumbling urgently at her bodice, searching for the fastenings on her dress.

"There are buttons at the back," she whispered. Then, without hesitation: "Rip it!"

His eyes shone with delighted laughter, and he tore the bodice from neck to waist, dragging the straps of her underslip from her shoulders to reveal her swelling breasts to him. "My love, my dearest love," he groaned, and alternately kissed and caressed their soft roundness. She lay on her back and drew him down on her, reveling in the sensation of his weight upon her. She was not at all afraid of what he would do to her, for not only did she not fear him in any way, she was also too weary to experience any strong emotion. It was as if she were floating, her body nothing but a delicious, weightless throbbing.

He drew her lips close to him and her body moved in unison with his in the preliminary movements of love. "At such a time I wish you were not quite so tall," she whispered, "for I long to kiss you."

He moved his body down a little so that he could fulfill her request. Then he laid his head upon her breast and she cradled it against her, overwhelmed with tenderness at the weight and warmth of it there. She closed her eyes, incredibly content. After a while, she opened them again, stirred by the aching desire in her loins. "Jusin," she whispered. There was no reply. "Justin!" She stroked the waving dark hair from his temples and, looking down, saw that his black lashes lay on his cheeks. He was fast asleep.

"Oh you—*devil!*" she whispered, stifling a laugh. Asleep! "Leaving me fraught with desire!" she would tell him when he awoke. But at the moment he exhibited not the slightest sign of so doing, even to the point of emitting a snore or two, and she was beginning to feel crushed by his weight. Slowly, she eased herself out from under him and stood up, uncertain what she should do. One thing was certain: They both needed sleep more than anything else, for tomorrow they would have to face each other and the ruins of his beloved library, unshielded by either liquor or fatigue.

Gathering together the bodice of her dress as best she could, she wrapped her shawl around her, trusting it covered her, and pulled the bell rope that hung by the mantelpiece. When a soft knock came at the door a few minutes later, she opened it to find Jarvis there, and slipped outside to speak with him, embarrassingly aware from his hastily concealed expression that she was probably now as smoke smeared as Lord Danville. "He is fast asleep, Jarvis."

"God be thanked for that, Miss Vernon."

"I think it best if you merely cover him with a blanket, make up the fire, and leave him there. He is greatly fatigued." She could not keep from smiling, which must have made her appear quite inane in the circumstances, but she was beyond caring.

"Very well, Miss Vernon. I shall do as you say."

"And I am unharmed, bar a few smears of black, I fancy," she said frankly, and met the twinkle in his eyes with a smile. "But I would dearly like to be able to wash and then to sleep."

"Mrs. Talbot has already anticipated your need for both, Miss Vernon, and has hot water ready in the chamber she has prepared for you. She chose one as far from all the noise as was possible."

"How very kind of her!" She hesitated and then said, "I realize it is not quite the thing for me to be staying here tonight, Jarvis, but in the circumstances—"

"Exactly so, Miss Vernon."

"Will you arrange for me to be called in the morning as soon as Lord Danville wakens, Jarvis?"

"I give you my word, Miss Vernon. May I presume so far as to say how happy I am—we all are—Miss Vernon?"

"Oh, no, Jarvis, you may not." She met his surprised look with a wry half-smile. "For you may heartily disapprove of the circumstances in which I remain with Lord Danville. We shall see what the morning will bring, Jarvis."

"Yes, indeed, miss." With a slight smile and a deep bow, he said, "I shall ask Mrs. Talbot to wait upon you immediately. I wish you good night, Miss Vernon."

"Good night, Jarvis." She held out her hand to him, and he took it and clasped it in his trembling, dry hand. "And thank you."

Chapter Twenty

When she arose the following morning, Katrina was extremely relieved to discover that Lady Helen had sent up a complete
change of clothing to the Hall, at Mrs. Talbot's request.

"For, as I said to Jarvis," explained that worthy lady as
she assisted Katrina to dress, "poor Miss Vernon, lying all
that time in the dirt and cold and her being so ill-treated by
that wretch Carlton, she'll welcome fresh clothing more than
anything else."

"You were quite right, Mrs. Talbot. I do indeed," agreed
Katrina, relieved that Mrs. Talbot blamed Carlton for the sorry
state of her dress. She had been too weary to think up an
explanation for the ripped bodice, when Mrs. Talbot had
carried it away the previous night.

She took great pains with her appearance, determined to
look her very best. Despite a dull ache in her head, she
looked and felt much improved, her eyes clear and sparkling
and a dash of color in her cheeks. She had been informed by
Mrs. Talbot that Lord Danville would join her in the breakfast
parlor in one hour or anytime thereafter at her convenience.
Katrina could see that Mrs. Talbot was bursting to say more,
but she contented herself with a sly look before leaving the

room. One hour gave Katrina more than sufficient time to curl her hair in a becoming style and put on her best black silk with the ruffle of white lace at the neck.

Her emotions at the thought of meeting him were extremely mixed. She was incapable of even guessing what his mood might be, and in the cold brightness of the morning the thought of facing him was far more daunting than it had been the previous night, when she had been fuzzy-brained with the headache and fatigue. It was with a certain amount of trepidation, therefore, that she trod down the stairs, past the dozens of servants scouring the floors and walls and statues, and was shown into the breakfast parlor, which had fortunately escaped the effects of the fire. She paused in the doorway, exclaiming, "Oh, how lovely!"

The room was most attractively decorated in a blue and white chinoiserie style. This, together with the abundant alcoved windows, which were lined with curtains of blue silk, gave it a refreshingly light and airy atmosphere.

"I am gratified it meets with your approval," said a voice from the end of the long mahogany table, and the Viscount set aside his one-day-old newspaper and rose to greet her.

He too had spared no pains in dressing elegantly: he wore close-fitting pale buff pantaloons, a white waistcoat, and a gleaming white neckcloth of intricate design, topped with a coat of blue superfine—a marked contrast to his wild dishabille of the previous night. He came forward and greeted her with the strictest formality, only shaking the hand she proffered him. Her heart sank when she saw the inscrutable expression in his eyes and the firmly compressed lips.

Having set a chair for her before the place that had been laid to the right of his, he waited until the footman had poured tea for her and more coffee for him, and then dismissed the man, saying that they would manage for themselves. The servant, trying to conceal surprise at this unprecedented announcement, retired, leaving them alone.

Neither of them chose to partake of the array of hot dishes on the sideboard, but Katrina did take a piece of crisp toast from the silver toast rack and buttered it. The Viscount set his elbows on the table and to her consternation and rising anger, put up his quizzing glass and surveyed her through it, without speaking.

Eventually, she set down her cup and said, "You know very well how much I detest it when you do that!"

"What? Ah, my glass. Forgive me. You are correct—a detestable habit, indeed!" He dropped the glass and leaned his chin on his clasped hands. "I have not yet made any inquiries as to your health, Miss Vernon. I trust you are feeling more the thing this morning. By the bye, I have asked Dr. Merivale to attend you at the parsonage at noon."

So, he intended to be rid of her before noon!

"Thank you, but there was no need to do so. Barring a large lump and possibly a bruise on my head, I do not think I have suffered any ill effects."

"I am glad of it. I—" He hesitated and then pushed back his chair, paced to the window and back again, to stand behind the chair. And she saw that his eyes were no longer inscrutable, but alight with a steely brightness. "What happened last night, Katrina?" he demanded.

She looked at him wonderingly. "You mean you cannot remember, my lord?"

"The fire, your arrival—yes, of course I remember. But afterwards—" For the very first time, she saw the faint red of embarrassment creep into his cheeks, and restrained a smile. He strode to her side and drew her up from her seat, clasping her hands tightly between his. "I beg you, tell me the truth. What happened—between us?"

She gave him a mischievous smile. "Why, nothing, my lord. Absolutely nothing!"

But he was not amused. "Damnation, Katrina! Be serious!" His eyes were now blazing. "Did I or did I not make love to you?"

"Why, yes, my lord. You did," she said softly, her eyes still teasing him.

"Completely?" he demanded.

"No, my lord. Not completely."

His chest rose and fell, and he dropped her hands and walked away. "Thank God!"

"I do not consider that altogether flattering, my lord."

"Do you not?" He turned sharply and returned to glare down at her. "Would you have me do—Would you have me behave as Carlton did toward you?"

"No, my dear lord," she replied, looking up into his face. "But there was no question of that, for I came to you willingly and was most disappointed when you did not, as you put it, 'complete' your lovemaking."

He grasped her by the shoulders and drew her closer to him. "Oh, my dearest, I was so beset this morning when I awoke to find I could not even remember. Good God, can you imagine how I felt! But what *did* happen?"

"You fell asleep, my lord."

"Fell asleep? You are roasting me!"

"No, indeed I am not. There we were, in the throes of passion—so I thought—and the next thing I knew you were fast asleep. Snoring, too!"

"The devil I was! You're certain you're not roasting me?"

"No, my love. Do you think I would invent such a thing?"

"What did you do?"

"I rolled out from under you—for you were dreadfully heavy, you know—and wrapping my shawl around me, rang for Jarvis, and left you to his tender mercies."

His eyes delved into hers, and then he stepped back and gave a great roar of laughter, exclaiming, "Trapped, by God! Trapped!"

"What on earth do you mean?" she demanded, bridling at his amusement.

"It was bad enough compromising you by making love to you and keeping you here—"

"You did not keep me here! I remained of my own volition!"

"Never mind! But you realize that if it were ever discovered that I fell asleep whilst making love to the woman I find desirable above all others, my reputation would be quite undone! I should be laughed out of town and put out to pasture with the senilities!"

"Who on earth would ever know?"

"Why, you, of course, my dearest love, and you could blackmail me with it. So I am forced to marry you."

"Forced!" She drew herself up, bristling with indignation, and then, seeing the teasing light in his eyes, relaxed. "Oh, Justin, how cruel of you to roast me about such a thing!"

He was immediately contrite. "Forgive me, my love. I could not resist it. But tell me, dear heart, why did you stay and risk your reputation?"

She looked away from him. "I must remind you, sir, that I have no reputation to lose," she whispered. "I stayed because I thought you would need me when you awoke this morning."

He gave her a wry smile and shook her hands a little to rally her. "Did you indeed, Miss Vernon? How very presumptuous of you—and how exceedingly considerate. Look at me, Katrina." She obeyed him and saw that the wry smile had vanished, and in its place was such an expression of glowing tenderness that she lost herself in its warmth. "Will you now give me your answer to my request?" he said softly.

"Your request?"

"Yes, my request that you accept my hand in marriage. For I love you, dearest Katrina, and I do indeed need you, not only this morning, but always."

She laid her head against his heart and whispered into his waistcoat, "You forget—about Carlton—"

"No, my love. I do not forget." He lifted her chin, forcing her to look up at him. "But I swear to you that I shall do everything in my power to make *you* forget Carlton, in *every* way! So much so that you will forget he ever existed, and so shall I!"

"Are you certain, Justin?"

"I have never been more certain of anything in my life!"

"Very well then, my answer is yes."

His face broke into a slow, sweet smile, and he bent his head and kissed her in the same manner, slowly and sweetly. It was not one of his passionate kisses, but warm and gentle, and she felt like a blossom in the early spring, slowly unfurling its petals in the warmth of the sun.

He brought her near the fire and, hand in hand, they sat on the high-backed settee, talking together in such a cozy domestic fashion that it might be thought they had already been married for years.

"You are certain you will not regret relinquishing the opportunity of a career as an opera singer?" he asked her, in response to her telling him of Mr. Kelly's offer.

"Why, no, my lord. But I do intend to maintain my voice in fine fettle, in case you ever grow weary of me!"

"Never, my love!" he responded with satisfying vehemence. "But as to our marriage, it will need to be a quiet, private ceremony, for you are still in mourning."

"With Mr. Standish officiating?"

"Of course. My erstwhile rival shall officiate at my wedding, and Lady Helen shall attend you. I should imagine that in itself would be fuel enough for the gossips for a fortnight, at the very least!" For she had already told him that Lady Helen had divulged their secret.

"You realize," she said, "that I suspected you of having seduced Lady Helen."

"Did you, by God! You really do not hold a very high opinion of me, do you, my dear Miss Vernon?"

"Of course not, my dear Devil! I even suspected that her first son might be your child!"

This sent him off into peals of laughter. "Oh, my dearest love. What an imagination you have! It's easy to see you are not yet acquainted with the Standish son and heir, for a more prosy, staid young pup it is hard to imagine! Had you met him, you would most certainly never have accused me of siring him!" His wide grin disappeared. "One thing you must not be thinking, love, and that is that I am still wearing the willow for Lady Helen. I realized many years ago that we would not have suited. I would have been bored with her within a month, so it was all for the best. Only my pride was bruised; my heart—after a period of mourning—remained intact."

"I am glad of it, my love, for they are dear friends, and I would wish us to be able to associate with them without reserve on either side. Speaking of friends, may I invite a few more friends to our wedding, only a few?"

"Not Letty or your aunt; I draw the line there!"

"Of course not! But I should like above all things to invite Uncle William, and Sir Matthew and Lady Bainbridge—who must have been wondering why on earth I should write to thank them for their great kindness in recommending me for the position of Lady Helen's governess!—and Desmond.''

''Desmond? Of course! And naturally your uncle will be giving you away at the ceremony. Besides, he will most likely be resident at the Hall.''

''He will?''

''Why, yes,'' he said lightly. ''I intend to have him down to assist me with the library.''

''Oh!'' she exclaimed, conscience-stricken. ''Oh, my poor darling. Your library! Pray forgive me. I—''

''Quite forgot?'' he interposed with a twisted smile. ''So had I, my love—for a while. Which only goes to prove that I value you even more highly than my books. And that, my little love, is high praise indeed!''

''Do you think Uncle William will be able to find replacements for most of them?'' she asked tentatively, reluctant to add salt to the wound.

''We shall see, but thank God the catalogs are still intact and less than half the books destroyed. I owe Dick Foster a huge debt of gratitude; had he not found you and given us the warning, the fire might have taken hold long before it was discovered—and you might be lying frozen in the park!''

She shuddered and thrust away the memory of the previous night. ''On the subject of Dick—''

''Yes, yes, my love. It has already been seen to. Dick will receive ample reward. He is already in my employ and is, I fancy, to be set to work on the stud records in the stable office.''

''You are too good!''

''Am I indeed? That is not what you were wont to tell me, Miss Vernon!''

''No, my lord. But then, you have changed.''

''Ah, I see. Softened by the love of a good woman!''

''Surely not softened, my dearest. Made more aware of other persons' feelings, perhaps?''

''Perhaps. Who knows what having you as my wife may do to me. I promise you one thing: I shall never again fall asleep upon you!''

"Despite the flush that mantled her cheeks, she met his laughing eyes with equanimity. "I am glad of it, my lord."

He bent his head to kiss her, and fleetingly she touched his dark, shining hair as her lips softened against the firmness of his. "Enough," he said, gently thrusting her away. "I must, I think, procure a special license for our marriage, for if I do not, I have the distinct feeling that this will prove a most frustrating period of time for us both. The sooner we can marry, the better!"

He took her hands and drew her back to the table. "Come, let us complete our breakfast, for I have suddenly discovered I am ravenously hungry. I shall ring for fresh tea and coffee."

Having pulled the bell rope, he held her chair for her and returned to his own seat, thus setting a distance between them. "Do you think your uncle will object to leaving your aunt for a few months, Miss Vernon?"

"I think it highly unlikely that he will raise any objection whatsoever to such an idea, Lord Danville."

He stood up and raised his cup of cold coffee. "I wish to propose a toast: to the future, the very near future, Lady Danville!"

She bowed in response and took up her own teacup. "To you, my dear, my very dear lord!"

A silent Jarvis, having quietly opened the door, stood watching as they toasted each other with cold tea and coffee. He then slipped out of the room, a smile on his lined face, to acquaint Mrs. Talbot with the glad tidings that Miss Vernon was to wed Master Justin; pausing on his way only to order a footman to take in fresh tea and coffee to the breakfast parlor.

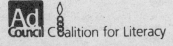